WEST
OF WANT

HEARTS OF THE ANEMOI
BOOK TWO

WEST
OF WANT

Hearts of the Anemoi
Book Two

Laura Kaye

Entangled Publishing, LLC
2614 South Timberline Road
Suite 109
Fort Collins, CO 80525
Visit our website at www.entangledpublishing.com.

Edited by Heather Howland
Cover design by Heather Howland

Print ISBN   978-1-62061-055-8
Ebook ISBN   978-1-62061-056-5

Manufactured in the United States of America

First Edition July 2012

You can't choose how or when you die,
but you can choose how you live.
This book is for the living.

CHAPTER ONE

Ella Raines knelt on the varnished deck of the sailboat's cockpit, her dead brother's ashes in her hands, and stared out at the dark green chop of the Chesapeake Bay. The cold March breeze kicked up sea spray and rippled through the sails, but all Ella could feel was the metal urn turning her aching fingers to ice. She had to let him go—she knew she did—but with everything else she'd lost, how could the world be so cruel as to expect her to give up her twin, too?

She twisted open the urn's brass lid and stuffed it in the pocket of her windbreaker. Sailing had been the passion over which she and Marcus had most bonded, not just as siblings, but as best friends. A day spent cruising on the bay, blue skies overhead and warm winds lifting the sails, had been Marcus's favorite thing to do. He wasn't a religious man, but said he most believed in God when he was out on the open water. So a burial at sea made sense, and it was time. When she'd woken up this morning and seen the clear forecast, she resolved today was the day. After all, it had been two months, and the first day of spring seemed a fitting time for starting over.

Leaning over the stern, Ella tilted the brass container by slow degrees until fine ashes spilled out, swirled on the wind, and blew away in a sad gray ribbon that blurred from her silent tears. Choppy waves splashed against the transom, soaking Ella to the elbows, and the boat heeled to the starboard. She braced herself on the backstay. The fixed steel cable bit into her hand but steadied her enough to empty the urn.

"Good-bye, Marcus. I love you." She barely heard herself over the sudden gusting of the wind that roared through the sails.

Ella locked down the grief and despair that wanted to claw out of her chest and climbed to a standing position. The boat heeled again, hard, the forty-five-degree angle nearly catching her off guard. She stumbled. The urn dropped with a brassy clang to the deck of the helm and rolled lopsidedly as the sloop tossed.

She turned, her brain already moving her hands and body through the motions of furling the mainsail and tacking upwind. A bright flash caught her gaze and a gasp stuck in her throat.

An enormous dark cloud sprawled low over the water to the southwest. Mountainous black plumes protruded from the top, creating a tower through which brilliant explosions of yellow-orange streaked. Inky fingers reached down from the storm's edge as the squalling winds lashed at the sea.

Where the hell had *that* come from?

A long growl of thunder rumbled over the bay. Ella felt it in her bones. The boat tossed and heeled. Waves pounded the hull, sloshed over the sides, and soaked her sneakers. A spare glance at her instruments revealed thirty-knot winds. Thirty-five.

A four-foot wave slammed against the port side. Ella slipped on the wet deck and went down hard on one knee. She grasped the wheel just as the boat lurched sideways. Thunder crashed above her, the sound vibrating through the whipping wind. Bitter cold rain poured down over the boat in a torrent. Tendrils of Ella's hair came loose from her long braid and plastered to her forehead and cheeks.

She needed to turn the boat and reach shore if she had any hope of escaping the wind. Ella wrestled the steering wheel hard to windward, the rudder fighting her every turn. Damn, how could she have been so reckless, so unobservant? Storms like this didn't just develop out of nowhere. A sailor never trusted the weathermen over her own eyes and ears. How long had she been kneeling on the deck giving in to her woe-is-me routine, anyway? And here she was, in the literal eye of a storm, sailing single-handed without life jacket or tether on. She locked the wheel into place. At least she could remedy *that* problem.

Ella reached for an orange vest and slipped her arms through the holes. A final glance at her instruments revealed forty-knot winds now. Dread threatened to swamp her. She disconnected the electronics, leaving only the compass to guide her. Her mast was a forty-foot lightning rod, so she did what little she could to combat the likelihood of a strike.

The windward course was a short-lived pursuit as the wind direction changed again and again. Eyes on the compass, she adjusted to the wind as best she could. She couldn't see squat through the deluge, and the hovering gray sheets of rain and spray and six-foot waves obscured the horizon. She'd have to ride it out. With shaking, bone-cold fingers, she connected the bottom of the three buckles on her vest. Small *clicks* sounded from overhead, got louder, more frequent. Hail pelted down the size of dimes, then nickels. Ella crouched against the wheel and shielded her head with her hands and arms. The falling ice ripped into the plastic of her jacket and bit into her knuckles.

Thunder crashed right above her and the storm-darkened sky exploded in ferocious jags of electricity. Rain and hail lashed her body, and wind and waves battered her ship like it had a personal vendetta to settle. With her. A tremendous wave crested over the starboard side, shoving her head against the metal spoke of the wheel. Spots burst across her vision. She cried out, the sound swallowed by the wind.

When she could focus again, her gaze settled on the lidless cremation urn wedged fore of the wheel pedestal. Marcus. What she wouldn't do to have him with her. She reached around the huge wheel to grab the container, just grasping for something, anything to make her feel less alone. She couldn't reach. Shifting her hold on the wheel, she stretched, her fingers straining, yearning to feel the cold brass. Not quite.

She lunged for the urn, grabbed it up, and hugged it to her chest.

Thunder and lightning blasted the sky above her. A wall of wind shoved at the side of the sailboat. It lurched. Spun. An ominous crack reverberated from below. A wave pounded Ella's shoulders and back, flattening her atop the urn onto the deck of the cockpit, holding her hostage with its watery weight. Seawater strangled her, stole her breath, and receded.

The boat reared over a peaked wave and bucked. Ella slid into a free fall.

Not releasing her death grip on the urn, Ella's right hand shot out and clutched the steel backstay. The ligaments of her shoulder wrenched apart in a sickening, audible pop just as her lower body whipped over the transom and hit the frigid water. The jolt stole her scream, allowed her only to moan long and low. Icy wetness soaked through her heavy clothes and the drag tugged and pulled at her destroyed joint.

Triple bolts of lightning illuminated the gunmetal sky in quick succession. Shaking nonstop from cold and pain and adrenaline, Ella stared up at her hand clutching the metal cable. One strike and she'd be done. Her mind laid out the choices. Ship or sea. Urn or ship. Drown or fry. Life or death.

A wave swamped her. And another. She choked and gagged. The next slammed her head against the fiberglass transom.

Her hands flew open from the impact. She plunged into the storm-tortured water, sucked down nauseating mouthfuls. Her body whipped feet over head, side to side. Impossible to determine which way was up. The violent churning of the sea ripped the lifejacket off one arm, but the orange padding held just enough to finally guide her head to the surface.

Despite her daze, survival instincts had her gulping oxygen, precious oxygen. Her successful fight against the urge to vomit left her shuddering, the sour bile almost a welcome respite from the cold salt. No matter. The next cresting wave forced her to drink more.

Panic jolted through her body, shook the drunken haze from her mind. Kicking and paddling, she spun around and around, until she'd done several three-sixties. The boat. Gone.

As her body crested the top of wave after wave, she strained to see some glimpse of white in the thick, dark gray. At thirty-four feet, the *True Blue* was not little, but the sea was too rough, the wind too forceful.

No. No, no, no. Not their sailboat, too. Not the last place

that truly felt like home, the last place filled with memories of laughter and love and honesty.

Deafening thunder rumbled over the world. Jagged electricity flared over the monstrous seascape.

Ella tilted her head back, squinted against the blinding rain, and screamed. "Is that all you got? Well, fuck you! Fuck you and the cloud you blew in on! I've got nothing left to lose, so take your best shot!"

A wave smacked her in the face. She gagged. Coughed. Laughed until sobs took over.

Exhaustion. Pure and utter. Like she'd lived a thousand lives.

Debris thudded against her ear. She howled as the jarring hit rang through her head.

Please don't let it be pieces of True Blue.

Her eyes focused on the sea next to her. Nothing. She propelled herself around. The urn. Ella gasped and irrational joy filled her chest.

She half-swam—a nearly impossible feat against the thrashing waves with one useless arm. Each leaden stroke sapped what little energy she had left.

She grabbed the urn. Held it in her numb hands.

"I knew you wouldn't leave me," she whispered against the brass, all she could manage. "We're true blue."

Together, the churn carried them up one side of a wave, then plunged them down the other. Ella's head slumped against the flat base of the upside down container. Her eyelids sagged.

And everything went black.

CHAPTER TWO

A life force was fading.

The sensation tugged at Zephyros's consciousness, embattled as it was as he raged over the sea. Caught up in his own thoughts, his own pain, his own loss, he writhed and tossed, howled and lashed out. The wind and rain—nature's very energy—were his to control, even when he was out of control. But, still, the wrongness of the sensation tugged at him, demanded redress. In his elemental form, he felt the call of life and birth and renewal most strongly. He could ignore it no longer.

He forced himself to embrace the calm that had once been the truest manifestation of his nature. Around him, the clouds dispersed, the rains thinned, the winds settled to a bluster. The sea, black and roiling a moment ago, eased into the early spring chop typical of the bay.

Zephyros allowed the tranquility of the open water to fuel the return of his composure. He focused. Scanned for the soul decrying its unnatural end. Commanding the West Wind to carry him down from the heavens, he soared on the gentle gusts. The only thing nearby was a lone sailboat, floundering in the wind.

He glided around the fine boat. No life resided on its decks or within its hull. A sour pit formed in his gut as he began to suspect what had happened.

Rising up to gain a broader view of the sea, Zephyros searched, the dwindling life a beacon he latched onto. Pursued. The thrum of its force vibrated within him. Closing in, he descended toward the surface, the waves passing under him in a blur. There! A flicker of orange upon the dark gray-green.

Flashing into corporeality, Zephyros assumed the form of a giant water kingfisher.

Slate-blue wings exploded twenty feet out on either side of his body. He plunged head-first toward the bobbing figure, the wind ruffling through the crown-like crest of blue feathers atop his head. Rarely did he ever have the need to shift into his sacred animal form, but it was a power all the Anemoi possessed.

Glaring down at the water, Zephyros braced himself. Extreme temperatures pained and weakened him, and he'd be lucky if this water was in the fifties. He skied into the water's surface, spread wings gentling his landing. No such luck. Mid-forties if it was anything. But this wasn't about him, was it?

Just ahead, the human bobbed face down, tendrils of long hair floating in strands of silk like a halo. He smelled blood. Best hurry. His senses told him time was short.

Zephyros plunged his regal, avian body into the water, came up with the dead weight draped over his neck. With a shove of a wing, he pushed the legs of the body up, resituating the length along his back. He took flight.

Frigid water shook off him in a fantastic spray as his

massive wingspan flapped and lifted them away from the bay. His gaze lit on the sailboat and he banked in its direction. He circled the boat once, twice. The metal cables connecting the mast to the deck would not accommodate his wings. He couldn't land on the boat.

Taking extra care not to jostle the victim, *his* victim, Zephyros landed behind the sailboat. Instinctively, he commanded the change and shifted into his human form. The biting chill of the water tormented his naked flesh, but more important matters demanded his attention. Grabbing onto one delicate hand, he ensured his hold on the person draped across his back before turning and cradling the body into his arms.

He sucked in a breath. Mother of gods. A bruise mottled the whole left side of her face, from cheek to eyebrow. A nasty gash along the cheekbone oozed a thin line of blood. Her bottom lip was busted open, swollen. But even the severity of her injuries couldn't hide her beauty.

That sour pit in his stomach grew, suffocated. He'd caused this. Damn it, could he never do anything right? Ancient turmoil roiled through him, threatening to turn him inside out. No, of course he couldn't.

Zephyros adjusted the woman's weight in his arms and reached up over the transom. His fingers searched for and found the release, and the swim platform folded out toward them. He lifted the woman above his head and settled her on the glossy wooden surface, then hefted himself up beside her. With solid footing beneath him, he gently lifted her again. He stepped around the massive wheel to the seating area to the fore, and laid her out on a long bench.

Her head lolled to the side. Wheezes morphed into a weak cough. Her whole body seized. Water expelled from her throat.

Zephyros supported her shoulders, held her up until she quieted. Her eyelids creaked open, revealing the rolling whites of her eyes. They sagged again, and her whole body went limp.

Zephyros released a breath as unexpected relief flooded him—followed quickly by guilt. His suspicions about what had happened to her were confirmed by an imprinting on her life jacket. The words "True Blue" matched the dark blue calligraphy painted on the back of the boat. She'd been thrown overboard in the storm. *His* storm.

He shivered, a combination of guilt, shame, and the wind against his wet body. Well, the latter problem he could address. He materialized jeans and a T-shirt and made himself decent.

Like a magnet, she drew his gaze. He reached out and stroked his fingers over the reds and purples coloring the side of her face. Her hair appeared deep brown, but he suspected the darkness was an effect of the water still drenching her.

Shaking his head, Zephyros debated. He should leave now. The Coast Guard would find her. The bay had patrols. He could even command the current to carry the boat, with her upon it, to shore. Even as he agreed with himself, agreed leaving her would be for the best, he searched the boat for information he could use to help her. Storage lockers filled the space beneath the bench seats. Empty. His gaze scanned. He'd look below.

Down the companionway steps, he descended into the cabin and stepped in a few inches of sloshing water on the galley floor. All warm wood and white accents, the space was surprisingly spacious and bright. Far forward there appeared to be a berth. Aft of that bedroom, a large sitting area centered round a table. To his immediate left, a small galley kitchen, and to his right, a chart table. Compasses and instruments hung above it on the hull wall.

Zephyros stepped to the desk and opened the top drawer. Maps and paperwork sat in skewed stacks. He flipped through the pages until he found a name and address. That the name was male brought an unexpected frown to his face, but at least he had a lead on where to take her. Surely someone so physically attractive had a significant other, someone who would care for her and see her mended back to health.

As he moved to return above deck, a small aft berth caught his eye and he reached in and yanked a blanket from the bed. Up top again, he tucked the red comforter around the woman. The loose strands of hair around her face had air-dried to a light golden-brown. Peaceful in her unconsciousness, her face appeared delicate and young, unmarred by cruelty or pain— except for what he'd done to her, of-fucking-course.

Ignoring the rock of guilt in his gut, he considered the problem of actually getting the boat to harbor. Sailing was a foreign language to him. He had no need for the knowledge. He could soar on the wind, even glide on the currents for short times. All he knew was a sailboat with furled sails wasn't going anywhere.

No matter. He stepped around the wheel and down onto the swimming platform. The clothing would just be a drag, so he disappeared it and jumped. The cold water sucker-punched him. He gasped and willed his muscles to cooperate. How long had the woman suffered with the freezing waves battering her damaged body? He bit down on his tongue to keep from roaring out. The pain focused him.

Arms extended beside him, he closed his eyes and called the current. As a wind god, Zephyros was most at home in the sky, but marshaling sea currents worked on the same principle.

The rush of water pushed behind him, just as he directed, and scooped up the boat's hull in the grip of its gentle forward motion. One hand on the platform, he floated behind the boat, guiding its heading, adjusting as necessary, shivering until he thought his bones might snap. Luckily, the storm had chased away other maritime traffic. The bay was wide open and empty. Nice to have one thing going for him. Occasional gulls cried out high above, their pale bodies nearly camouflaged against the gray-white sky.

Within an hour, they were in sight of Annapolis. Above the town proper, a large steeple and a tall domed cupola framed the colonial seaport. But Zephyros's destination was a bit closer. The address he'd found should be on the neck of land just south of the town.

An inlet emerged up ahead. All along the shore, clusters of masts stood up together, sentinels on the water. He guided the boat toward the creek. A sailboat with a large blue mast sail glided past. Zephyros submerged into the cold, but not before noticing the confounded expression on the other captain's face. Of course. The boat he guided moved without aid of sail or motor.

He resurfaced long enough to see the other boat coming about, the captain on the radio. Damn it all to Hades.

This situation was about to become shit meets fan. For gods' sake, he currently didn't have clothes, and until he warmed he'd be lucky to hold a conversation. Naked, nearly incapacitated, with no ability to dock the boat, and with a gravely injured woman on board, he had little likelihood of contriving a convincing story about how they'd gotten that way.

His presence was a liability here. He was useless. Again.

As the blue-masted boat neared, the captain called out,

asking whether the *True Blue* was in distress. No one answered, of course.

And it was time for him to go.

Zephyros released his grip on the platform and eased the created current until it dispersed altogether. He sank beneath the surface, shaking nonstop, and hesitated just a moment. His gut clenched. He hated the idea of not seeing her to safety. Okay, in truth, he'd done that. But what he *wanted* was to see her to health—awake and conscious and warm and happy.

Happy? What did her emotions have to do with anything? Fluttery panic ripped through his chest. The fact he was even thinking about her feelings was a major get-the-hell-out-of-there red flag. Getting involved was the last thing he needed. Hadn't he learned that? Again and again and a-fucking-gain?

No more.

The rescue sailboat came alongside the *True Blue*. A man's voice rang out above the water's surface. There. *He* would make sure she was safe, cared for, got everything she needed. The thought had Zephyros grinding his teeth in frustration. In self-defense.

In want.

No.

He wanted nothing and no one. And, in truth, no one wanted him either. So didn't that work out just perfectly, thank you very much.

Zephyros turned and, without looking back, swam to the opposite shore.

He broke the icy surface gasping for breath and shaking so hard his bones hurt.

"Job well done, Zephyros. Very good. And on the first day of your season, too," came the last voice Zeph wanted to hear in that moment. Or any moment.

Zeph wiped the water from his eyes and climbed the small embankment opposite the marina where he could hear a small crowd gathering. The clothes he materialized didn't begin to compensate for the consequences of over an hour of exertion in a forty-degree sea. Grinding his teeth together to keep them from chattering, he faced his younger brother Eurus, Supreme God of the East Wind and Harbinger of Misfortune. Evil in a pair of $900 dress shoes. Zeph ignored the comment intended to pluck at his guilt and rile him up. "You have no business here, Eurus. Leave. I don't have anything to say to you."

Standing on the shore in his I'm-dark-and-mysterious black leather getup, Eurus stared across the water through the black wraparound sunglasses he always wore. His lips twitched. "Be that as it may, I have something to say to you." He turned away from the drama unfolding across the inlet and faced Zeph, but didn't speak.

Striking a careful indifference as emergency vehicles poured into the marina parking lot, Zeph glared at his brother. He'd paid his debt to Eurus, and then some. Not that Zeph truly believed he owed that fucker anything, but he'd wanted to make nice, keep the peace. Problem was, Eurus didn't agree. And never would. "For the love of the gods, Eurus. What do you want? I'm freezing and don't want to stand here arguing with you."

Eurus laced his hands behind his back. "Fine. I'll get right to the point. I plan to submit a petition."

Gods, he hated how Eurus made everything so damn dramatic. "About?"

"I will propose that, lest you beget an heir by the end of your season, my son Alastor be installed as your heir." Zeph gaped as Eurus plowed on. "Only Boreas and I have addressed issues of succession." He shook his head and tsked. "And it's very dangerous, Zephyros. Very dangerous indeed not to have an heir in place."

Maybe Zeph's ears were frozen and the words had gotten garbled. No way his brother had just proposed— "You can't be serious."

Eurus arched an eyebrow.

"You're out of your mind." As if that wasn't stating the obvious. "A god of the East could never do the job of a god of the West." Not to mention the fact Alastor was a complete recluse and, more importantly, Zeph would never trust anyone of Eurus's line with…anything.

"Alastor could."

Zeph turned away and climbed the rest of the way up the embankment. "Whatever. I'll get around to having an heir when I'm good and goddamned ready." When that might be, he had no idea. After all, someone had to stick around long enough first. "Besides, Father would never approve an eastern god as the heir of my line."

"He would if he had the blood of spring in his veins."

Going stock still, Zeph heaved a breath. Icy fingers crawled up his spine. He schooled his expression and turned on his brother. Glared, but kept his mouth shut.

Eurus's smug expression went glacial. "Oh, come now. I know you want me to explain."

Despite the way his skin crawled and his gut squeezed, he'd freeze out here before giving Eurus the satisfaction of asking.

Leaning forward, a smile that could only be described as wicked curled the edges of Eurus's lips. "Your *wife*, Chloris," he sneered, voice dark and satisfied. Then he was gone.

The words cut through the air and crashed into Zeph so hard he couldn't breathe.

CHAPTER THREE

Words disconnected from meaning. Sounds out of context. Numbness like floating. And always the darkness.

Sometimes she surfaced. Nauseating light played behind eyelids she couldn't force open. Shooting pain accompanied the smallest shift in her position. A world-spinning ache throbbed beneath her face and ear. An odd, distant keening sounded in those moments, bringing a rush of relief through her veins that would pull her under into merciful oblivion once more.

Consciousness returned in the quiet of night. Ella blinked her dry, crusty eyes again and again. The dim room took shape before her. Sage-green walls. A mounted television. A movable tray. Gentle, rhythmic beeps entered her consciousness. Rolling her head just a little, she found the source of the sound. Monitors and medicine drips on metal stands lined the side of her bed. A hospital, then.

She opened her mouth, but knew instinctively she wouldn't be able to talk. Her tongue lay thick and unused. Her lips burned with dryness. She tried to lick them.

"Here. Take a sip."

Her gaze tracked the new sound, setting off a wave of dizziness. Her lips found the straw first, held right where she could reach it. She sucked the life-giving water into her mouth. It was the best thing she had ever tasted. She could've cried.

"Welcome back," the deep voice said.

Ella had almost forgotten someone was there. She released the straw and with effort made herself look up.

The nurse stood next to the side of her bed. She blinked and squinted. Focus slowly returned. He towered above her. His hair was short and dark, unruly curls just at the ends. Close-trimmed facial hair set off an angled jaw and lips pressed in a concerned line.

"More?"

She frowned. The straw stroked her bottom lip. She opened, eagerly drank more of the water. Her throat rejoiced.

"Thank you," she mouthed, no sound emerging.

"Don't try to speak. Just rest. And be well."

She sighed. And slipped into nothingness.

In the early morning gloom, she awoke again. A man, all broad shoulders, stared out through the slats in the blinds. Green scrubs. Her nurse again?

"Water," she croaked.

He was at her side so fast, she must've blinked. A couple of times. She hadn't seen him move.

This time when she offered her thanks, she could manage a rasping whisper.

His lips curved up, the smallest bit. "You're welcome." Intense slate-blue eyes stared down at her. "How are you feeling?"

"Dunno." She licked her lips. "What happened?"

His brow furrowed. "You don't remember?"

She closed her eyes and concentrated. A lump formed in her throat and swelled. "Marcus." Flashing images of a ferocious storm joined the memory of her brother. "Dead." She swallowed hard, the sound thick and tortured in her own ears.

"He died?"

Something in his voice begged her attention. She blinked up at him. He'd gone totally still next to her, his expression grave and alarmed. Ella frowned. "Yeah."

"When this happened to you?"

She opened and closed her mouth. The hair on her arms raised, the air taking on a warm, electrical quality. Obviously, some good drugs dripped into her veins. Still, his intensity did seem weird. Why was he so upset?

He grasped her hand. "Ella, did he die when this happened to you?"

Her gaze fell to his engulfing grip on her fingers. So warm. Her skin tingled where they touched.

The big man leaned across the path of her vision to capture her attention. "Gods, woman, answer me."

Her head swam. From the effort of remembering the question. From exhaustion. From the roiling power behind his piercing blue eyes. She shook her head once. "No, not then."

His whole body sagged. The air in the room cooled and calmed. He stood up and turned away, lacing his hands on top of his head. Ella missed the warm connection immediately, but was equally consumed with watching him. For a moment, he muttered and paced along the length of her bed, roughly scrubbing his palms over his face. He had the slightest sprinkling of gray at his temples.

His every movement radiated power. The green scrubs

pulled across the muscles of his shoulders, back, and thighs with each step. His very presence took up the whole side of the room in which he paced. He exuded a raw masculinity her body recognized, even if she was in absolutely no position to respond to it.

"You okay?" she scratched out.

He whirled on her, eyes guarded, muscles tense.

The movement was so unexpected, she gasped. Her heart raced, unleashing a series of throbs in her shoulder, neck, and head. She groaned.

"Damn it!" he bit out. He rushed to her and pushed a button on the side of the bed. A big hand smoothed over her forehead. "I'm sorry."

Ella's eyes clenched shut against the pounding torment rooting itself behind her eye and ear. But his touch helped. How amazing the power of human touch.

Then it was gone.

Her gaze scanned the room. Empty. A ball of panic bloomed in her gut. Where had he gone? And why had he left?

The door to her room pushed open and a woman with brown skin and pink scrubs breezed in. "Well, welcome back, Ms. Raines. It's good to see you awake."

Ella could only manage a drawn-out moan. The nurse was pretty, her smile open, and she wore her black hair in a curly natural style. The woman made pleasant small talk with her while she checked her vitals and entered her findings into a computer on a swivel stand.

"Don't you worry, now, we'll get you feeling better in no time. Can you tell me your pain level on a scale of one to ten, with ten the worst pain of your life and one pain-free?"

Licking her lips again and forcing herself to focus, Ella

considered the question. How did one judge pain? Her shoulder was a good solid six. The throb vibrating through her skull, a seven. But her heart, oh, her heart might never recover. A ten for sure. But Ella supposed that wasn't the kind of pain the nurse was asking her to describe. "Maybe a seven," she rasped.

"Okay, honey. Let's see what we can do about that." The woman inserted a needle into the IV. Cool solace slid into her veins and tugged at Ella's consciousness. She almost gave in, before she thought to ask. "The man? The male nurse?" she slurred.

The woman smiled and shook her head. "Musta been a good dream. Only us ladies on this unit." She went right on, explaining procedures to Ella in case she needed anything, but Ella's attention drifted away, stolen by the pain medication and the memory of a man who didn't exist.

ℝ℞℟

Zephyros hovered outside the woman's hospital window, a moth to a flame. He couldn't explain it, but every effort to leave her since the ambulance crew had carried her off the boat throbbed deep in his chest until he nearly suffocated.

He was just so damned drained. Guilt over hurting her sat like a weight on his chest. Being immersed in freezing water all that time had weakened him to the point he should've returned to the Realm of the Gods to be restored. And, if those weren't enough, Eurus's lie about Chloris, Zeph's ex-wife and the first woman he'd ever loved, picked at his brain until he'd driven himself nearly crazy worrying holes into the ridiculous story. Just more of Eurus causing chaos. Had to be. And damn if it hadn't worked.

Still, he'd have to talk to Father about whatever scheme his brother had in the works.

Zeph's gaze scanned over the woman sleeping in her bed. The conversation with his father could wait. He just wanted… what? To see her conscious. To know she'd be okay. So he waited. Part of him believed he'd be able to leave when her family showed up. Even if he couldn't see her awake, he could at least stay until those who would take care of her arrived.

Three days passed.

And she hadn't awakened.

And no one had come for her.

So Zephyros stayed. He refused to leave her alone, even if she didn't know he was there. He'd caused this, and he wanted to make it right. Though he couldn't do a true healing in such a public place, he infused what energy he could into the air of her room, directing it to surround and ease her.

But it wasn't enough, not nearly enough. His uselessness roiled in his gut, squeezed his heart.

Damn it, he should've returned to the Realm of the Gods after his nephew's anniversary party last week. Even as he'd hovered on the fringes of the partygoers, grief and loneliness had him grinding his teeth to keep his turmoil to himself. Never should he have come into the human realm feeling that way. Clearly, he'd had no business being among mortals.

For that matter, how he'd thought an anniversary party would've been anything other than salt in his ancient wounds, he had no idea. He was pleased Boreas's son, Owen, had found his happiness after so long. The god deserved it and his wife, Megan, was completely worthy of him—Zeph saw that the first time they met. But he couldn't handle stepping inside someone else's happily-ever-after, especially when he'd never have one himself.

So he'd raged.

And this woman had paid the price for his torment. Ella, he'd heard the nurses say. Just thinking the name calmed him.

Lingering around the hospital for three days, elemental during the busier daytimes, more often human during the quieter nights, Zephyros had studied the woman, wondered about her. He'd overheard the nurses say she had no family, no husband. How was that possible? Even bruised and battered, with tubes and wires and monitors crisscrossing her body, her youth and beauty shined through. With her eyes wide in her face, dark circles beneath, and bottom lip fuller than the top, hers wasn't a conventional beauty, but it appealed to him, made him want to know more. How one such as her could be all alone in the world, he simply couldn't fathom. Or maybe it was just that he didn't want to, that imagining what caused her solitude just might make him examine the reasons behind his own.

When she'd finally awakened, he'd been torn. Her emergence from unconsciousness should have freed him to depart. But he found it oddly appealing to take care of her, to bring her a drink or hold her hand. His whole existence was about bringing life and marshaling the rebirth of nature after winter's slumber, and yet those small acts in the dark of a hospital room somehow felt more meaningful.

And then she'd asked him if he was okay. When was the last time someone had expressed care for him instead of contempt? Instead of betrayal? So unexpected, the two words had jolted his heart. Blanketed him for a long moment in a rare sensation of peace.

All of this explained why, three days into the very season his lineage fated him to usher in and oversee, Zephyros, the

Supreme God of Spring, Master of the West Wind, found himself haunting a human hospital, standing watch over a mortal woman.

When the female nurse left the room, Zephyros sighed and snaked through the gap in the window frame. Each hour, nurses came in to do routine checks, until finally Ella's eyes blinked open in the late afternoon. Her awakening heralded a parade of hospital personnel through the room. A doctor gave her a thorough exam. A nurse removed various tubes her conscious state no longer required. A nutritional aide delivered a plastic tray of covered food.

Ella eyed the food and licked her lips. The aide positioned Ella so she could reach everything, and removed all the lids and covers since Ella only had one useful hand. Her right arm, injured somehow in the storm, sat immobilized in a sling. Zephyros grimaced at the watered-down sauce covering limp pasta noodles, but his bigger reaction was an intense desire to feed her from his own hand, to provide her the nourishment that would return her to health. Regardless, she ate with gusto like, well, like a woman who hadn't eaten solid food in three days. When everything was gone except a container of lime Jell-O, she wiped her mouth, pushed the tray away, and dropped her head back against the pillows.

"Bet you think this is hilarious, don't you?"

Zephyros's disembodied gaze cut to her, startled at her speech though there was no way she could know he was there.

"I can just hear you, going on and on about how this is proof positive you're such a better sailor than I am." She chuckled ruefully and shook her head. "But I'm still not the one who took out a whole section of dock. I don't care if you were sixteen." The smile dropped from her face. Her breathing hitched. "I brought her back, though, Marcus. Somehow I got her back to the marina."

Zephyros frowned at the mention of the man's name, but couldn't deny he was mesmerized by her words and the expressiveness of her face. When she fell asleep again, he stayed. Not because he had to, or felt he should. But because he wanted to. It probably wasn't in his best interest—and certainly it wasn't in hers—but where else did he have to be, anyway?

CHAPTER FOUR

Two mornings later, Ella woke to the smell of pancakes and sausage and the chatter of Janet, one of the friendlier nurses. The heaviest fog of pain and drugs had finally lifted from her brain, though she still felt a bit slow, a bit disconnected from reality. As the nurse took her vitals and spoke, the only words Ella really seemed to hear were "released later today."

"Today?" Ella asked, her voice sounding more like itself.

"Yep," Janet said with a smile. "Doctor has to check you out, and you have a PT consult, but we should be able to get you out of here later this afternoon." The nurse raised the back of the bed and rolled the food tray closer.

Ella cooperated as the woman resituated the pillows to help her up, being very careful to move her right arm as little as possible. A spot of bright color caught her attention from the corner of her eye. Flowers. An enormous arrangement of springtime blooms of every color sat on the windowsill. "Where did those come from?"

Janet glanced over her shoulder and smiled. "I don't know,

but they sure are beautiful, aren't they? Florist left them at the reception desk without a card, but no one noticed until after the delivery man was gone."

Ella stared at the gorgeous bouquet. A rush of warmth flooded her chest. For the life of her she couldn't imagine who they'd be from. And how sad was that? Still, they were stunning, and proof that someone had thought of her, even if she didn't know who.

Janet looked at her. "Doctor's gonna want to know if you have someone who can take you home, stay with you for a few days. Just to be on the safe side. You didn't have any ID on you when you came in, so we only had the name and information the marina provided the EMTs. They said you didn't have any family here, and we didn't have any way of contacting anyone."

Ella nodded, wondering which of her longtime buddies had found her on the *True Blue*. She wasn't looking forward to facing him, whoever he was. "I'll have to take a cab home, but if I can make a call, I have someone who I can arrange to come stay with me. Would that work?"

The nurse frowned for a minute, but finally said, "Should. Go ahead and make your call, though, and get those arrangements set up. You really ought to have someone with you." She moved the room phone to the tray next to Ella's breakfast.

"Thanks," Ella said as she picked up her fork. "I'll call right after I eat. I'm *starving*."

"An appetite's a good sign." Janet smiled and left.

Ella groaned and the fork sagged in her hand. She had no one to call. Parents were gone. Marcus was gone. Craig…she scoffed…no way she'd ask him for help. Not after everything. Among her friends, most lived an hour away in D.C. and had families and jobs of their own they wouldn't be able to walk away from to come play nursemaid. Not to mention, she had no desire to see the pity in their eyes, to watch them tiptoe around all the landmines in her life.

No thanks.

She'd be fine. What choice did she have? She'd been one of two her whole life, literally, now she needed to go it alone. If everybody else could do it, so could she.

Resolved, Ella pressed the edge of her fork into the pancake. It slipped, splattering syrup onto the tray. "Damn!" She cleaned up the spill, but couldn't wipe all the stickiness off the fork handle. Cutting pancakes one-handed with your weak hand was a lot more difficult than it seemed. She sighed and attempted it again and again until she finally managed to free a few mangled bites. Giving up on cutting her food, she speared the whole sausage patty with her fork and ate it that way. She shoved the rest of the tray away.

She wanted to sleep, but found she couldn't get her mind to stop churning. Every worry demanded airtime in her thoughts until she simply itched to get the hell out of there.

Maybe getting out of bed would help. Ella threw the light covers back and shifted one leg at a time over the edge. Keeping her immobilized right arm against her chest, Ella held onto the bed with her left hand and rose to her feet. Her back muscles ached and her head swooned, but she kept herself upright as she shuffled to the bathroom door and flicked on the light.

Her gaze went immediately to the mirror and the horror show that was her appearance. "Holy shit," she murmured. The whole right side of her face was swollen and bruised from cheekbone to eye. She had a nice gash on her cheek with three—she leaned in closer—no, four stitches. Her lips looked like she could use a whole tube of Chapstick and never get them soft again. And that wasn't even mentioning her limp, messy hair or the dark circles under her brown eyes. The latter she couldn't really blame on the accident.

Relief flooded through her when the doctor arrived a little before noon. She was ready to be back in her own bed. Well, it wasn't really hers, but as close as she had, right now…

"I see Janet left a note in the chart that you were making arrangements for company at home for a few days." He looked up from the computer where he'd been entering findings from examining her.

"Oh, uh, yeah. Yes, I did. My, uh, a friend from D.C. will be over after work tonight. She's going to stay with me a few days at least. She can telecommute, so it works out good."

The doctor, an older man with a kind face and bushy eyebrows, nodded and smiled. "Good to hear. We'll get you out of here as soon as the physical therapist can see you. In the meantime, a nurse will be in to go over your discharge instructions. You should follow up with your regular physician within forty-eight hours, and don't hesitate to call the number on the discharge paperwork if anything worsens."

A nurse came in just as the doctor left, a sheaf of paper in hand. In addition to the home-care instructions for her injuries, Ella also received a bundle of forms from admissions and billing. Normal people had loved ones who could take care of those things when you arrived in the ER, but, of course, she wasn't normal. Not in that way, at least. And she couldn't even use filling out the forms as a means of busying her hands and mind, because her right hand was largely immobilized and her left hand produced scrawl no better than a kindergartener. She set the paperwork aside.

In the afternoon, a gentle rain shower pattered against the window. The relaxing sound made her sleepy, so of course the physical therapist finally chose that moment to make an appearance. A young guy with far too much pep for her current mood delivered the disturbing news that she was going to have to use her injured shoulder and begin therapy right away. The ripping sensations that shuddered through her right side as he examined her nonexistent range of motion made his order seem frankly ludicrous, but injured muscles and ligaments apparently couldn't sit idle too long without causing other problems down the line.

Begrudgingly, Ella agreed to the regimen he laid out before her and accepted the referral to a physical therapist who could see her day after tomorrow. Even without the sling, she found herself cradling her arm under her breasts.

As the therapist departed, a nurse breezed in and settled a bundle of fabric on the foot of the bed. "They cut your jacket and top off when you came in the ER, so here's a fresh set of scrubs. How 'bout I help you into them?"

"No, that's okay," came Ella's knee-jerk reaction.

The woman arched an eyebrow. "I wouldn't risk your shoulder by attempting this yourself right now."

"Oh, right. Guess I wasn't thinking."

"No worries, hon."

Dressing was a torturous affair. Clearly, she'd be wearing a lot of button-up shirts for a while. She couldn't have gotten the top over her head alone if she'd tried all day. She chuckled when she wondered how she would get it off again, but couldn't share her thoughts with the nurse, who was under the false impression she'd have help at home this evening. Guess she'd cross that bridge when she came to it.

After sitting around all day, her departure from the hospital went comparatively quickly. An orderly wheeled her from her room, through the front lobby, and out to the circular drive, while a second man carried her bag of personal items and flowers. A taxi already waited, so with the men's assistance, she slipped from one seat right into the other. The gentle drumming of the rain and the rhythmic thump of the windshield wipers filled the silence as she stared out the window.

The driver took her the back way to home. Down the busy strip of West Street, past fast food restaurants and car dealerships, to the historic part of Annapolis. At Church Circle, he veered right, then right again to head down the hill toward Eastport, her neighborhood that was really its own separate enclave within the town. Over the drawbridge they went, the metal surface a loud *whirr* under the tires, and Ella's gaze couldn't help but be drawn to the masts clustered together everywhere along the shorelines. A pang squeezed her chest when she thought about *True Blue*. She didn't know her condition. And, likely, it would be a few days before she was up to checking her out.

A few quick turns later, the driver pulled up in front of the little yellow cottage that had been her brother's home for the past three years. Now it was hers.

She dug into the bag with her ruined clothes and found her keys zipped into a side pocket of her windbreaker. Thank God. The cabbie carried Ella's things to the front porch and waited while she ducked inside and grabbed some money. Ella threw a few extra dollars in when the older man offered to bring the flowers to her coffee table. It wasn't like she could lift the heavy vase, and she'd become rather fond of them. So she agreed. The driver took the money with a smile and a "good-night," and then Ella was all alone.

For the first time in the almost two months she'd resided here, she was truly alone. Marcus wasn't here any longer. Not even in the form of his ashes. She didn't even have the urn—

She shuffled over to her bag and yanked her tattered jacket onto the coffee table. Holding her breath, she grasped her right pocket. Sure enough... She grinned so wide it hurt her chapped lips. Somehow, the urn's lid had stayed in her pocket through everything. With a groan, Ella reached up and settled the brass cover on the mantel. It was stupid, really, but having it there made her feel better. She could almost imagine she wasn't alone.

Moving like an eighty-year-old, Ella grabbed a drink from the fridge and wandered around enough to turn on a few lights and her iPod. The light and music filled the house, feeling like company on the cold, rainy night. Her evening consisted of a dinner of chicken noodle soup at the table and reading the last few days' newspapers that had piled up on the front porch, and even that was more than she probably should've done. When her eyelids drooped, Ella left her dinner mess for the morning and retreated slowly through the house, turning everything off on the way to the upstairs bathroom.

Once there, the idea of bathing took root, and sounded so delicious she gave in despite her exhaustion. What she really wanted was a shower, but her bandages made that impossible. She filled the tub with warm water, then turned to undress. No way she was getting her top off. Not by herself. She dug into a drawer and found a pair of scissors. Careful to hold the material out from her skin, Ella cut the shirt from V-neck to hemline and gingerly slipped it off her shoulders.

Washing her long hair one-handed proved a frustrating

task, but she felt so much better when she was done she could hardly regret it. The water was warm and soothing, luring her to doze off. In the quiet stillness, she had the strangest sensation she wasn't alone, but knew it was just the wishful thinking of her grief playing tricks on her. She sighed and pulled the plug with her toes before she really did fall asleep.

As she stumbled into her bedroom afterward, Ella decided to skip the bother of trying to get a shirt on. Instead, she simply slid under the thick pile of covers. Cold at first, they warmed quickly. She arranged the pillows as the nurse had suggested to keep from rolling onto her right side. Achy as her shoulder was, though, Ella was pretty sure even the slightest movement in that direction would wake her right back up.

Her body melted into the inviting comfort of the big bed. She lingered for long moments right at the cusp of unconsciousness. A smile tugged at the corner of her mouth.

"I feel you watching over me. Thank you for being here. I love you," she murmured, thoughts of her dead twin the last she had before finally drifting off to sleep.

CHAPTER FIVE

Zephyros stood, stunned.

He was ancient. He was immortal. He was a god. Yet this slip of a mortal woman pulled the ground out from under him over and over again. And she didn't even know he was there.

Or maybe she did?

Every time he convinced himself to go, she said or did something that intrigued him. Or, worse, concerned him, and he'd find himself negotiating for just a little more time. Her pleased reaction to his flowers, her lie to the doctor and nurses, her pain at seeing her own reflection, at having that young doctor poke and prod her ruined shoulder. He couldn't leave.

In truth, he didn't want to.

His interest was stupid—and dangerous—but how many other times had he ignored the warning signs and plowed straight ahead? What his brothers said about him was true. He was apparently hardwired to fall, and fall hard. He couldn't help it, though. Something to do with the interconnectedness of love and life and all that bullshit. Fat lot of good it had done him.

And then, as if each of those earlier moments hadn't intrigued him enough, her words as she fell asleep nailed his feet to the floor. Did she really feel his presence? Surely, her expression of love wasn't intended for him. But he was here, even if only in his elemental form, and he was real. And he was, in fact, very much watching over her.

As compelling as all of those reasons were, they paled in comparison to the one that kept him rooted to her side since she'd fully regained consciousness. When he was in her presence, a fundamental sensation of peace flowed through him. The first time he'd felt it, he'd nearly gone to his knees in sheer relief and surprise. For long, wondrous moments, the ancient pain and sadness and humiliation lifted. Sheer ease of heart, mind, and body surged through every molecule of his being. He couldn't fathom an explanation, but the fact it kept happening when he was in her presence quite clearly meant it had something to do with her.

He had to learn more. And, in the meantime, he had to soak in every iota of her life-giving energy. It had been eons since he'd felt anything like it, and who knew when he would again. Maybe never. Definitely never.

But as the night passed and Ella slept, Zephyros resolved to right what he had wronged once and for all, before any further damage was incurred, before she became any more interesting. Now that she was at home, he had enough privacy to heal her, and then he would depart from this situation. Difficult though it would be to leave whatever it was about her that soothed him, he certainly couldn't lurk around the edges of her life for however much of it she had left.

In the morning, he'd do a full healing and settle his debt.

Until then, he could give her something. Enough to get her through the night peacefully. He held his right palm up before him. The healing energy manifested in a diffuse ball and Zeph released it, sending a part of himself to surround and cover her in a blanket of soft, ambient light. The tight dip of her eyebrows eased, relaxed. Unfamiliar satisfaction snaked through his chest in a ribbon of warmth.

He sank into a large, overstuffed chair in the corner of the room. Head reclined against the soft cushion and hands clasped over his chest, he let himself soak in her influence and rest. In truth, he was weary. Just tired and drained and weighted down. But, even without her mysterious power, taking care of Ella in the smallest ways lifted a bit of that weight, made him feel lighter, buoyed. Useful. Good.

Good enough.

Well, maybe that one was a stretch.

Zephyros smiled ruefully and shook his head. Some things never changed.

ಋೞ

Ella stretched as the gray morning light finally drew her into consciousness. The uninterrupted night of sleep had been so wonderful. To be sure, her shoulder throbbed with a stiff, hot ache, and her head pounded all down the right side, but for all that, she still felt about a thousand times better than last night. The full night's rest left her feeling like someone had topped off her gas tank. And, miraculously, no dreams had intruded on her peacefulness. No terrifying thunderstorms, no gasping awake at the image of *True Blue* descending beneath the waves, no hauntingly desperate and ceaselessly fruitless searches for Marcus, no mortifying confessions from Craig, only to wake up again and realize it had only been a nightmare. A nightmare based on reality, anyway. Weren't they all.

Easing up on her good elbow, Ella yawned and opened her eyes.

She inhaled a hard breath that almost choked her. And then she screamed.

A man sat in the dark corner of her room.

At her alarm, he flew to his feet, shoulders hunched, fists clenched, as if braced for battle. His gaze cut to her and the scream died in her throat. From where he stood in the shadows, his eyes glowed. She could swear they did. The odd blue light swept over her body, stole her very breath. Her flight instinct roared to life, but his presence paralyzed her. Not to mention her body wasn't much capable of sudden movements at the moment.

"Who are you?" She shook her head. "What do you want?"

He held out his hands, relaxed the slightest bit. "Ella—"

She gasped. He knew her name. "How do you…"

The man stepped toward the foot of the bed, into the dim morning light. "Be well. I mean you no harm."

"You!" Ella gaped at the male nurse from the hospital. Well, apparently not a nurse, given what the *real* nurse had said. "You were in my room!"

He nodded, hands still up in an unsuccessful gesture of reassurance. "Yes."

"What do you want from me? Why are you here?" *Did he follow me? How did he even get in?* Ella's mind formed new questions faster than she could ask them.

"I will explain everything. Just don't upset yourself."

"Upset myself? You're in my house. You're sitting there…

what, watching me sleep? Please...please leave. I promise I won't tell anyone." Oh, God, and she was naked under these covers. Her gaze dropped to her lap. "I didn't get a good look at you. It's still too dark in here and I was too loopy at the hospital. Please, please just go."

"I promise I have no intention of hurting you. In fact, just the opposite."

Ella shook her head. Craziness. This was utter craziness. "Look, mister, I don't know who you are, but you have to go. My"—she forced normalcy into her voice—"husband will be home from a trip early this morning. Get out now while you can still put this behind you."

The man slowly stepped around the foot of the bed and settled onto the corner of the mattress. Ella's heart took up root in her throat, making it hard to breathe, to swallow. He clasped his big hands on a muscled thigh. Damn, why was she noticing these things? Who cared if he was handsome. Gorgeous, even. He was totally crazytrain, and he was in her house.

"Ella, I know you have no husband. And I promise you, it's okay. If you'll just let me explain."

His expression of false concern threatened to lure her in. Not taking care to avoid her arm, Ella scrabbled back on the bed until her spine met the headboard. She clutched the sheet's edge to her neck. Adrenaline flooded her system, provided a cushion against the pain, but she was going to pay for her reckless movements later. If she had a later. *Please, God, let there be a later.*

He reached out a hand. "Don't! You'll hurt yourself. Damn it, Ella, listen to me!" His voice echoed around the room, deep and resonant.

She couldn't restrain the whimper his shout unleashed, so unexpected after the calm tones he'd used earlier to create a false sense of safety. Pulse pounding in her ears, her gaze skittered around the room, looking for something that could serve as a weapon. Something on her side of the room she could get to first. Something she could lift and swing with one hand. In her mind's eye, she saw Marcus's lacrosse stick in the utility room and nearly groaned in desire of it.

His extended hand dropped to the bed. The man sighed, a loud, troubled sound, and shook his head. "I'm messing this up. I'm sorry. This wasn't how I should've gone about this. I see that now. But if you'll just give me five minutes to explain. I wanted only to help you. And then I'll leave."

Trapped against the headboard, trembling from adrenaline and barely suppressed pain, Ella stared at him. Man, she must be a complete sucker, because something about the defeated set of his broad shoulders had her almost agreeing. His eyes pleaded with her. She found him hard to look at. Everything about him was physically beautiful in a totally powerful, masculine way, but that didn't keep him from exuding a hurt that resonated somewhere deep in her chest. She recognized the aura of pain and loneliness that surrounded him.

She shook her head. This was such a monumentally bad idea. But, really, what choice did she have? Meeting his observing eyes, she said, "Five minutes."

He sat up straighter and nodded. His shoulders eased beneath a dark gray T-shirt pulled taut across his chest and around his biceps. "I'm sorry for what happened to you."

"Uh, okay. Thank you?" There went her hope he'd get right to the point.

"Gods, I don't know what I'm doing." He shifted away,

leaned his elbows on his knees, and dropped his head into his hands. Ella watched him for a long moment. The scared side of her almost snarked that time was a-ticking, but something held her back. The thought to wrap an arm around his bent shoulders, to offer comfort, was just the same urge anyone would have when witnessing someone hurt or upset. Right? But what did *he* have to be upset about? She was the one who woke up to a stranger watching over her.

Watching over her. The hair raised on the back of her neck. A feeling like déjà vu had her frowning and trying to figure out the cause of the odd, niggling sensation.

She sucked in a breath. Last night. "Oh, my god." The tension in her muscles was sapping her strength. As the initial rush of adrenaline wore off, the freshness of her injuries made its presence known with the force of a jackhammer. She couldn't control her body's shaking. "You…you were here last night."

He lifted his head and laced his hands where they hung between his knees. "Yes."

Ella's mouth went dry. The weirdness of the situation ratcheted up her alarm. A single tear spilled down her cheek. Through everything that had happened to her—her parents' deaths, her inability to conceive, Craig's betrayal, the stroke that stole her brother in the middle of the night—she had never once wished for an end to it all. And she sure as hell didn't want to die, now, not after she'd survived all that.

The man rose, hesitated for just a moment, then stalked around the bottom of the bed toward the side on which she huddled. His movement opened up a direct shot to the door to the hallway.

Ella bolted.

Nakedness be damned, she scrabbled across the mattress and flew to the floor. Her foot slipped and she went down to one knee, but she forced herself to ignore the bone-shattering agony and keep moving. She cursed her habit of sleeping with the door closed, even when she was alone in the house. Obviously, that wasn't the case, was it? If she survived this, she'd start locking the damn thing, too.

Without thinking, she reached out with her right arm, grasped the knob, and flung the door open. Lancing pain tore through her from shoulder blade to fingertips. White spots danced behind her eyes and a cold, tingling sweat broke out across her naked body. Oh, no, no. She was going to faint. She shook her head, attempting to defy unconsciousness's grasp. Swayed. Crashed into the hall wall, knocking a picture frame to the floor in a spray of glass.

Warmth wrapped around her belly, supported her, cradled her. A soft shushing sounded in her ear. Embraced by the man and the fog of pain, Ella surrendered.

Her feet left the floor. He folded her body in his arms and tucked her against his broad chest. She felt almost sheltered, and a tingling warmth infused her wherever his skin touched hers. Forcing her eyelids open, she finally focused and found the hard angle of the man's jaw. He looked ahead, toward wherever he was carrying her.

"What's your name?" she whispered, wanting to know all the details of her demise, including at whose hands it would occur. She was getting to see death barreling at her in a way Marcus never did. She wondered which was better—obliviousness or awareness.

Blue eyes cut down to her face and stayed there. "Zephyros Martius," he said in a deep rumble.

She tried to repeat what he'd said, but she wasn't sure she heard him right. "Zeph," she managed finally.

He stopped and gently settled her back on the bed. Soft cotton fell across her skin, covering her.

Her lethargic brain churned, processed the significance of his actions. He'd kept her from falling, carried her back to bed, shielded her nudity from his gaze, his touch. Someone who meant her harm wouldn't do that, would he?

"Who are you?" she rasped.

He smoothed a big hand up her forehead and back over her hair. "I am the one who can take the hurt away."

CHAPTER SIX

Restrained power made Zephyros's hands tremble. At first, he'd wanted to help Ella because he owed it to her. Now, *want* bloomed into *need*. When he'd held her soft curves, the strength of her life force soaked into him. Seldom did he have any cause to interact with humans, let alone touch them, but the soft yellow aura that surrounded her body told him this woman was good, pure, true. A rare character, in his experience.

And then she'd said his name. Whispered it, really, but that didn't keep him from fully enjoying the way her lips wrapped around the sound.

Silently, he summoned the ancient, elemental power, the one that flowed through him, that made him what he was. His palms warmed. Soft white light spilled from between his clasped hands.

Ella's eyes cut to his glowing hands, went wide. "What? Don't hurt…" She swallowed thickly. A tear leaked down her temple into her hair.

He met Ella's barely focused gaze. "Fear not, I promise to

hurt you no more."

Her only answer was a shiver that racked her whole body.

Normally, a healing of this magnitude required sacrifice. It was how the gods worked. *Quid pro quo*, and all that. But, in this case, Ella's case, that was hardly appropriate. After all, she wouldn't need to be healed if he'd kept better control of himself.

Words in his native tongue spilled into the quiet of the room. He parted his hands, held them over her prone form, and let the healing energy cover her. The pale, white glow infused her aura, which absorbed the curative force, distributed small doses of it throughout her body.

Ella sucked in a breath.

"Be well, now," Zeph whispered, knowing from experience the surprising jolt one felt when this process first began. At least, he assumed it was the same for humans.

He focused first on her shoulder, sensing her greatest pain and damage centered there. While he didn't need to touch her for the magic to work, he couldn't resist letting his fingers skim the small patch of bare skin just above the bandages. Passing over the joint once, twice, three times, Zeph finally felt the restoration of the tissues' health. The pain and damage left her body and entered his. He gritted his teeth against the agonizing sensations. Then, slowly, they passed from him and into the nothingness. Gently, he removed the bandages, wanting to see the effects of his labors. The skin beneath was unblemished and whole. He caressed her again, just to be sure, just to feel a bit of connection.

Zeph focused next on the injuries to her face. Alarm threatened as he sensed the hematoma under her ear, but dispelling it was an easy matter. The cuts on her eyebrow and cheek bone knit together, then the bruises faded, revealing the full extent of her beauty. That Zeph had ever been responsible for marring something so exquisite twisted his gut, but he forced the feeling away. Focused. There'd be plenty of time for guilt trips later.

He let his fingers drag over her cracked lips. The sore-looking dryness gave way to a healthy, plump softness. He clenched his teeth, resisting the way even the slightest touches of her body made him feel. The yellow of her aura flared, intensified, pumping that pain-relieving peace into his soul once again. His gaze cut to hers and found her eyes filled with wonder and bewilderment. She looked at him and the corner of her lip quirked up. His chest swelled. Oh, how pitiable that the smallest morsel of kindness or friendliness affected him that way. For a god, he was truly pathetic.

No wonder no one wanted him.

Breathing her calming influence into him, he pushed the tormenting thought away. As her pain decreased, the field of energy around her strengthened. He swayed at its goodness, a balm to his long-battered soul. Leaving was going to be its own torture, but at least he'd always have the memory of this feeling. It was more than he'd had in a long, long time.

He shook his head and looked away from her observation. His hands cast the energy over the rest of her, focusing on the injuries he'd seen on her, dealing with bruises here and lacerations there. Lifting the pain out of her, into him, through him. He paused over the knee she'd fractured, he now realized, when she fell from the bed. Gods, he couldn't even heal her without hurting her, without fucking up.

Well, he'd be gone soon.

The thought rolled his stomach.

He scanned over her one final time, but found nothing. Good as new. Good as before him.

Clenching his fists, he recalled the power, drew it back into himself, and turned away. He didn't want to see the fear or rejection that would surely usher his departure. Not that he deserved anything different. After all, she thought him a stalker, a common criminal. Someday that would be funny.

But not today.

A few fatigued steps led him to look out the window into her backyard. Early morning sunlight sprinkled through some tree branches and fell on a garden that ran along a picket fence separating her yard from a neighbor's. At the rear of the yard, a cluster of early spring greenery caught his eye, and he cursed under his breath. Well, if that wasn't a perfect fucking end to all this. From one end of the flower bed to the other, the stiff leaves and unopened blooms of hyacinths poked up through the mulch. Even in the human realm, he couldn't get away from Hy.

If Zeph wasn't a god, he might've thought the gods were laughing at him.

He crossed his arms over his chest and sagged against the window frame. It had been a long time since he'd last used his power to heal, and he'd nearly forgotten the draining effect of it. He focused on a rosebush near the window and directed a burst of energy at it. The bush greened and budded. Brilliant pink petals unfurled into full blooms. There. One last small, good thing, for her.

The sound of shifting bed covers told him Ella had recovered from the healing. He tensed in preparation for the command to leave, which this time he would follow. He breathed in a slow, deep breath, filling himself with her peace, and steeled himself.

"You said your name…was it Zephyr?" came her small, feminine voice.

He turned his head just enough to see Ella from the corner of his eye. She sat on the edge of the bed, blanket clutched around her, watching him. He frowned, confused. "Er, Zephyros."

"Zephyros," she repeated.

He swallowed, hard. When she said his name, this time stronger, clearer, with more certainty, he felt it like an incantation. It made him want to go to her. To fall to his knees between hers.

"It's unusual," she said after a long pause. "Cool, though."

He cocked an eyebrow and directed his gaze fully at her. Her beauty, and the hesitant way she looked at him, set off a longing deep in his chest. Gods, he was such a sucker for the slightest bit of attention. He turned away from the window and faced her. "I'll go now. I'm sorry for the trouble I caused."

Without waiting to be rejected or for her to respond, Zeph crossed the room and entered the hall. Shattered glass from the picture frame glinted in the morning light. Yet another thing he was responsible for ruining. Zeph frowned and flicked his hand, a preternatural wind sweeping the shards into a pile in the corner. He jogged down the hardwood stairs. Each step placed more distance between them and made his insides feel as though they were being torn asunder. So? What was new?

"Wait!"

Footsteps followed behind him. Zeph bit out a curse, wanting to disappear on the spot, blink into his elemental form, but he'd really rather do that without a witness. He crossed the living room, grasped the doorknob, and stopped as a hand settled on his shoulder.

"Please, wait."

Zeph's whole body went rigid. An intoxicating mix of their energies flowed into him where they touched. If he tried, he would be able to sense her from anywhere with the signature of his essence still flowing through her system. This elemental connection made it damn difficult not to turn to her, pull her into his arms. Instead, he heaved a deep breath and commanded his feet to remain planted where they were. Her hand fell away. Zeph nearly groaned from the loss of her warmth, her touch, her energy.

"Please. I don't understand."

He shook his head. "It is not for you to understand," he managed.

"Why not? What does that even mean?"

He debated, fought the urge to face her. But her voice already tugged at him to share himself, and he felt certain he'd never hold out against the mix of her voice and eyes. "Just what I said." He twisted the knob and pulled.

She grabbed his shirt. "Don't go, please? Just…can you just wait a minute?"

Her plea, her aura, their connection—it all let her sneak through his defenses, or what there were of them anyway, and that pissed him off.

He whirled on her and stepped right into her space. "What do you want from me?"

Staring up at him, her lip trembled, but she didn't back down or move away. "Answers."

Oh, was that all? He scoffed and shook his head. "How I healed you."

"Yes."

He clenched and unclenched his fists. "What is it you want to hear, woman?"

"Ella."

"What?"

"I know you know my name. It's Ella."

He closed his eyes and blew out a breath. Some of the fight drained out of him. He was tired and feeling it now that she was cured, now that his purpose here had been fulfilled.

"Are you okay?

His eyes flashed open. Her sincere question glanced right off his chest, sct his heart to beating harder, faster against his sternum. It was the second time she'd asked him that. That made it twice as much as anyone else. In a quiet voice, he said, "That's the question you really want answered?"

She nodded once. "To start."

He couldn't resist the urge to smile, just a little. An hour ago, she'd been hurt, weakened. Now she stood up to him, proved his equal.

No, not his equal. His *better*. It wasn't even a question.

"I will be okay."

She tilted her head. "Does that mean you're not okay now?"

Dangerous hope ballooned within his heart. He narrowed his gaze. Warning bells went off in his gut. It was like she was made for him with how much she appealed to him. Her comforting energy aside, he could easily become addicted to her caring concern, but could he trust she really meant it? His eyes raked over her face, her body. That soft yellow glow remained, proved her guileless nature.

The thought she worried for him dispelled the last of his urge to resist her kindness. Zeph's shoulders went slack. "I am tired," he said simply.

"From what you did, up there?" She thumbed over her shoulder with the hand not holding the blankets closed in front of her.

He forced himself to ignore how easily her lovely body could be revealed and met her concerned stare. "Yes, from that."

Ella looked at him a long moment. An obvious thought process played out across her face. She inhaled a deep breath. "Are you going to hurt me?"

Meeting her eyes, he shook his head. "No."

"Do you have somewhere to go?"

Zeph frowned. "I don't understand—"

"Friends? Family?"

His mouth dropped open. "I...not really, no." While he greatly admired his older brother Boreas, he hated the thought he might be ashamed of him, of all that had happened to him. So Zeph tended to stay away rather than risk seeing disappointment in his eyes. And you could barely get to his youngest brother Chrysander through the throngs of admirers. The attention was totally deserved, though, because Chrys was fun and carefree. The sun personified. But all that feel-good was hard to be around sometimes. As for Eurus, the third-born, Zeph wasn't sure he'd ever felt close to him, and certainly not since they'd come into the full power of their godhoods. And how many eons ago was that?

"Me neither. I don't know about you, but I wouldn't mind a little company. So"—she shrugged—"you could stay, rest here, for a while. If you wanted. And, well, maybe later, we could talk." She shrugged again and the deep red comforter shifted with the movement, hung around her like a robe. The morning sun gleamed off the golden highlights in her light brown hair, which fell in soft waves around her face and over her shoulders.

Zephyros went still on the outside as he processed her invitation, but on the inside, his heart thundered within his chest, his brain erupted in a cacophony of disparate thoughts. She... *wanted* him to stay? After all he'd done?

"Why"—the words stuck in his throat and he had to swallow the lump formed there—"why would you want me to stay? After everything?"

Ella twisted her lips and studied him. "I just...when I look into your eyes, I see something there that reminds me of myself." A slow blush pinked her cheeks, and she ducked her head. "Sounds stupid. But..."

Competing urges made every one of Zeph's muscles go rigid. He wanted to hold her gently for her kindness. To tear that blanket away and kiss her until she yielded to his darkest desires. To flee. This woman seemed to know exactly what to say to get to him. Red flags flapped in his mind. If it wasn't for that beautiful yellow glow around her, he would've bet this kind of too-good-to-be-true setup had his brother written all over it. Eurus just loved to play with Zeph's too-damn-open emotions. Sadistic bastard. And that was no exaggeration. Well, maybe the bastard part. They did share a father, after all.

Ella shuffled and took a step back, away. It was the first time since their doorside conversation began that she'd shown dis-comfort. Zeph frowned and scanned her face, saw the uneasiness there. Realization hit him. He'd been caught up in his own thoughts and hadn't responded. Good gods, he was a misfit. "No," he rushed, "not stupid. Kind." It was all he could manage. Emotion gripped his throat.

A shy smile curved her lips, all pink and soft now. She grasped his hand. "Come on. You rest. Then I'll make us some food later." She led him across the living room and up the stairs. He tugged her to the side as they passed the pile of broken glass, not wanting her to get hurt. Just inside her bedroom, she paused and dropped his hand. "Wait here for a minute."

Zeph watched as she retreated down the hall, blanket dragging behind her, and disappeared into what he knew was the bathroom. The door clicked shut behind her. For a long moment he stood still, debated. His head dropped and he rubbed the heels of his hands into his eyes. He groaned. "Gods," he murmured to himself, "what the hell am I doing?" He should leave. Now.

"Why do you say it that way?"

Zeph's gaze flew up and found Ella leaning against the doorjamb in a long-sleeved T-shirt and a pair of sweats rolled at the ankles. She held a ball of blankets in her arms. His head tilted. "Say what?"

"Gods." She emphasized the 's'.

Observant thing, wasn't she? Consternation made him frown, but her direct gaze challenged him. Dared him to answer. Soon, good humor warmed him, and what a wonderful, long-lost feeling that was. How long since he'd last felt such amusement? He shrugged. Lied. "Habit."

"If you say so." She walked around him to the bed, spread the blanket out. "You rest for a while."

He arched an eyebrow. Now she commanded him?

"Well?" she said, her gaze full of expectation.

Damn it all to Hades, he *was* tired. Weary and exhausted. Some of it was the healing. Most of it was his isolated life these past centuries, not to mention always keeping one eye trained over his shoulder. Even gods had enemies, after all. Plus, the relief his soul felt in her presence put him at such ease inside he felt he could truly heed the restful call of sleep like never before. He ran a hand through his hair and looked at Ella. "Yeah, okay."

The brilliance of her smile lit up the whole room. He basked in it.

Sitting on the edge of his bed, he kicked off his worn boots—a favorite when in human form—and yanked the T-shirt over his head, tossed it to the floor.

A gasp drew his gaze across the room. Ella's cheeks had gone bright red.

"I'll uh, sorry, you rest. I'll go." She turned.

He bit back a smile. That he affected her felt all kinds of good. He wondered how her heated skin would feel against his fingers, would taste against his tongue. "Ella?"

Door nearly closed, she stopped and looked over her shoulder. "Yeah?"

"Thank you."

"Yeah." The door clicked behind her.

Zephyros collapsed against the pillows, tugged the covers over his legs. He debated removing his jeans, but didn't have the energy. Heaving a deep breath, he inhaled the scent of Ella that infused the bedding all around him. He went hard between his legs, making him rethink his decision on the jeans. Almost. The soft cotton was so comfortable, he couldn't move. Didn't want to.

Deep down in his gut, he knew it was a bad idea to stay, to linger in her presence, to accept her hospitality. To enjoy it as much as he did. But he couldn't make himself reject it, either. Why couldn't he have a little peace and companionship? Maybe even a little friendship? At least for a few hours.

So, he'd get some rest, share a meal, and then he'd leave before he got in any deeper.

CHAPTER SEVEN

Ella's head was spinning, but not from the head injury. Because, of course, the odd, beautiful stranger sleeping in her bed had, uh…healed her…with a magic light that shot out of his hands.

Uh huh. That didn't sound crazy and delusional at all.

She shuffled into the kitchen in a bit of a daze. Her hands didn't require concentration to make coffee—she could do that in her sleep. Was it possible she *had* imagined it? Maybe she'd lost consciousness, just as she'd feared she would, when she went careening into the hallway wall. Maybe everything she *thought* happened afterward was actually a dream, the last of the pain meds working their way out of her system.

She plucked a nearly too-ripe banana out of a bowl on the counter, peeled it, and frowned at the brown spots on the fruit. She braced her elbows on the counter and took a bite.

A dream wouldn't explain the fact that her shoulder didn't hurt anymore, that it felt like it had never been hurt in the first place. She leaned to the left and peered into the metal of the toaster's side. The reflection that came back at her was a bit like what you might see in a funhouse mirror, but it was clear enough to show the bruises were gone, too.

So, not a dream, then.

But…how?

She tossed the empty peel into the garbage and her thoughts turned to the man in her bed. Zeph. Zephyros. An odd name, but it also sounded vaguely familiar, like she should know it from somewhere.

If she'd ever seen him before, though, she had no doubt she would remember him. After all, the guy had to be six-three, six-four. Craig had been six-one and Zeph was definitely taller. The comparison was unwelcome. She didn't want to compare the two men because, despite the fact she really didn't know Zephyros—and only an hour before thought he might kill her—there was no comparison. Her stranger was fierce masculinity personified, where Craig was all things metrosexual—a total clotheshorse and a brand snob. He even got manicures. What had she seen in him again?

She twisted her lips and wandered into the living room. She wasn't being fair to him, or to what they had shared—or, at least, what she *thought* they'd shared, but she wasn't in the mood yet to enumerate his good qualities. Maybe she would never be. Not after the lies he had told, the depth of his betrayal. Not after he'd taken her love and her trust, ripped them into tiny shreds, and thrown them in her face.

Which was why she wanted to get to the bottom of who Zephyros was and what he had done. Not that he owed her, necessarily, but that didn't keep her from wanting the truth. Badly. It didn't seem so much to ask from people.

Ella opened the front door and sucked in a deep breath

of chilly spring air. She retrieved the "Crab Wrapper"—
Annapolis's affectionate name for its local newspaper—from
the covered porch and rolled the rubber band off. She flicked
it open, perusing the headlines as she absently walked back
inside and kicked the door shut behind her. Coffee brewed, she
headed straight to the pot and poured herself a fragrant mug,
stirred in a little cream and sugar, then settled at the little two-
seater table with coffee and paper in hand. By the time she'd
read from cover to cover, sleepiness made her eyelids heavy.
After spending nearly four days in bed, though, the last thing
she wanted was to be horizontal again.

Though, her bed was a good bit more attractive right now.

She gaped at the thought. Last thing she needed was
to get involved with another man. Geez. It had only been
three months since she'd discovered Craig's dirty little secret,
otherwise known as her former best friend.

Still, she couldn't stop her brain from resurrecting the
image of Zeph tearing off his shirt as he sat on the edge of
her bed. As if the man's broad shoulders and bulging biceps
weren't impressive enough. As if the ridged muscles of his
abdomen didn't just call out to be traced. She had absolutely
never seen with her own eyes, on a real man, that incredible
cut of muscle just above his hips. But, yeah, he had it, and then
some. Her mind wandered. If she wrapped her arms around
him, would he feel soft or hard within her embrace? She shook
her head and sighed. She'd never know, but…damn. It sure was
fun to think about.

As she cleaned up her mess, she chuckled at herself.
The sound stopped her short. When was the last time she'd
laughed?

That she couldn't pinpoint a specific month or season

spoke volumes.

Then again, winter couldn't have been shittier for her. The final rounds of testing in November confirmed what they'd feared—she couldn't have children. Just before Christmas, Craig announced her infertility was for the best, because he was gay and wanted out. The bombshell revelation hit her hard, and for weeks she grappled with a rage she couldn't express. After all, a person couldn't choose his or her sexual orientation. And though she didn't understand why he hadn't recognized it about himself before they'd married—it had been three years, for God's sake—she had no intention of harassing him about it.

But then, she'd found him in bed with Teresa, her best friend. Or so she'd thought. Craig had been forced to admit he'd only said he was gay "to let her down easy," whatever the hell that was supposed to mean. He was in love with Teresa, who was four months pregnant. And that delightful bit of math meant he'd been sleeping with her while Ella was still trying to conceive.

Ella's whole life had caved in around her. Dreams of mother-hood gone, her marriage a farce, her friends feeling the need to choose sides, or too uncomfortable to figure out what to say. She didn't think things could possibly get worse.

And then the phone call that proved just how wrong she was.

Sitting alone in the house she'd once shared with Craig, she received the news that Marcus had been found dead in his bed. His cleaning lady had discovered his body. He'd apparently already been gone a few days when she did. Dead of a stroke at thirty.

That was the moment Ella knew what loss was. Compared to Marcus's death, losing Craig had been relatively painless.

"Enough," Ella said out loud. The time for wallowing was over. Marcus wouldn't want that for her. And she didn't want it for herself.

Problem was, she had no idea what she *did* want. Somewhere along the way, she'd lost herself, lost track of what was important, what made her happy. But she had to figure it out. Marcus might not be alive, but she still was. She owed it to the both of them to live—for real, not just go through the motions—and now was the perfect time to begin. Spring was the season of rebirth after all, and she intended to give it an honest effort. Even if she had no freaking idea where to start.

She threaded through the house and paused at the closed door to her bedroom. After hesitating for a moment, she gingerly turned the knob and pushed the door, wincing as it squeaked.

Ella moaned under her breath at the image that appeared on the other side.

Zephyros was sprawled on his stomach across more than half the bed, his massive shoulders and arms curled around a mound of pillows. Even in rest, his thick muscles appeared ready to spring.

She tiptoed closer, holding her breath as the floorboards creaked here and there.

In sleep, the harsh contours of his face relaxed, casting a peacefulness over his features that wasn't there when he was awake. That he apparently carried around some heavy unnamed burden made her heart squeeze. Sleep provided escape for her, too—when she could manage to quiet her heart and mind enough to actually nod off.

Standing there in the cool stillness of her room, her own exhaustion reared its head and demanded she cave in to the desire to rest. The urge to join Zeph in bed gripped her. Ridiculous. She padded over to a laundry basket near her dresser and chose clean clothes from the folded pile. With one last look at her mysterious guest, she slipped back out into the hall.

A shower would revive her. Plus, it had the added benefit of not landing her in bed with a total stranger. At least she thought that was a good thing.

Plopping her clothes on the bathroom counter, Ella peered in the mirror and confirmed her earlier impression from the toaster. She was healed. Totally and completely. The hair on her arms raised and she shivered. What he'd done…it was a miracle. Truly. What else would you call it?

Ella reached into the shower and adjusted the water. The house was old, and it took forever for the hot water to come up, so she'd need to let the shower run for a while before she could get in. As she waited, one question repeated itself in her mind: *How?* How had he healed her? How was something like that even possible?

After a few minutes, a thin mist of steam told her the shower was probably warm enough. She grabbed the hem of her T-shirt and pulled.

A knock sounded at the front door. Hard and insistent.

Ella frowned. Who could that be?

The doorbell rang once, twice, adding to the ruckus.

Damn. She tugged her shirt back into place and dashed downstairs. She didn't want anything to awaken Zeph.

In bare feet, she skidded to the front door and opened it.

All the breath whooshed out of her.

The man on the other side was enormous, big as Zeph, but dark. Spiky, dark charcoal-gray hair. Wraparound black sunglasses that didn't offer even the slightest glimpse of the eyes behind the lenses. A fierce, harsh mouth, beautiful but cruel. Black leather gloves and a black leather coat so long it swept over a pair of gleaming black leather shoes.

"Hello," he said, voice full of amusement.

Ella blinked and shook her head. "Uh, hi. Sorry." A cutting breeze ruffled her hair, raising gooseflesh down the back of her neck. "Um, can I help you?"

His smile did nothing to put her at ease. "Is this the Smith residence?"

The words wrapped around her throat, making it hard to breathe. Ella's knuckles ached from gripping the edge of the door so tightly. There was nothing overtly threatening about him. He smiled. He maintained a socially appropriate distance. His posture seemed relaxed, easy. Still, her fight-or-flight instinct was making all kinds of noise in her mind. "Um, no. I'm sorry." She swallowed, trying to find a bit of moisture in her suddenly dry mouth.

"Bill and Linda? They don't live here?"

The most primitive part of her brain screamed for her to get the hell away. She fought the urge to slam the door shut and pile every piece of living room furniture against it. "No. I don't recognize those names." She gripped the door harder and narrowed the opening.

One corner of his mouth quirked higher, then he gave a small bow. "Oh, well, then I'm sorry to have troubled you."

"It's okay," she said, stomach turning. "Good luck finding them."

"Luck." He shook his head and chuckled. The sound crawled over her skin. "Aren't you precious." The words seemed full of an innuendo she couldn't understand, but then he turned for the steps, the leather coat billowing out behind him. A cold gust of wind swirled around her, seemed to play with her hair, caress her skin. She shuddered, flooded with relief to see him leaving.

Jesus. What the hell was that?

With him gone, the air was almost easier to breathe. Ella didn't realize how scared she'd been—after all, he'd been perfectly polite. But as she watched him start down her street toward the main part of Eastport, her heart sprinted in her chest until cold prickles broke out all over her scalp.

Hands shaking, she closed the door and locked it, throwing the dead bolt for good measure.

Zephyros came flying into the room, still half undressed from his nap.

Ella screamed and fell back against the door, her arms braced in front of her as if warding off an attack. She blinked up at Zeph, who stood right in front of her, towering over her.

"Who was here?" he growled.

Ella gulped air. Her mouth fell open, but she couldn't manage a response. Her brain struggled to catch up.

He grasped her arms and squeezed. "Ella, who was here?"

"I...I don't..." She shook her head. What was wrong with her? Her body was acting like she'd just barely escaped an accident.

"What did he look like?"

She frowned. "He...he..."

"Damn it all to Hades." His hands slipped up over her shoulders to cup her face. "Take a deep breath. Come now."

Ella sucked in a halting breath.

"Again."

She did.

"Focus on my breathing, Ella. Breathe with me."

Her gaze dropped to the bare, broad chest right in front of her, noted the soft rise and fall of the taut muscles. After a few moments, she calmed.

"Look at me," he said quietly.

Her eyes flashed to his. The anger of a moment ago remained, but his expression was mostly one of concern.

"Tall? Salt and pepper hair? Dark glasses? Melodramatic leather duster?"

Apparently the incessant knocking had woken him, after all. He described the man to a T. "Yes."

The next thing she knew, she was pressed against his chest, his arms strapped tightly around her. Words in a language Ella had never heard spilled from his lips. They started out sounding like a prayer, but ended with the biting tone of a curse.

CHAPTER EIGHT

Rage, icy and violent, flooded through Zeph's veins. Ella had no idea what she'd just encountered, how dangerous the situation had been.

But *he* did.

His body had sensed him while still unconscious. His sleep, moments before among the most peaceful and restful he'd had in, well, he couldn't even remember, had turned restless and troubled. At once, he was thrust into a nightmare, pulling Ella's limp body out of the bay, but finding her dead. Her open, lifeless eyes mocking and accusing him.

Zeph tried to wake, but found himself trapped in his subconscious, held down upon the bed by an unseen force.

And he'd known. He'd known exactly what the hell was happening. And worse than his fury over Eurus getting the jump on him like that was his knee-jerk belief that Ella somehow played a part in it. Only her body's blind terror convinced him otherwise, but long moments existed between that recognition and the old specter of betrayal attempting to knot itself around his throat. Guilt over his suspicion flooded his chest, but he shoved it aside in favor of much darker emotions. Revenge fantasies ran rampant in Zeph's mind, wicked and relentless. He was going to enjoy acting a few of them out.

First, he needed to make sure Ella was really okay.

He buried his face in her hair and breathed in her natural, feminine scent. She was safe. Warm and unharmed and alive in his arms.

Her incredible calming aura, the one that brought him such unusual peace and comfort, was gone, revealing that her body recognized the threat even if her mind didn't. Even without the balm of her unique energy, Zeph was attracted and interested. He didn't want to just take from her, he wanted to give in return. Undeniably, there was some connection between them, and he found himself flirting with the most dangerous emotion there was—hope.

Ella's heart thumped against his abdomen, proof of life. He squeezed her against him, needing to feel every beat. He knew he'd surprised her when he'd tugged her into his embrace, but he couldn't hold back, couldn't staunch the relief coursing through him. And holding her was the only thing keeping him from hunting his brother down, destroying him where he stood—or die trying.

Slowly, Ella's arms raised and curled around his lower back. Her hug was full of comfort and reassurance. A moment ago, he'd been trying to calm her. With her touch, it felt like she was trying to ease him. As her focus apparently shifted to his well-being, her peaceful aura returned and slowly wrapped itself around him. His heart expanded in his chest. Between his legs, his erection stirred.

Gods. What was it about this woman?

He held her one last minute, absorbing everything about the feel of her in his arms, then stepped back. He didn't want his body's reaction to scare her. Still, he kept his hands on her arms, unable to release her entirely.

She looked up at him, her eyes wide and glassy. "Are you all right?"

He closed his eyes and centered himself. By the gods, she said the damnedest things—things that went right to the heart of him, that landed like a salve on the long-damaged parts of his psyche.

"Are you?" he managed. He opened his eyes, needing to see what he knew to be true.

"Yes."

He released a deep breath. "Then so am I."

She nodded, licked her lips. "Zephyros, who was that?"

It was probably too late, given his reaction, but he didn't want to alarm her further with the details, especially as he hadn't yet shared those about himself. "My brother," he said simply.

Her eyebrow arched. "Your brother? But…but how…"

"I don't know what he was doing here. But I intend to find out. Later. For now, I'd just like to stay close to you."

"Okay. I'd like that, too." She reached up and rubbed her arms, her fingers brushing his at the top of her biceps. She looked across the room and her eyes went wide. "Oh, shit."

He tensed. "What?"

"Nothing to worry about." She patted his chest, the touch full of calming warmth again. "Just realized I left the shower running all this time."

Zeph looked over his shoulder, the rush of water through the house's plumbing clearly audible now that he wasn't preoccupied. His muscles relaxed. He released Ella and stepped out of her way.

"Now that you're up, I'll just go shut it off." She smiled at him as she rounded the love seat, then tripped over the edge of the living room carpet and only stayed upright by bracing against the entertainment center. "Oof. Damn." Her face was pink when she glanced back, clearly checking to see if he'd witnessed her. Zeph frowned as she disappeared into the hallway and started up the stairs.

Thumps sounded from the top of the steps.

"Ow! Ow!"

Zeph's stomach clenched, and he reappeared at Ella's side. She was curled on the floor, sitting on the top step, clutching her left foot. He knelt down, his eyes trained on the trickle of blood pooling at the corner of her big toenail.

"What happened?" he asked in a quiet voice.

She pouted and chuckled. "Tripped and stubbed my toe. I'm not normally this much of a clutz. Ow."

He held back a growl, suspicion blooming. "Here. Let me see." He pushed the leg of her sweatpants up the strong curve of her calf, out of the way of his exploration. Her skin set his fingertips to tingling. Forcing himself to focus, it became clear something jagged had taken a small chunk out of her big toe.

Shaking her head, she gingerly prodded the skin above the toenail. The flow of blood already slowed. "I've never understood why something so small hurts so bad. Seems like a design flaw to me." She gave him a shy smile.

Zeph met her gaze, held it. "I don't see a single, solitary flaw."

Blushing, she ducked her head.

He rose, and helped her up. She limped into the bathroom. Wary, he followed her to the doorway, the steam hanging thick in the air, way warmer than what was comfortable for him.

She grabbed a tissue and blotted the blood from her toe, then reached into the stall. Hissing, she yanked her hand back without turning the water off. "Damn. How did that get so hot?" She sucked her fingers into her mouth.

In an instant, suspicion morphed into certainty. Zephyros's soul filled with a roiling desire for vengeance against Eurus, who clearly was toying with Ella. No one had this much bad luck all at once. Except after meeting his brother. Then one's chance of misfortune skyrocketed, especially if Eurus was in a mood. And when wasn't he?

Gods, this was his fault. He'd lingered, he'd stayed, he'd healed her. And now Eurus knew about Ella, probably suspected Zeph cared for her, which put the beautiful woman before him between a rock and a hard place, between the East and the West. His brother enjoyed nothing more than taking away the things Zeph cared about. One by one. Slowly but surely.

With family like that, who needed enemies?

"I need to ask you something, Ella." Even to himself, Zeph's voice sounded deep, strained.

Her narrowed gaze cut to his. "Okay."

"When he left, did you feel a gust of wind?"

Her brow slashed downward, wary. "Well, yeah, but—"

"Damn it. He marked you." Why did he have to know his brother so well?

She folded her arms around herself. "Marked? Meaning?"

Zeph sucked in the cool air of the hallway, then stepped into the steamy room. "My brother's calling card is unluckiness. I know how that sounds, but he, well—"

She tilted her head. "He's like you."

"No!"

Ella gasped and retreated one step, another. "I only meant—"

Zeph rushed to her, rubbed her shoulders. Dropped his forehead against hers. "I'm sorry. I know what you meant. It's just, I am many things, and far from perfect. But where my brother takes pleasure in others' pain, finds amusement in causing chaos, I prize life, Ella. I value goodness." He let out a long breath, aching for her to recognize the goodness in him.

For a long moment, she held his stare. She spoke quietly, carefully. "I can tell, Zephyros. You are a good person. I can almost feel it coming out of you, the way you care, the way you bear the weight of responsibility." She shook her head. "I don't even know if that's the right way to say it, but I…I like the way I feel when I'm around you. It's just"—she clenched her eyes shut and shuddered—"your brother…your brother totally creeped me out." She opened her eyes and shrugged. "Sorry."

Her words wrapped around his heart, made it pump harder, or maybe that was the clinging heat in the room. He wanted to reward her assessment of Eurus by telling her she was a good judge of character, but that would mean praising what she'd said about him, too. As much as he needed the affirmation she'd voiced, he found it hard to accept about himself. So, he kissed her forehead, allowed his lips to linger. An electrical charge rippled from his lips down his body.

"Don't be sorry. And thank you," he finally said in a shaky voice. Finding it harder and harder to breathe in the heated air, Zeph flicked on the exhaust fan and reached into the stall to shut off the shower. Scalding water streamed over his arm. He hissed, cranking the nozzle with his injured hand, and the shower cut off. His stomach flirted with nausea. Good thing it was just an extremity.

Frowning, Ella leaned around him and gasped at the angry red mottling his forearm. "Oh, I'm so sorry. We should run that under some cold water."

Zeph attempted a small smile. "It'll be okay, but thank you. Right now, you are our first priority."

She looked doubtful, but finally nodded. "Okay, so, about this marking thing."

He stepped back. "Right. It will likely wear off, after a time, though there's no telling how many small misfortunes will befall you in the interim. My brother's a death-by-a-thousand-cuts kinda guy."

She swallowed audibly. "Uh-huh. And option B? Please tell me there's an option B."

Of course there was. But how could he expect her to agree to it? He pressed his lips together and inspected his arm. The skin already felt cooler, the burn fading from red to pink.

"Zeph?"

She really had no choice—so neither did he. The marking ensured things would continue to get worse, much worse, before they got better. "There is," he finally said. "A cleansing."

"A cleansing. As in, get a shower? I was going to do that anyway, before all this." She waved her hand between them.

Zeph crossed his arms over his steam-dampened chest, hiding the fists clenching and releasing as he imagined running his hands over her body. "That's the basic idea. Though it's a bit more involved."

Fuck if this wasn't probably part of Eurus's plan, too.

She gestured as if drawing the words out. "Okaaay."

"First, a bath, then a shower. I must wash you with my hands. Only a g—" *Good gods.* He'd nearly divulged his identity.

He shook his head, regrouped. "Only *I* can remove my brother's...influence."

"Why is that, Zephyros? What were you going to say?"

He turned away, focused on his distorted reflection just visible through the condensation on the mirror.

"Please tell me what you were going to say." She grasped his shoulder. Skin-to-skin, the strange, wondrous elemental connection they somehow shared flared. Zeph sucked in a breath. "I hate not knowing the truth."

He sighed and glanced at her. The humidity in the air made the soft cotton cling to her body. The outline of her bra became just visible through the fabric. He'd already revealed so much that must seem strange, could it really hurt to fill in the gaps for her? "Cleansing first, my story second. Please. It's imperative I take care of you as soon as possible." He turned and grasped her hand.

Her gaze followed the gesture and she gasped. "Your arm. It's...all better. How..." Her face paled. "You heal?"

No sense holding back, really. The evidence was right before her. "Yes."

"Jesus. I guess that shouldn't surprise me, given what you did for me." She carded the fingers of her free hand through her hair. "But will you explain that later, too?"

"Yes."

"I want it all. How you got in my house. The healing. The deal with your brother. What you were going to say. All of it."

The thought of such a conversation made him weary, but it was also one full of potential—for acceptance, for sharing just a little of his load. Assuming he didn't scare her so bad she banished him forever. He nodded once. "Okay, all of it."

She pressed her lips together, twisted them. "And it will be the truth," she stated. Demanded.

"Yes. Always." Her insistence on the truth piqued his curiosity and tugged at the center of his chest.

Sagging back against the counter, Ella released a long breath. "Okay. Thank you." She braced her hands behind her. Jumped right back up. "Ah!" She flew forward, cradling one hand against her chest and pointing at the scissors on the counter with the other. "I just cut myself on these," she growled, showing him the angry red mark just blooming with blood. "Your brother?"

He scowled at the shears, as if they were responsible for attacking Ella's hand all by themselves. "Yes," he bit out.

"Zephyros, I want this cleansing. Whatever it entails, I want you to do it. Now."

CHAPTER NINE

Ella was down the rabbit hole. No doubt about it. A beautiful and presumably gifted man with impossible powers. A miracle healing. Some sort of fraternal feud that had apparently put the crosshairs of a curse on her back.

And the weirdest thing? It all felt real. The oddness was as exhilarating as it was frightening. But she was going with it, for now. After all, he'd eased her pain, healed her injuries, and offered his protection against his own brother—what more would a man have to do to earn her faith? So, she believed Zephyros, believed *in* him. She just hoped she didn't live to regret putting her faith in him. But at some point, she had to listen to her gut again, start trusting it.

Not everyone was Craig.

She returned the scissors to the counter, pushed them far from the edge. Everything looked like a mishap waiting to happen, now. She had no idea how someone could make you have bad luck, but something had to explain how she'd tripped and almost fallen, busted her toe, burned herself, and cut her hand, all in the past fifteen minutes.

She whirled on Zeph. "So, will you do it?"

He studied her face. "Perhaps you would like to hear what it entails first?"

Ella released a shallow breath. "Okay." She shifted feet. "What do I—"

"You must be in water, and I must bathe you." Ella gaped. "First in a salt bath, and then I must rinse you off in the shower."

She scoffed. "Oh, that's all?"

"Yes."

Ella thought to argue, but now that Zeph had described her as "marked," she was sure she could feel it. The memory of that cold, slick wind surrounding her made her shiver. It almost felt as if her heart had to work harder to pump normally. Maybe it was just her anxiety, or the weirdness of…everything. She met his waiting gaze. "Okay, I guess."

"You're sure?"

"This is really the only way besides just waiting to see what else happens?"

"I'm afraid so."

She twisted her fingers together. "Then let's get it over with."

He nodded and started filling the tub. "Now, can you bring me as much salt as you have?"

"Like, regular table salt?"

"Yeah."

"Sure. I'll just, uh…" She thumbed over her shoulder, then left.

"Ella?" he called.

She swung back around the doorjamb. "Yeah?"

Intense gray-blue eyes stared at her. "Be careful."

She nodded and retreated. Her mind went mechanical. *Salt. Salt. Salt.* Thinking about anything else threatened to unleash a serious case of nerves. Shaker off the table, canister of Morton's from the pantry. Of course, when she reached for the latter, it slipped out of her hand and spilled on the floor. Bad luck on top of bad luck. Just great. Eager to be free of whatever was happening to her, Ella returned to the bathroom, shut the door, and plunked her findings on the counter. "Please tell me this is enough."

"Should be." He unscrewed the lid from the saltshaker and emptied the granules into the filling tub. Repeated the process with the canister, pouring what was left of it in.

"So, er, I suppose it's too much to hope this will work with clothes on, right?" Heat infused her cheeks, but the thought of baring herself to him got her hot and wet in a way that had nothing to do with the steam the shower had thrown off earlier.

He turned and raked his gaze down the front of her. "I'm sorry."

"Uh, don't be. Somehow, I knew." She nearly asked him to turn around so she could undress, but any attempt at modesty was pointless if he had to bathe her. Besides, this was simply a clinical procedure. Like being at the doctor's office.

Uh-huh. Right.

Well, Dr. Zeph, here goes nothing.

Before she allowed herself another second to consider her actions, she whipped her shirt over her head, then shoved her sweats to her ankles and stepped out of them. She wasn't ashamed of her body—she bore no resemblance to Barbie, to be sure, but her body was strong and curvy, and she liked how the wide flaring of her hips made her waist look smaller than it was. This body let her handle the rigors of sailing a ship all alone, and she liked that about herself. Still, her muscles went tight with nervousness, and moments passed before she gathered the courage to check Zeph's reaction.

His eyes bulged, then narrowed. An odd, reflective quality played behind the blue, like they were backlit.

No doctor had ever looked at her like that before.

That she affected him eased her anxiety, made her bolder. Holding his gaze, she swallowed hard and reached behind her back. Her bra fell loose and she dropped it. With a deep breath, she shimmied out of her panties.

Adrenaline surged through her. She clenched her fists to restrain the trembling. The reaction wasn't from nerves or embarrassment, but from a growing desire for the near-stranger before her, from the sense something rare and magical was about to happen—was already happening. Instead of the self-consciousness she expected, Ella's arousal surged, then spiked when Zeph's eyes started to glow that tense, beautiful light she remembered seeing upon waking this morning. A quiet, needful moan sounded from the back of his throat, and he licked his lips. Ella's gaze dropped and locked onto the huge bulge filling up the front of his jeans.

Jesus.

Ella's nipples, already peaked from baring herself to his observation, went tight. Warm heat slicked the place between her legs. *Holy shit.* In all the years she'd been with Craig she'd never once felt this kind of crazy animal attraction.

His jaw clenched and his chin gestured her toward the tub.

Oh, right. Good thing one of them still had their head about them. Though she didn't love the proof that he affected her more than she did him.

She stepped into the tub with one foot, then the other, and promptly slipped. Her arms shot out to brace herself against nothing, but Zeph caught her around her waist, his hands clutching just below her breasts.

He growled out a string of words she didn't understand, but totally got the gist of from his tone. She could only suck in a deep breath and try to calm her racing heart.

"Let's do this," she finally said, "before I kill myself." She sank down into the bath, almost glad for her most recent incident because it bolstered her resolve. "Ooh, it's a little chilly."

"I'm sorry. It, uh, it needs to be."

"Okay." Sitting up, she clasped her arms around her knees and glanced at Zeph. He towered over her, that strange glow lighting up those incredible eyes. "You with me?"

There was a flaring of blue, and then he knelt beside the tub.

The image of his masculine bulk, bare from the waist up, on his knees… Ella dropped her gaze to the water to try to rein her body in. "Okay, so, what do I—"

"My hands will draw the curse out of you, and the salt will render it inert." He tilted his head to meet her lowered gaze. "All right?"

She nodded, and her shoulders relaxed. That he took the time to explain what was going to happen made her feel less out of control.

"I'll start with your back. Stretch out as much as you can, and face the wall."

Ella blew out a breath and obeyed. In allowing her the modesty of facing away, he showed her respect and earned her trust, which wasn't something that came easily to her, not anymore. She concentrated on the lapping of the water against her skin, on the chill of her exposed shoulder.

His hands burrowed under the length of her hair and cupped the back of her neck. A tingling like static electricity danced off her skin, seemed to conduct through the water even where they didn't touch. Meticulously, he glided his palms over her, from neck to shoulder to spine to ribs. A deep yearning erupted within her. How she wished this wasn't just some ritual. How she wished a man like this would tend to her and worship her because he *wanted* to. But that wasn't what this was about.

Words spilled from his lips. She'd only ever heard him say a few utterances in that foreign language before, but as his speech flowed now, it sounded reverent and plaintive. As his hands reached the swells of her rear, she held her breath, trying to restrain the trembling brewing beneath her skin.

He switched into English. "In the names of my ancestors, my gods, and myself, I call upon the elements of good and the forces of righteousness. Come forth and cleanse Ella of all evil and alien magic, and restore her to balance and health. By our wills combined, so be it."

The words mesmerized her so much that his hands were on her lower thighs before she realized. He slipped back into the other language, and she knew in her gut he'd purposely distracted her as he'd touched her more intimately. Her heart squeezed and released. A delayed ripple of pleasure surged between her legs. Her body was hyper aware of his touch, even if her mind had been temporarily diverted.

As his charged touch caressed the backs of her feet, she kicked, sloshing the water. "Sorry, it tickles," she said.

A low chuckle rumbled out of him. "Turn over onto your back."

She shivered as she turned, and not just because the water was cool.

Except for her face and nipples, most of her was submerged. She'd never felt more vulnerable in her life.

"Be at ease," he rasped.

How often his words seemed to respond to her thoughts! Her gaze cut to his. That blue light was back, studiously fixed on his hands' journey. His mouth hung open, his chest expanded and contracted at a faster pace than before.

"Tilt your head back," he whispered, cupping the nape of her neck so her head didn't go all the way under. "Your hair needs to be wet through."

She tipped her head and nearly purred when he stroked his fingers through her hair. He combed his nails against her scalp, and the combination of his touch with his energy turned her body liquid all over.

Zeph sucked in a breath. "Good. You're doing so good. Can you hold your breath and go under? Let the water cover your face."

Ella sucked in a breath, closed her eyes, and pressed her head backward into the water to comply with his request.

His fingers traced her features and drew that odd static sensation over her face. "Okay," he said a little louder.

Breaking the surface, she let out her breath, and found she could think more clearly than before, as if a cottony fog had disappeared from her brain. Was she imagining the difference or did this mean the cleansing was working? She blinked and clenched her eyes, the salt stinging as if she'd been swimming in the ocean. Soft terry pressed against her brow, her eyes, her mouth.

"Thank you," she said. It was like he could read her needs.

His caring attention added another layer to her growing arousal. It wasn't just his physical perfection to which her body responded.

Chanting the prayer again, he repeated the same process as on her back side. The light that shone from his palms was softer than the one that had healed her this morning, or maybe that was the impact of the water or the mid-day sun coming through the slanted blinds. Over her neck, shoulders, down the length of her arms and hands and back up, across her chest. "I must touch you here," he said in a low voice, hands hovering over her breasts.

"I understand," she said.

And then he was touching her, cupping the swells of her breasts, palming her nipples. God, his hands were so big, so warm, and felt so right on her. The little moan she unleashed mortified her, but she'd been powerless to hold it in. If he made her feel this way when he wasn't even trying to seduce her, she could only imagine…

His hands smoothed around the underside of her breasts, then back up to the middle. Supporting her weight in the water, his right hand pressed firmly against her heart. Lingered there. "We are doing it, Ella. Your heart already beats lighter, freer."

He needn't have told her. The tightness in her chest receded, making it easier to draw a deep breath, and her heart rate calmed. Again, he was healing her. "Thank you," she said in a shaky voice.

He shook his head. "Don't thank me. None of this would be necessary if I'd left you alone."

Ella shot into a sitting position. Water splashed over his arms, onto the golden skin of his chest. "Don't say that."

Zeph's expression turned surprised, but Ella couldn't stand the idea of never having met him. Not that she knew him, or understood exactly what was going on. But the rightness of his presence here? She felt that. Bone deep. "It's just…I'm *glad* I met you."

Zeph stared but remained silent, like he didn't know what to do with her declaration. The words were soft when they finally came. "Why? I've caused you nothing but trouble."

Ella drew a wet picture against the tub's edge with her finger. "I can't tell you the last time I felt this alive. I may be confused and mystified and curious as all hell, but I'm also engaged and interested and eager. And those are things…I haven't felt this way…" She got tangled in emotions, in memories. She swallowed around the knot in her throat. "Like I said, I'm just glad, is all."

His wet knuckles caressed her cheekbone, her jaw. "In truth, so am I."

Ella smiled, absorbing the warm impact of his admission.

Zeph retained his serious façade. "We should finish this," he whispered.

"Right." She reclined.

His hands smoothed over her belly, her hips, the top of her pubic hair. Ella fought the instinct to part her legs. Was he going to have to touch her there? *Jesus.* Probably. She couldn't look at Zeph, didn't want him to see the desire she felt. But he leapfrogged to her thighs, and, ridiculously, disappointment swamped her.

"I will have to touch you there, too," he murmured.

Her gaze whipped to him, but he was looking away, watching his hands, chanting the prayer in low tones. He caressed her feet, the sensation almost as good as a foot massage. She bit back a threatening moan.

Fingers tapped against the insides of her ankles. "Open,"

he commanded, his voice a rough scrape.

Ella swallowed hard and spread her legs.

His big hands caressed upwards, carrying that strange, wonderful tingle over her skin as he went. Ella's heartbeat took off at a sprint, anticipating his touch. There. She could feel his approaching heat, the hint of the energy. In that moment, every nerve ending in her body seemed to congregate between her thighs. She held her breath. *Oh, just do it already! Do it!*

With one big hand, he palmed her mound. Didn't move. Didn't rub. Didn't stroke. Which was good, in a way, because she was certain the slightest movement would make her come.

She bit down on the inside of her cheek, fighting the rising swell of sensation, the congregating pressure, the instinctual need to rock her hips. One half of her brain begged him to stop touching her, the other side pleaded for more. The debate raged within, adding to the feeling she was going to split wide apart.

His hand left her.

She gasped, then moaned out loud. The sound didn't embarrass her this time because she wanted him too much.

"Good gods," he growled, then heaved her out of the tub. Water rained off her body, over him, over the floor. Carrying her, he sidestepped them into the shower and turned on the water. Cold to start, it heated to a just tolerable lukewarm. He lowered her feet. She stood, wobbly at first, but steadier after a moment. The good thing about the shower, it hid how loud she was panting. For him.

A rustling of fabric behind her caught her attention, and she didn't turn to look, because she knew. He'd taken his jeans off. Her imagination went wild. He was magnificent from the waist up—cut stomach, taut chest, broad shoulders, arms so muscular the veins popped. No way the scenery on the bottom half was any less impressive. If she let her eyes confirm the details, she'd be done for. All over him. Any pretense that this was just about removing bad magic would go right down the drain.

Wet denim slapped against the floor. The door slid shut.

Instinctively, Ella felt Zeph's presence behind her. Looming. Promising to touch.

Her mind resisted what her body wanted. Ella didn't do this. She was analytical and levelheaded. While she enjoyed adventure, she wasn't a risk taker and she wasn't a by-the-seat-of-her-pants kind of woman. These were traits developed through sailing, traits that made her a good sailor. Recent debacle notwithstanding.

"Almost done now, Ella," he whispered against her neck. His lips skimmed under her ear. The action was just a brush, not a full kiss, but it ignited the blood in her veins just the same. She tilted her head away, exposing her throat to him, inviting more. Fingers stroked her, from jaw to collarbone. "You are so lovely. I could touch you forever."

She sagged back against him and gasped. He was completely naked. And fully aroused. *Oh, my God.*

He grunted and froze. "Ella, Ella," he rasped. "We'll never finish this if you do that." He retreated enough to part their skin where they'd touched below the waist.

"Sorry," she whispered. But she wasn't. Not in the least. In fact, it took all her willpower not to grind back against him. Maybe it didn't make sense. After all, she'd only known him a few hours, days if you wanted to be generous and count the times they'd talked in the hospital. But what she wanted, it didn't feel like sex with a random stranger. It felt deep and meaningful and right. And, God, did she want it. Want him.

Zeph reached around her and grabbed the bottle of

shampoo, poured a dollop in his palm. He washed her hair, a mix of relaxing scalp massages and gentle, circling scrubs. When he was done, she turned and tilted her head back to keep the suds from rinsing into her eyes.

"Oh, gods, so damn beautiful."

Despite the cool water, the shower went hot and steamy, the glass fogged, and the air condensed like the gathering low pressure of a spring storm. Their eyes met, and Ella's mouth dropped open at the raw hunger of his gaze.

He leaned in. Close. Tight. And reached over her shoulder for the bar of soap. Without stepping away, he lathered it between his hands, returned it to the rack, and washed her in soft, circular strokes that made her nearly beg for more. This time, he didn't ask permission to touch her most private parts, but he also didn't linger. She wasn't sure whether to be relieved or disappointed.

Either way, she felt the tension building between them, electric and relentless. Something was coming for them.

"Turn," he rasped.

She gave him her back. He washed her gently, efficiently. Then turned her and made sure every last sud rinsed away. His soapy hands flew over his own body, and her hands fisted, itched to replace his. How ridiculous to be jealous of him touching himself.

He pressed in beside her and rinsed off. When he looked up, eyes full of relief and accomplishment and need, Ella couldn't resist. She grabbed Zeph's shoulders and launched herself at him.

CHAPTER TEN

As his back hit the cool tiles of the shower wall, Zeph's mouth fell open on a gasp. Ella was all over the front of him—hands clutching his shoulders, breasts crushing against his chest, hips grinding on his erection—and it was fucking heaven. Her mouth found his bottom lip and sucked. Hard.

The shock of her sensual assault wore off, and his hands finally got in the game. One arm curled around her waist, hiking her more tightly against him. The other grasped the back of her neck, tilted her head so he could control the kiss. His embrace didn't keep her from writhing against him. Her body moved in great, needful undulations, creating the most maddening friction. Her incredible passion nearly drove him to his knees. He dove in deeper, twirling his tongue with hers, pursuing, exploring. Good gods, she tasted sweet and feminine and full of life.

Zeph's thighs quivered with the desire to squat down, just enough to align the swollen head of his cock with the graceful slit between her legs. He'd touched her there. Knew her warm perfection. Felt the slickness of her invitation.

It would be so easy. And so fucking good.

Of course, his brain chose that moment to parade out the images of the people for whom he'd felt this way before. Chloris—the wife he'd loved and lost, the relationship that started his centuries of torment, the fraternal competition-turned-feud with Eurus he didn't deserve and couldn't defuse—their most recent conversation with all its treacherous revelations proved that. After Chloris, there was Maia, Hyacinthus, Dion, Andreus, Eirene, Skiron. Some were unrequited crushes, others brief dalliances, others longer, more meaningful affairs. But they all had one thing in common: he'd been betrayed or abandoned in the end. Every fucking time.

Which was why it had been a great while since he'd last allowed himself to wind up naked and panting and wanting against another's warm, willing flesh.

His heart kicked into a higher gear as a layer of anxiety blanketed the sharpest, neediest edges of his arousal. He loosened his grip, calmed his kisses. Withdrew.

Panting, Ella looked up at him, brown eyes on fire, lips wet and swollen.

Don't stop! In his head, the debate raged. Want versus fear. Need versus self-defense. Fantasy versus the likely reality this would blow up in his face.

But she made the decision for him. "Oh. Oh, God." She pushed herself out of his arms. "I'm"—she wiped the water from her face—"I'm really sorry. I don't know…" Ella shook her head and turned.

"Ella."

"No, I get it." She wrenched the water nozzle into the "off" position, yanked the shower door open, and rushed out.

He knocked his head back against the tile. "Ella, wait, it's not—"

"Listen." She reappeared in the opening of the shower door, blue terry cloth wrapped around her. "Let's just pretend this didn't happen." Her eyes flickered to him and away again.

Zephyros dropped his head. When he heard the bathroom door open and close, he clenched his eyes shut and cursed.

Damn it. He could feel the gut-kick of rejection rolling off her. He knew that emotion too well not to. He hated hurting her, but deep inside, he feared getting hurt worse.

No hero material here, that's for goddamned sure. Fuck.

Zeph stomped out of the shower and found his own towel, tucked it around his waist. Hands on his hips, he sagged, the ancient weight pressing down on him. This woman appealed to him, even before what had happened in the shower. Her words, her aura, her invitation to stay, her little acts of kindness that probably meant nothing but felt damn good anyway—all of it. And now he'd seen her naked, touched her, held her, tasted her. He *wanted* her.

But history had proven he was a piss-poor judge of what was in his own best interest, of what—and whom—he could actually trust.

He scrubbed his hands through his hair and spat a curse under his breath. He turned and faced himself in the mirror. Time to make things right with Ella. His heart was already making decisions his brain was going to have to deal with, like it or not.

Head hanging, he left the bathroom and rounded on her bedroom door. Knuckles met wood twice and he waited.

Nothing.

He knocked again. "Ella?"

"Go away, Zephyros," came her muffled voice.

A rock took up residence in his gut, but he found himself rubbing the muscles over his heart. "Ella, please."

"Not now, Zeph. Okay? Just…"

He waited, but she didn't finish the thought. She didn't have to. "Okay."

The sadness came first, but quickly morphed, darkened, roiled into a dangerous storm of rage.

Zeph willed himself into the elements and vanished.

೮つಛ

Some time later, Zeph materialized in the Realm of the Gods wearing human street clothes. Because they made him feel closer to Ella.

When he'd first left Ella's, he'd needed space to vent his turmoil, but then, his energy flagging, he needed the rejuvenation being in his own world would provide. From his elemental form, he'd simply visualized his private chamber and focused on the compass rose mosaic with its calligraphic W tiled into the wall.

With a sigh, he lifted his head and found the beautiful design of the mosaic. It had always helped center him. Except… this wasn't…

"Sometimes you get what you need, not what you want," said a deep voice.

Zeph smiled. "Is that so, brother?" His gaze traced over the stylized N at the top of the compass rose before he turned and laid eyes on Boreas. The oldest of the four Anemoi, he was the Supreme God of the North Wind, and the one who understood Zephyros best. Only problem was, Zeph respected him so damned much, he felt ashamed for Boreas to see him this way, for him to know just how bad he always fucked things up. He hated the thought of disappointing him.

"Indeed." Boreas shoved off of the wall he'd been leaning against and held out a hand.

Zeph grasped it, gladly, and braced for what he knew was coming.

Boreas yanked him into a brotherly embrace and clapped him on the back. The other man had a good eight inches on Zephyros—it was the only time he ever felt small—but he didn't mind.

He returned the hug, stepped back, and threw Boreas a wry smile. "Is this where I get the 'ya never call, ya never write' speech?" Generally, he steered clear of hanging here as much as he could—there were just too many damn people to avoid. He'd either end up in a fight with Eurus, get his heart ripped out all over again by Hy, or end up in bed with Dion—none of which were particularly good for him.

Boreas's silver eyes flashed with mirth. "Apparently, there's no need. You already know. So, instead, tell me what has you so wrapped up in knots."

He couldn't restrain the groan. Zeph's elemental powers might've been the strongest among them, but Boreas had intuition a mile wide and twice as long.

"Let me rephrase the question. What did Eurus do that has you so tied up in knots?" Boreas asked, leveling an intense stare at him. Long white hair and a beard framed his unexpectedly young face. As younger gods, they'd actually borne some physical resemblance until Boreas's hair went white from the shock of his wife's sudden death. Though he wore his grief in the Father Time getup and deep creases around his eyes, he'd never stopped being a father to his children. Just another thing to admire about the man.

Zeph hesitated for just a moment, then unloaded. "By the gods, Boreas, I can take his misplaced vengeance no longer."

Boreas paced his chamber, well, more like floated over the surface of it, but the effect was the same—he'd long ago given up any pretense of humanity and now wore the magic of his godhood the way mortals wore their skin. He was the only one of the four of them who really couldn't pass in the human realm. Finally, he heaved a great breath. "If only Mother had lived."

"We all lost her."

"Yes, but he was the only one Father made feel responsible for it."

Zeph crossed his arms, not wanting to fight with Boreas. And he knew his brother spoke the truth. But Zeph found it damn near impossible to see Eurus as the victim. After everything. Instead, Zeph shared some of his own truth. "I've met someone. I care for her." He shoved his hands in his jeans pockets.

Boreas's eyebrow flew up. "A human?"

"Yes. Ella."

He nodded. "Beautiful name."

"That's all you have to say?"

"I have to no censure to offer, brother. I am curious, of course. I cannot recall the last time you interacted with humans with any manner of substance. She must be special."

"I nearly killed her."

Boreas whipped around, his fur robes whirling. A blast of cold air shot out from his body. "I do not believe it."

"It's true. As if the anniversary party wasn't hard enough." He glanced at Boreas. "Don't get me wrong, I am happy for

Owen. But, you know, I don't really do the whole happy-couple thing very well. Anyway, afterward, Hy tried to summon me back here."

"Did you go—"

"No, of course not," Zeph said, hating this.

Boreas's silver gaze narrowed. "For someone who supposedly made his choice—and chose someone else—he sure keeps close tabs on you. It's not fair to you, brother."

The protective tone in the older man's voice felt like what home and family were all about. Zeph needed such care and concern like mortals needed food and water, but that didn't make him any more comfortable with it. He shrugged and scrubbed his hands through his hair. "Anyway, I just felt suffocated at the party, but couldn't come back here, and I lost it. And Ella got caught in the crossfire."

Boreas frowned. "But you saved her."

"Yes."

"Then, good gods, Zephyros, give yourself a break."

Zeph cut his gaze to Boreas.

"I have never known someone who tormented himself as much as you. Everyone makes mistakes, but not everyone shoulders them like Atlas carrying around the weight of the world. Not everyone bleeds for them."

"That so, brother? And what are your mistakes? You are the most righteous god I know." Zeph meant that, from down deep. His respect and admiration for Boreas knew no bounds.

"Do not place me on a pedestal. I cannot stand there. No god can."

"I'm waiting." He cupped his hand to his ear, knowing he was being a sarcastic asshole.

"Next time you see Owen, you ask him if I'm perfect. Or

ask Chione. Oh, wait, she's off bed-hopping, providing fodder for another round of warfare between Ular and Koli. What a great job I did there. Shall I go on?

"Shit, Boreas."

"You have a way with words, brother."

Zeph chuckled. "I'm sorry."

"Don't be. So, now that we got all of that out of the way, what exactly did Eurus do?"

Zeph inhaled a calming breath before he spoke. "He came to Ella's house and marked her. Invaded my dreams and restrained my body while I slept."

Boreas's expression darkened. "Damn it all to Hades. You must walk away. Or guard her well."

"I know." Restlessness shot through him. Talking about Ella made him want to get back to her.

"I fear some of this is my fault, Zephyros."

Zeph frowned. "How do you figure?"

"Last year, I didn't invite Eurus or his sons to Owen's wedding, nor to his anniversary party last week."

Holy shit. He gaped. Not that he really blamed him. Nothing like the Supreme God of the evil and unlucky East Wind to throw a damper on a happy celebration. And his sons hadn't fallen too far from the old evil tree. "And he knows?"

"He does. I couldn't do it, not with a new grandchild growing in Megan's womb. I just couldn't risk it."

"She's pregnant again?"

His brother's eyes crinkled in mirth. "She is."

"That's good. Real good." Zeph smiled and ignored the empty ache that took root in the center of his chest. He'd always liked Owen, and the guy deserved this happiness, but damn if it didn't highlight everything Zeph lacked. He clasped Boreas's shoulder. "I certainly don't blame you for being cautious. No one would."

"Eurus does."

"He's the only one. And he earned it, fair and square."

Boreas grunted.

Cracking his neck, competing thoughts rose up for attention in Zeph's head. Only one thing he knew for sure. "I should go. I want to get back."

"I'm glad. Don't give Eurus the power to choose for you, Zephyros."

Zeph nodded, but didn't know what to say. If he was going to give this a real shot with Ella, it wasn't only him he had to worry about getting hurt.

"Thank you, Boreas. I'm glad you summoned me here."

The god chuckled. "Don't stay away so long next time."

"I'll try." Zeph closed his eyes and focused, saw *his* compass rose in his mind's eye. Just as he dematerialized, Boreas offered a last parting thought:

"Sometimes what you want *is* what you need, Zephyros. Don't forget it."

CHAPTER ELEVEN

Boreas's words filled Zephyros with resolve. He had no idea what, if anything, might happen with Ella, but he wanted the chance to find out. He wanted to know if that peaceful aura would continue to affect him, if the kind look in her eyes could bloom into true affection, if the passion in her kisses would be lasting or fleeting.

She dominated his thoughts. Excited his body. Eased that dull ache filling his chest just left of center. He felt drawn to her in a way he didn't fully understand, but damn it, how he wanted to.

But he couldn't explore any of that while Eurus played his games.

Zeph concentrated and allowed his mind to travel in search of his brother's unique energy signature. As polar opposites, their energies were connected. Yin and yang. Life and death. West and East. So he found Eurus, easily. Within blocks of Ella's house. Thunder rumbled around him as he flowed through the air in pursuit.

Corporeality returned in a blaze of light, his seething rage crackling around him.

"Ah, brother. I've been expecting you," Eurus said. In the gloom of twilight, he lay prone on the dock in the middle of the marina where Ella's boat had been taken that first day. Ankles crossed. Fingers making lazy designs in the air as if he were conducting a symphony. Cold wind whipped up around them, turning the calm waters of the inlet choppy, jostling the sailboats in their slips.

His brother's calm, casual repose was more disturbing than if Zeph had found him petulant and ranting. Because it meant he was planning. "What the fuck are you playing at, Eurus?"

He sprung to his feet and tugged the lapels of his leather coat. "You see? I offer civility, and what do I get in return?"

Zeph squared off and braced, ready for anything. "You don't have a civil bone in your body."

Eurus pinched the bridge of his nose, shifting the wraparounds up the smallest bit. Though not enough, Zeph was relieved to see, to reveal his dead black irises. "If what you say is true, brother, whose fault exactly would that be?"

"Not. Mine." It was a fruitless conversation, but it was their little dance, and Zeph's own special corner of hell.

"Of course not yours. Not perfect Zephyros. Not the god of life and renewal. Gods forbid."

Zeph ignored the barb. Perfection was the last thing he believed of himself. Eurus was jealous of a figment of his imagination. "What do you want?" he finally bit out, hoping to defuse the other man, to delay the confrontation long brewing between them.

Eurus whipped off his glasses and drilled his disturbing, blank gaze into Zeph's very soul. "Leave the woman alone."

Rage filled Zeph's chest with white-hot pressure. "Why the fuck do you even care? It's nothing to you—"

"Ah!" He chuckled and held out his hands. "You see, that's where you're wrong. It *is* something to me. Because it's something to you." He jabbed his long, elegant finger in the air.

Warm wind whipped around him and rain pattered down in heavy drops, alleviating the smallest amount of the volcanic build-up within Zeph's human manifestation. Prudence dictated he maintain a façade of calm. The more he revealed his interest in Ella, the more Eurus would latch on to the idea of her. "You know what? I'm not doing this with you anymore. You've built up this list of imagined offenses and there's no reasoning with you." He slashed his hand in the air. "Be gone."

Eurus's body stumbled back, like an invisible hand shoved at his chest. He went elemental as his body flew off the edge of the pier. A short moment later, his caustic voice came from behind. Zeph whirled as Eurus ranted. "I did not imagine you insinuating yourself into Chloris's life. I did not imagine you taking her away, joining your godhood with hers." Thunder rumbled around them, shaking the boards beneath their feet.

"For the thousandth time, she did not love you—"

"Because you interfered and never gave her the chance!"

Rain slashed down in stinging, jagged lines, chasing away the last of the daylight. "Don't you ever tire of this merry-go-round? I didn't know you felt something for her. And whatever wrong I might have done, you inflicted your vigilante justice several times over. She *left* me, remember? You blackened something good and true until she broke under the weight of it."

Eurus had accused Zeph of abducting Chloris from him, raping her, keeping her hostage in their new home. He'd run right to their father, Aeolus, and when the powerful storm god wouldn't take the charge seriously, Eurus spread the lies to any god who would listen. After a time, Chloris couldn't stand the whispers and furtive glances, and she'd left in tears, unintentionally giving credence to the rumors. Zeph didn't blame her, and still couldn't bear the memory of her pain. Muscles rigid, he shook the rain from his face. "Truth be told, at the time I didn't even know you to be capable of love. The way you treated her proved I was right."

The wind howled around them, dueling cold and warm drafts driving the rain sideways. "Any goddess who would stand between two brothers was not worthy of either," Eurus spat.

"Do not speak as if you ever felt the least fraternal affection toward me. I blame Father for much of that. But what you do—what you've always done—serves you and you alone."

"You will not mention *him* in my presence."

Zeph shook his head and swore under his breath. All gods excelled in stubborn righteousness, but perhaps none more than their father. Grieving over his beloved's death in childbirth, Aeolus had blamed Eurus for her loss and refused to show him the least parental affection ever after. As much as anyone or anything, Aeolus's treatment had seeded the resentment, bitterness, and hair-trigger rage so central to Eurus's godhood. And he'd rubbed salt in the wounds by showering his new wife's youngest son, the Anemoi Chrysander, with love and acceptance.

Zeph got it. He did. But none of it was his fault, and he was tired of paying for it. "He did you wrong, Eurus. There's no questioning that—"

Eurus scoffed, a black light flashing from his inhuman eyes.

"I don't want your false pity."

"And I'm not offering it." Zeph tugged his hand through his wet hair. "Enough of this. It's the same shit, different century. Nothing I say or do makes any difference. You will not dictate my life to me. You will not dictate who I love."

The buffeting wind caught the length of Eurus's coat, furling and unfurling it around him, giving it the appearance of a live being struggling to break free. "Perhaps if you didn't spread your love"—his fingers curled into air quotes as he sneered the word—"around so indiscriminately, I wouldn't have to step in. For the love of the gods, first Owen cavorts with human vermin, and now you. At least his indiscretion can be excused by his lack of true pure Anemoi blood. You, however—there's no excuse for your dalliance here. Humans are beneath even you. Do not sully our godhoods with any more of this nonsense."

"Your view of humans is an abomination."

He released a sigh, like he was unjustly tormented by Zeph's defense of humanity. "No, my view upholds the natural order of things. Fuck her and get your rocks off if you must, then leave her."

Lightning slashed across the sky, highlighting in stark relief the roiling clouds their confrontation had unleashed. Zephyros's hands curled into claws and he nearly vibrated with the ancient need to put his brother out of his misery, out of all of their miseries. But Eurus *was* his brother and that connection—however damaged and distorted it had become—was hardwired into him. It meant something, something very hard to give up on. Moreover, killing an Anemoi would upset the balance of nature, and who knew what disasters would befall the human realm should that happen.

But it was truly difficult to keep all those rational, logical reasons in mind when he talked about Ella that way.

Ella. Lovely, sweet, and strong Ella. Filled with passion and life. Someone to be cherished, protected.

The old fear rose up. Urged caution. Demanded self-preservation. Memories barraged him. Maia's face in the mask of death. Hyacinthus walking away, choosing another. The easy, careless way Dion would roll out of bed, the sweat not even dried on their sated bodies, and treat Zeph like what they'd shared meant nothing at all. The expression Andreus wore as he left, refusing to say why he ended their still-new relationship...The list went on and on. Did he really want to add Ella to it? For his memory of her to be tainted by melancholy?

Don't give Eurus the power to choose for you, Zephyros.

The baritone of Boreas's voice splintered the dark spiral of Zeph's destructive thoughts. He heaved a deep breath.

He wanted this chance with Ella. He could almost believe he deserved it. Almost. Either way, it was no one else's business. Resolve settled over him like a warm, comforting blanket.

He stalked forward. "Just stay the hell away. None of this is your concern." Zeph plowed past him, shoulder checking him as he went.

Eurus returned the shove and whirled. "Fine. You want her? You think she's worthy of an Anemoi? Prove it. You have until New Year's End to plant your seed, Zephyros. Make an heir with her, and do it now, or I'm submitting this petition on Alastor's behalf. And make no mistake, it *will* be approved."

Turning on his heel, Zeph got right up in Eurus's face. "This again? I will not hear you spread such malicious lies about Chloris—"

"Wouldn't think of it." Eurus's smile was so smug it dropped Zeph's stomach to the ground. "Because it's not a lie. Alastor is Chloris's. And mine. What a night that was…"

Unthinkingly, Zeph's fist crashed into Eurus's jaw. Thunder cracked overhead as Eurus stumbled back a hard step. Zeph's brain was already running a mental calculation. Alastor's birth date, when Chloris left him. Nausea twisted his gut.

Eurus's tongue snuck out and licked blood from the corner of his lip. "Believe me now, do you?"

Damn it all to Hades, the dates were close, so fucking close to making what Eurus said possible. No way Chloris would've… Was there? No. *No.* Oh, gods. "What did you do, you sick bastard? What did you fucking do?"

"Nothing she didn't want."

Zeph barely withheld the moan as the pieces clicked into place. "That's why she left, isn't it? You. What you did." His knuckles throbbed from how tightly he clenched his fists. If he swung again, he wouldn't stop until one of them breathed no more.

"You were better off. The fact she so easily foisted the kid on me, just threw him away, shows what kind of trash you were mixed up with."

Zeph sucked in a breath and forced a calm façade. "You and me. We're done." Within his chest, something deep and fundamental strained and frayed, threatening to sunder Zeph's very psyche.

"Don't test me, brother." Eurus growled. "You know what I say is true. And you know that means Aeolus will approve it."

"Don't call me brother." Zeph pointed, glaring. "And don't make me prove I'm the stronger god."

"You don't have it in you," Eurus spat.

"Maybe not before this conversation because a part of me didn't want to let you go. Even after everything you've done. You were still my little brother. That earned you my loyalty, my protection, a place in my heart from day one. But no more. The resolve I needed to make good on my threat? Nay, my vow?" Zeph shoved Eurus back with a burst of energy. "You just gave it to me."

Before his brother had the chance to escalate their conflict further, Zephyros shot into the air. Agony ripped through his chest as their strained connection severed. Once and for all. In the freedom of his elemental form, his psyche unleashed the pent-up emotions, railed against the injustice of his brother's revelation, against the torment of his brother's inexorable slide into damnation. Memories battered him, and the spring storm raged around him. This time, at least, he had the presence of mind to assess the sea below, to assure no one would suffer the same fate Ella had.

Ella.

Just the thought of her name, the memory of the softness of her skin in his hands, the lovely warmth in her words and her expressions—she wrapped around his heart and soothed him. Calmed him. What or who had ever achieved that for him before?

A magnetic force pulled him toward her. Her body would warm him. Her acceptance would be life-giving, a balm to his soul. But he wouldn't go to her like this, carrying all this rage and guilt and unease. He didn't want to scare her. Or disappoint her. Or risk ruining his chances in any way. He needed to pull his shit together.

And he also needed to decide how to take Eurus's threat. Dead seriously was probably the only way to play it safe. Zeph calculated. By the old calendar, New Year's Day passed two days before. Centuries ago, people observed the dawn of the new year on March 25th, with a week of celebrations, festivals and gift-giving, all culminating on April first. That meant he had well less than a week to explore this thing with Ella, to see if it was worth exposing her to Eurus's madness. Less than a week until his brother's threat might lead them into all-out warfare.

April 1st. April Fool's Day. The origins of that day lay in the medieval derision toward those who failed to adjust to the new calendar. Adherence to the old ways was met with tricks and pranks meant to tease and instruct. Those who didn't learn were deemed April's fools.

Maybe he was a fool to clutch at the hope and potential he felt around Ella. But, by the gods, some things were worth being foolish for.

But even if things did work out between them, how could he think she'd ever entertain a child in so little time? He couldn't. Aeolus would answer for whatever Eurus was plotting. No way he was seriously considering it. Zeph would make sure of that.

He could only pray that, if a relationship with Ella didn't work out, taking a hit to his ego was as bad as things would get.

CHAPTER TWELVE

Ella had searched the whole house, not that there was that much of it. Zephyros was nowhere to be found.

Well, what did you expect? You told him to go away.

After dozing off in her room, Ella had come out ready to talk, ready to explain. Or, if that didn't seem to be the right way to go, ready to act like a whole lot of nothing-at-all had happened. Whatever it took to make things right between them.

Now, it seriously looked like she'd never get the chance. She had no idea how to find him, where he lived. She vaguely remembered him saying his last name, but even if she could get it right, something visceral told her she wouldn't find him in the phone book. Because Zephyros wasn't any ordinary man.

Maybe. But she still wanted her answers. And he'd promised.

Plus, she wanted him.

She hung her head in her hands. *Oh, God. What a mess.*

Despite the nap, her earlier fatigue returned. Maybe food

would help. She never had gotten around to making him anything to eat. She wandered into the kitchen. Nothing really appealed to her. She threw a pizza into the oven because it was easy.

While she waited, she dug into her junk food stash and pulled out a half-pound bag of peanut M&Ms. Peeking into the bag, she shook it until her favorite color emerged at the top. She reached in and plucked two green candies out—she swore the green ones tasted the best—and popped them in her mouth.

Zephyros. Such an unusual name. Maybe she *could* find something about him on the Internet?

Glancing at the oven timer, Ella shrugged. She had twenty-two minutes to kill and nothing better to do. M&Ms in hand, she headed upstairs and settled into the comfortable leather chair at the desk in the spare bedroom. The green banker's lamp cast a soft glow over the room. Against the far wall sat a futon, but otherwise Marcus had made the house's second bedroom his home office. Floor-to-ceiling bookshelves lined one wall and a nearly new computer system with a huge twenty-four-inch monitor dominated a corner of the wide desk. Marcus had run his financial planning business out of this office, so he'd spared no expense to make it comfortable and workable.

Ella particularly enjoyed the room because, in the afternoons, light spilled in from the windows and the glass door that led to the balcony over the front porch. She couldn't wait for warmer weather to arrive so she could curl up on the chaise lounge out there with a good book.

Ella fished out more green M&Ms while she waited for the computer to boot up. Finally, she was logged on and surfing the Internet. She'd managed to type the letters "Zephyr" before Google very helpfully started suggesting matches. She scrolled down.

An HVAC company, a baseball cap manufacturer, a paintball store. No, no, no. Wow, the word had a whole Wikipedia entry. She clicked on it. Her options here weren't much better: a light or west wind, a mythological Greek god, a type of lily, a New York graffiti artist. There were also a lot of brands of planes, trains, and cars named Zephyr. That's where she'd heard that word before—it was a famous train.

Back at Google, she finished typing the name, and tried it with both an "os" and an "us" on the end. Either way, one result headed the top of the lists—Greek gods called the Anemoi who, according to legend, controlled the winds and seasons. She got sucked into reading. So much intrigue and drama. Greek myths were like the world's first soap operas, filled with star-crossed lovers, infidelity, secret babies, and backstabbing.

But these stories being mythology and all meant, by definition, they were made up. They were the urban legends of the ancient world. And since Zeph's hands had been all over her—and she'd been all over him—she could say without hesitation that he was real. Very real.

Through the stillness of the house, she heard the oven dinging its one-minute warning. Ella brought up a people search window and, just to rule it out, looked for Zephyros several different ways in the Annapolis area. She broadened it out from there. Nothing. The oven timer went off for good.

Ella closed her web browser and scooped up the bag of M&Ms. In the kitchen, she grabbed the oven mitt and pulled her pizza out to cool. The rich, zesty smell of spicy sauce, baked crust and savory pepperoni filled the room. Her stomach rumbled.

She plated two slices and grabbed a can of soda from the

fridge, but she couldn't get comfortable at the table. Her insides felt restless, confined. She picked up the paper she'd read this morning and discarded it as quickly. *Wow, had that really been just this morning?* Wind gusted through the tree behind the house, drawing Ella's attention. She slid out of her chair and slipped into one of her brother's old and way-too-big fleece jackets hanging on a hook by the back door. Despite the early evening gloom and the promise of rain, she grabbed her dinner, flipped on the porch light, and went outside.

The air had that special cleanness she associated with spring. You could smell the stirrings of new life. She sucked in a deep, cool breath and let some of her stress pour out on the exhale.

The back porch was small—only enough room for a two-seater iron table and chairs and a covered grill. Ella got settled, much more comfortable than she'd been inside in spite of the chill, and enjoyed her pizza with slow bites. The more she ate, though, the hungrier she felt, and she realized just how long it had been since she'd had a decent meal.

The image popped up unbidden—her and Zeph on a date at a nice restaurant. Maybe Carroll's Creek, where they could sit surrounded by the marina and see the lights of the Naval Academy across the water. She'd start with the cream of crab soup, so decadent in its richness. Or maybe they'd go to Carpaccio's. Despite the pizza she was eating, her mouth watered when she thought of the incredible pizza bread they brought to the table as an appetizer. Crispy on the outside, but soft on the inside, and covered in an incredibly savory sauce. Oh, and their pasta alla vodka...

The thought of her companion was even more delicious. She had no idea what he would wear, since she'd only ever seen him in scrubs, jeans, and T-shirts, but her mind put him in a suit jacket and collared shirt, open at the throat. God, he would look even more broad-shouldered, and that close-shaved beard of his would give him a dashing appearance.

No sense daydreaming about what she'd never have.

Shoving the thought aside, Ella wandered from the porch into the backyard. She wrapped her arms around herself, shielding against the gusseting winds. Above her, dark clouds gathered. Still, she took her time, ambling from one group of plantings to another.

The person who owned the house before Marcus had clearly loved gardening. Though her brother had let the beds grow largely unattended, the small fence-enclosed space was a riot of color by late springtime, and Ella felt like a symphony-goer awaiting the orchestra's arrival. While only the daffodils and forsythia shined their pretty yellow faces now, soon the yard would be a rainbow of life. The gardener had chosen plantings that would keep the beds in bloom at all times. The flowers would grow in waves and stages, like instruments joining in on a melody, and peak in brilliant bursts of color, just as music crescendoed. Tending this neglected garden, restoring it to its former glory—now, that would be a nice goal on which to focus. Having a plan, even a small one, filled Ella with a sense of hope.

Thunder rumbled close by. Fat drops of rain pelted down. One hit her throat and slid under her collar, snaking its icy tendrils over her. She shivered and dashed across the yard as the intermittent drops turned into a driving rain.

Lightning flickered and illuminated a spot of color off to the side. Ella stopped so quickly she skidded in the slippery grass. Her favorite rose bush, the one with the bright pink blooms, looked as if it was the middle of summer. Full, heavy blossoms sagged as they collected the falling rain. She glanced around. Everything else was as she expected except for this single, beautiful rose bush that had no business blooming. Heart thrumming in her chest, Ella stared until her clothes nearly soaked through, then jogged into the house.

She didn't know what to make of it, but somehow felt even more inspired for having seen it.

Inside, Ella grabbed a kitchen towel, swiped it over her face and hair, and dried her hands. She stripped off the fleece jacket and her wet jeans and chucked them into the dryer in the utility room. From the junk drawer, she grabbed a pen and a piece of paper. Time to make a plan. A real one.

She settled at the table. At the top her page, she wrote *Ella Gets a Life* and underlined it three times.

She wrote *1)* and paused, her pen hovering over the paper. She had all this time now, but no idea what to do with it. Her old job as a paralegal had been just that. A job. She'd thought she wanted to go to law school someday, but working at the firm had disabused her of that idea. Then she'd met Craig, got engaged, got married, and unthinkingly placed her career ambitions—or trying to determine what they were—on the back burner. Marcus had made her the sole beneficiary of his belongings and his insurance, leaving her financially secure for a long, long time. So few ever had an opportunity like this. To do what they *wanted*, what *mattered*. Now she had to figure out what that actually was, for her.

What did she love? What made her happy?

Zephyros.

"Oh, get a grip, Ella," she murmured.

Sailing.

Yeah, that was more like it. She could breathe when she

was out on the bay. Her soul almost took flight when the wind caught the sails and carried her across the water. But what could she do with that?

She scooped up her list, blank as it was, and grabbed the bag of M&Ms for good measure. Back at the computer, she typed "Chesapeake Bay" into the search engine and waited. The first results were like a revelation.

Of course. Why hadn't I thought of that?

The country's largest estuary, with a watershed encompassing tens of thousands of acres over six states, the Chesapeake was a body of water in trouble. You didn't have to be a tree hugger to know it. You saw it every summer in the fewer local oysters and crabs available to pick, in the beach closings due to water-quality issues at various waterside parks. She clicked on the link for the Chesapeake Bay Foundation and it was like a lightbulb went on. With a storm raging outside and the sound of rain pounding on the roof and windows, an hour passed before she realized it.

Grinning, she looked down at her list and jotted in all caps:

1) VOLUNTEER WITH THE CBF

God, if Marcus were here right now, she'd totally give him a bear hug. The thought set off a bittersweet pang in her chest. His loss made this possible, but she also knew in her heart he'd love the idea. Man, she hadn't felt this keyed up about something in, well, a very long time. She blinked the threatening tears away and added more goals to her list.

After a few moments thought, it read:

ELLA GETS A LIFE
1) VOLUNTEER WITH THE CBF
2) Restore the garden

3) Get True Blue repaired
4) Look into adoption and foster care

That last one was a biggie, and by no means an afterthought. Just because she couldn't conceive didn't mean she could never give a mother's love to a child who needed it. She wasn't ready to do anything about that desire now, but she ought to at least learn her options. Was it even possible for a single person to adopt or be a foster parent? She just didn't know.

What would someone like Zephyros think of her inability to have children? It was a ridiculous thought and she rolled her eyes at herself, but the question was always on her mind now where men were concerned. Craig had left her over it, so she couldn't help but fear other men would find it a deal breaker, too.

"Stop it," Ella said, turning back to the CBF's website. The feeling of having a mission drove the worries from her mind.

She had a plan now, and it was good.

And the best part of all? No man required.

CHAPTER THIRTEEN

Several hours sitting at the computer left Ella achy and bleary-eyed, though her mind and imagination were alive, energized, ready to dive into her to-do list, now taped squarely in the middle of her refrigerator door.

Desire to do something, to take that next step forward, gripped her with a restlessness that was as maddening as it was exciting. Tomorrow morning seemed a lifetime away.

Comfortable in pajamas now, Ella pulled the fleece she'd worn earlier from the dryer and slipped it on. Nearly groaning from its warmth, she sank into the couch and propped her feet on the coffee table. The room was masculine—all taupes and browns—making the enormous bouquet of spring blossoms stand out all the more. Especially since…she sat forward and brushed her fingers over the bouquet—they were some of the nicest flowers she'd ever received. They were still so healthy, you would've thought she'd just received them. She smiled and sat back again.

Who could've sent them? She couldn't imagine. But they

reminded her of her goals, and she smiled. Maybe the next time flowers decorated the house, they'd be from her very own garden.

Outside, the storm had finally ebbed and now a steady shower created a calming lull. Too bad she'd napped earlier. Sleep wasn't coming for her any time soon.

A thump sounded from upstairs.

Ella startled, craned her ear in the direction of the noise. But there was nothing. Maybe a branch had fallen on the roof?

She leaned forward and inhaled the perfume from the flowers, then pushed off the couch and went upstairs to check things out. The noise sounded like it came from the front of the house, so she started in the office. Through the darkness, she made her way to the desk and pulled the chain on the banker's lamp. Movement caught her attention from the corner of her eye.

Someone stood on the balcony, their large silhouette darkening nearly the whole door.

She sucked in a rasping gasp and stumbled back against the bookshelves. Her racing heart pounded blood through her ears. She screamed and bolted toward the hall door.

The wind knocked out of her as she crashed into something big and solid and unmoving. Something that wasn't supposed to be there. Arms wrapped around her waist.

"Ella. Shh, Ella. It's just me."

Shock and relief twined through her veins. Zephyros.

Zephyros was…here. In front of her. When, seconds before, he'd been outside on the balcony. On the far side of a locked door. A door that was still closed and still locked.

Trembling from the surge of adrenaline, she peered up at him. His astonishing good looks struck her anew. Jesus, he was rugged and kind-faced, masculine and tender. In the diffuse light of the hallway, his slate-blue eyes glowed, warming her from the inside.

It was the eyes that brought it all back in a rush. He'd gotten in her locked house before. Healed her with his hands. Seemed to move in ways and at speeds impossible and incomprehensible. Removed a curse—now that she thought about it, she'd not experienced a single instance of clumsiness or bad luck since he'd…done whatever he did.

A thousand questions vied for airtime. She shook her head and shivered—this time because the whole front of her, where their bodies pressed together, was wet through and cold. The state of Zephyros's appearance finally registered. He was soaked to the bone, like he'd gotten caught in the storm.

"You're all wet," Ella managed, realizing how stupid it sounded as the words left her mouth. Undoubtedly, it was the least important observation she could make in the moment, but it was the one with which her mind was most ready to deal.

Zephyros smiled, and his face took on that easier, open expression she remembered from when he slept. It soothed the last of her fright and tugged at a place deep in her chest. He rested his forehead against hers. "I missed you. And I'm sorry."

Ella breathed him in. He smelled of spring rain and night air. Her nipples tightened where she pressed against him. "Sorry for what?" she breathed, distracted by his encompassing presence.

"For earlier."

Heat infused her cheeks. "Oh." She shrugged. "I understand."

Zeph's arms gripped her tighter, yanking her fully against him. The rigid line of his erection pressed into her belly. "No, you don't. You don't understand how much you intrigue me." His head dropped so his lips caressed her ear. "You don't understand how much you attract me. You're in my head. All the time. You make my heart beat faster, my body ache with want." He kissed the shell of her ear and moved sinuously against her.

Her body came alive, tightening, opening, preparing. Ella gasped as he nipped and licked down her neck.

Then he growled. "What is this?" He tugged at the fleece collar around her neck.

"What?" she asked, trying and failing to keep up through the haze of lust.

"This…is this a man's shirt?"

Ella looked down. "Oh, yeah."

"I cannot abide it." His mouth dropped open and the dark blue of his eyes flared. "Please," he rasped.

Ella frowned. "I don't understand," she said, but she stepped back enough to pull the fleece over her head. She tossed it to the futon. "It was just my br — "

Zeph's mouth crushed to hers. His big hands buried in her hair. He pursued her, devoured her. His passion overwhelmed and overpowered. She stumbled back a half step here and there, until her shoulders hit the hallway wall.

Male spice filled her nose and tantalized her taste buds. Jesus, she couldn't get enough of him. She met him kiss for kiss, stroke for stroke. She sucked his tongue until he groaned deep in his throat, and then she did it again.

He grabbed her hands in one of his and braced them over her head, against the wall. He pulled away from the kiss, but kept their faces pressed together. They were both panting, chests heaving, their clothing wet everywhere they touched. He stroked her face, her neck. "I'm sorry. I didn't mean…I…" He pressed his lips to her cheek. "I couldn't stand seeing another man's belongings on you."

Ella's panties dampened at the possessiveness of his words, of their position. "It was my brother's," she whispered. "Just my brother's. No other man." She sought and found his lips. "Promise."

He groaned. "Thank the gods." Slanting his mouth against hers, he kissed her until she was dizzy and languid. Until his body was all that held her upright. Until she was half convinced she could live without oxygen.

But part of her brain demanded to voice its concern. She tugged her face to the side and looked up at him. "Can you say the same? Is there a woman in your life? Because I won't share." Given her recent experience, she didn't think it so unreasonable to clear up that basic expectation at the beginning.

Zeph cocked an eyebrow and licked his bottom lip. "No. There's no one else. Not for a long, long time."

"Good," Ella whispered. "Good."

"There's just me." He kissed her ear. "And you." Her eyelid. "In this moment." Her nose. "There's just this lost soul." His lips lingered over the corner of her mouth. "Who wants the most beautiful woman he's ever seen." He plunged in with his tongue for a short, searing kiss. "I want you, Ella," he breathed into her mouth.

The world narrowed to the space between them. Zephyros was all Ella could see, all she could smell, all she could feel. Her body responded to his words as if on command, and she could barely stand still against the urgent need to pull him down to the floor and straddle him.

Another part of her worried about the all-in approach. This man…he was different. And…maybe not just a man?

God, with all his male flesh pressing against her, that sounded ridiculous, but a weighty pile of evidence was accumulating she'd so far managed to compartmentalize and ignore. Could she really give her body to someone about whom she had so many questions?

Not to mention her more run-of-the-mill concerns regarding whether she should trust him not to hurt her. Whether she *could* trust him, given her recent experience. Her heart was the new poster-girl for gun-shy. She'd come by that shit honestly.

But it doesn't have to be about that, her body chimed in, ready, willing.

"Too fast?" he whispered against her lips.

His words tugged her out of her head. She met his concerned gaze. He released her hands and stroked her cheek with his knuckles.

"No." She shook her head. "Maybe. I'm sorry."

"Don't be." His brow furrowed and he stepped back, her body chilling at the loss of his masculine heat. "Hell. I just came storming in here. I should just…" He shook his head and turned.

"What are you?" she blurted. The words hung in the air, awkward and demanding, but she was glad she asked. She needed to know. Before anything else happened, she had to understand what made today's long list of impossibilities possible.

∞

Zeph froze with his back to her. He turned his head to the side, considering her in a sideways glance. *Damn it.* He hated the likelihood that this was the beginning of the end.

By why shouldn't it be more bad news? First Eurus's bombshell, then Aeolus's refusal to grant him an audience. Par for the course.

Cautious footsteps sounded behind him, and every step she came closer eased the ache his plans to leave had unleashed. She stopped short of touching him, but her heat and her aura warmed his back, tugged at his heart, blanketed him in calm. "I need to know, Zephyros. I can't not know the truth."

Gods, he understood that. He really did.

A light weight fell on his arm. She squeezed, her touch connecting them as it always did. "You can trust me," she whispered.

It was like she knew what he needed to hear.

Trust. Honesty. Such rare qualities. So few prized them. Having been denied them over and over again, though, they were like air to Zephyros. Just one relationship he knew he could trust. Just one person he could count on to be honest. He needed that from her. He wanted it.

And he wanted to give it in return.

He turned slowly. "I shouldn't tell you. I shouldn't even be here."

Hurt flashed across her eyes.

He grasped her chin in his fingers and lifted it to meet his gaze. "But I will, Ella. I fear it, but I will."

"You have nothing to fear from me, I promise." She tilted her face into the palm of his hand.

She was so wrong, though. The way she soothed and attracted his body and appealed to his heart—she could be the most dangerous person Zeph knew. To him, anyway. He released a deep breath and took a leap of faith—and damn how he hoped she leapt with him.

He nodded once. "I understand how this will sound. But

what I'm going to tell you is the truth. And I'll prove it if I must."

"Okay."

"Er, would you like to sit down, or something?"

"No. Just tell me."

He took a deep breath and looked her in the eye. "I am Zephyros Martius, Supreme God of the West Wind, Guardian of Spring, and one of the four Cardinal Anemoi."

Ella blinked. She opened and closed her mouth. Then her dark eyes went wide. "A god? An Anemoi?" She slapped her hand to her forehead and rubbed.

Zeph watched her, wary, waiting. His gut twisted and tensed.

"The freaking Internet was right. Holy shit, Wikipedia was right." She started pacing the short length of hall between where he blocked the stairs and the office door. "A god. A *god*. I can't believe it. Well"—she chuckled, a slightly hysterical sound—"I *can* believe it. I mean, come on, light comes out of your hands, and you healed me, and you poofed in here."

He quirked an eyebrow. "Poofed? I don't *poof*."

She stopped, as if just noticing him again. "Well, what do you call it?"

"Uh…materializing? I guess. I don't really call it anything."

"You just do it."

"I just do it."

She tucked golden brown strands behind her ears and closed her eyes. In the darkness, her shifting expressions were clear. He could see her thoughts playing out on her face, not that he knew what they were. And it was driving him crazy.

Curious brown eyes peered up at him. "So, then, the creepy guy, from before?"

"Eurus. The Supreme God of the East Wind and the Harbinger of Misfortune. My younger, estranged brother." *Yeah, that was prettying it up a bit.*

Ella sagged back against the wall. Slid down to her butt. "A god." She craned her neck to look up at him. "For real? Oh, never mind. I believe you, I do. But, Jesus, it's hard to wrap your brain around."

Her expression of trust made the distance between them, small though it was, feel far too great. He settled down on the floor next to her. It was a tight fit, his boots resting against the far wall, but he needed to be near her. "Thank you."

She shook her head. "Well, what are you doing here? Not *here*"—she rushed to add—"but on earth, down with us mortal types. Do you like...I mean...where do you live?"

He wanted to share himself, yearned for her to truly know him, but he couldn't help fearing that every revelation would be one revelation too far. "I come from the Realm of the Gods, but I spend much time on earth, just not usually in this form."

She froze next to him and frowned.

"Fundamentally, Ella, I am a force of nature. I spend much of my time in the elements, *as* the elements, protecting life, guiding spring's renewal. That is my purpose."

"Oh." She traced an invisible pattern against the cotton covering her knee. A soft pattering of rain sounded against the windows. "What is that like?"

The lack of judgment. The lack of skepticism. If he'd been intrigued by her before, now he was downright fascinated. The courage her open-minded curiosity demonstrated astounded him. He leaned his shoulder against her, craving her touch, needing to borrow just a little of her innate calm. When she returned the gesture by pressing herself against him, he closed his eyes in relief and delight.

He shrugged and met her patient gaze. "Mostly, it just

is. It's why I was born. Why I exist. But, as I sit here with you and think on it, it feels lonely and isolated. Don't get me wrong, what I am empowered to do is unquestionably important to this world. And there is satisfaction in that. But, there's an impersonality to it, too. What I do caters little to matters of the heart or body, yet I want…" He couldn't find the words, but he felt the yearning for connection and belonging soul deep.

"What do you want?" she whispered.

When they came, the words were unthinking and terrifying but true. "A chance. With you."

CHAPTER FOURTEEN

His words echoed in the stillness of the hallway and made her stomach flutter. She didn't need to ask for clarification—what he asked for was the very thing she wanted, too. A chance to know him. A chance to understand how he was even possible. A chance to explore the restrained chemistry dancing between them.

She shifted onto her hip, knees tucked under his thigh, and met his unwavering gaze. Jesus, he was so damned gorgeous. And the fact that he apparently wanted her amplified his appeal by about a thousand. "But, you're a god. I'm just a woman. You said it yourself. You live in a different realm, have a whole different existence. How can we—"

Fingers fell gently against her lips. "I know. I do. But there is something about you, Ella. Something I can't resist. And I don't want to. If there is something here, something we both want, we will figure out a way."

"But, aren't you busy right now? You know, with the whole spring thing?"

"I am always aware. And I have help. All is as it should be, for now." He chuckled, and the sound made her smile.

"You should do that more often."

"What?"

"Smile. Laugh. It looks good on you." She ducked her chin.

"Gods, Ella." He shifted and dug his hand into her hair, around her neck. "Say yes. Say you'll give me a chance. Tell me you feel it, this thing between us."

She nodded, loving the possessiveness of his grip. "I do. I feel it." She pressed a kiss against his forehead. "So, what now?"

The corner of his mouth lifted. "Is that a yes?"

His cautious enthusiasm made her chest go warm and tingly. "Yeah." Then his smile fell and she frowned. "What is it?"

"I have to be honest with you, though."

"Okay." She held herself still when self-preservation wanted her to draw away. She wanted to reward his honesty, whatever it was he felt the need to say.

"My brother is not happy that I'm here." He shook his head. "No, that's not strong enough. Ella, unlike the rest of us who prize life and humanity, Eurus…something happened to him…he thinks of humans as, well, subservient inferiors at best, worthless and inconsequential at worst. He's warned me away from you, and I think you should know that. What he did to you earlier? It was a drop in the bucket compared to what he's capable of." He squeezed her neck reassuringly. "I'm stronger, and I can protect you. But I'll understand if that's more than you want to take on."

Anger made her stomach go hot. She hated the thought of someone threatening this man who could show passion, then tenderness in turn, who seemed to value honesty the way she did, whose eyes shone with an ache that felt familiar. And she resented the idea that someone wanted to take her choices from her. Again.

Infertility. Divorce. Betrayal. Loss. None of these things she chose or wanted, yet they'd been forced upon her by circumstance or fate.

Zephyros? She wanted him—at least the chance of him. And she refused to be bullied into walking away, or telling him to do so. Plus, if he hadn't ever told her about Eurus, she wouldn't have known otherwise. His honesty gave her heart the confidence to take the chance her body so desperately wanted.

"Thank you for telling me. It is something to consider. But, you know what?"

"Hmm?"

"Fuck him."

Zeph's eyes narrowed and flared that deep blue light.

"I want a chance, too, and I refuse to run scared." Her stomach flip-flopped, revealing the hearty dose of bravado in her words. But, *damn it*, enough was enough. She was putting the world on notice—she was done with the bad luck and tragedy. *We're all full-up at the inn*, she thought wryly.

"So, fuck 'im?"

Ella blushed and nodded. "Yeah."

"Say it." He grinned.

"No."

"Come on."

God, she loved this playful side of him, so she rolled her eyes and humored him. "Fuck. Him."

She wasn't sure what happened or, rather, how it happened. But the next thing she knew she was flat on her back, Zephyros's huge body atop hers. The kiss was consuming and filled with gratitude, promise. His hands tangled in her hair, little appreciative and totally sexy groans echoing deep in his throat.

Desperate for more contact, she spread her legs, and he slid into the cradle of her thighs.

The earlier heat between them returned and went molten. Her body remembered her unsated arousal, which surged anew with every suck of his lips, stroke of his tongue, and shift of his hips.

"Say it again," he whispered against her lips, a sensual smile playing around his mouth.

"Fuck him, Zephyros. I mean it."

"Gods," he groaned. "That word, out of your mouth."

She kissed his cheek, his jaw. Leaning up, she licked his ear. "What word? 'Fuck'?"

His hands tightened in her hair, hips rocked against the jangling nerves of her center.

"Fuck," she whispered again, totally stunned at her own boldness. But she was too aroused to censor herself, and teasing him—and being teased in return—was just too damn much fun.

He bit out what sounded like a curse in a language she didn't know, and she went hot and wet between her thighs at the desperate, sensual tone of it. Cradling her head, he buried his face in her neck. He licked, nipped, and sucked his way down to the collar of her shirt, sliding against her, creating delicious friction against her nipples, her core. But not enough.

"God, I need more of you."

He kissed up the other side of her neck, dragging his weight over her in the most maddeningly delicious way. She drew her knees up, adjusting him so he fell closer to where she needed him.

"Ella," he groaned and traced the shell of her ear with his tongue. "What do you want? This time, you tell me. I don't want to make any mistakes here, and I"—he swallowed thickly—"I can't...I have to..."

She whimpered. Heart, body and mind aligned, she didn't need to think about it. "In me. Need you in me."

His weight disappeared. Then so did she. For a split-second, her physical self seemed to vanish. And then they were on the bed in her room.

Dazed and awed, she laughed. "What just happened?"

Heavy-lidded eyes traced over her face. "I don't have the patience to act human right now."

"Mmm, I kinda like the sound of that."

"Gods, woman, you are driving me crazy." He sat up, straddling her thighs, and helped her remove her shirt. That flaring light returned in his gaze, and she swore she could feel it drag over her breasts. She bared them to his observation, and he caressed them with light fingertips that made her shiver. "Such exquisite perfection."

Her breaths coming in faster, shallower draws, she grabbed the hem of his damp shirt. "So, you can move us with your mind, but can't remove our clothes? Not an all-powerful god, then?" Biting the inside of her lip to restrain the threatening smile, she looked up at him with what she hoped was innocence.

He blinked once and the cotton disappeared from her fingers. "Are you questioning my godhood?"

Mouth gaping, Ella dragged her gaze down Zeph's completely naked body. She couldn't restrain her huge grin. "Not...um, not anymore."

Zeph threw his head back and laughed, the warm and

totally delighted sound filling the room, surrounding her. Every so often, something happened and he seemed momentarily free of the weight his shoulders normally carried. Ella's chest went tight—what satisfaction she would feel to do that for him, always.

Starting now.

As his humor died down and the light of his eyes colored her skin once more, Ella focused on the impossible-to-ignore erection standing out from Zeph's body. That ridged stomach and fascinating cut of muscles above his hips weren't the only amazing thing about his physique. Jesus.

She wanted to take care of him. To please him. And she knew just how to begin. She leaned forward and licked the swollen head of his length. He sucked a sharp breath in through his teeth and groaned deep in his throat, urging Ella on and emboldening her. Still sitting before him, she scooted her body until she could reach him more easily.

In her hands, he was soft and rigid, thick and warm. Gripping him in one palm, she nuzzled the smooth skin against her cheek, then turned her head to kiss along his shaft from base to tip. His hand fell gently upon her hair and petted her, encouraging, rewarding. Ella smiled and breathed in the musky maleness of him, then opened her lips around his head.

"Ella," he rasped. "My Ella."

Two little words. They planted themselves into the rapidly moving organ in her chest. Ella closed her eyes and sucked him in, slowly, teasingly. As she moved, she wrapped her tongue around one side of him, then the other, still exploring. She found a rhythm and dropped her hands to his hips, using only her mouth to pleasure him. God, she'd always loved sharing this with a man—it seemed one of the few times a man truly made himself vulnerable, emotionally and physically, and she adored the connection that created.

Zeph's grip tightened in Ella's hair. Still, he allowed her to set the pace, but with that single touch he communicated the effect she was having. Words in that foreign language spilled from him again, his voice filled with gravel and need. He cupped her face and pulled back from her.

Biting her bottom lip, she peered up at him. "I want to take care of you."

He kissed her, short but deep. "You are. Phenomenally. But how about we take care of each other?"

She smiled and nodded around the kisses he showered over her face, and allowed herself to be laid back. His weight blanketed her and she reveled in it—she'd always loved the encompassing, secure feeling of a man atop her. She drew up her knees and welcomed him in.

He drew lazy circles over her hip and thigh with dragging fingers. "Later, I plan to explore every inch of you. But now, now I just need to be in you."

Ella nodded. "I need that, too."

He reached between them and stroked gentle fingertips over her folds. He hummed as he dropped his head against hers. "So wet for me," he murmured, lips hovering just above hers. "I want you, Ella. Can I please have you?"

CHAPTER FIFTEEN

Zephyros could barely restrain the energy flowing through his body, but it wasn't the dark maelstrom he was so used to feeling. Light suffused his whole being, filling him with a new and nearly unbearable sensation of goodness that hovered just on the edge of true, unqualified contentment.

It was Ella. It was all Ella.

"Yes," she finally replied, her hips tilting up, searching, inviting.

A warm pressure expanded within his chest until he thought he must surely burst. He kissed her, trying to communicate with his lips, with his every touch, how very much this moment meant to him.

Gods, how he hoped he wouldn't be forced to pay for this bit of happiness.

This time could be different. This time *would* be different.

He shook the thought away and took himself in hand just as prudence intruded through the haze of desire. Zephyros froze. The gods had no diseases they could pass, but they certainly had the power to procreate. Eurus's threat flashed through his mind, but no way he was letting that intrude into the righteousness of this moment. "Ella? Protection?" The fantasy of maybe one day not needing any—or wanting any—ricocheted down his spine. Good to know he wasn't packing too much into this.

Her gaze snapped into focus. "Oh. Um." She rolled her head to the side for a long moment, then turned back to him. Her whole face had changed. Warm and engaged before, her eyes had gone wary. Now she appeared uncertain, even a little scared. She shrugged with one shoulder. "I don't have anything because, um, well, I wasn't expecting this…and"—she sighed—"in the spirit of all the honesty you shared with me, I can't conceive, so…"

Zeph's heart clenched at the flat tone of her words, at what she shared. "I'm sorry," he said automatically. Where a moment ago he'd successfully shut Eurus from his thoughts, now his brother burst in uninvited. Could it really be a coincidence that his brother would stake his ultimatum on an infertile woman?

Ella shrugged again, her eyes skittering over his face but not meeting his gaze for long.

"It's okay," Ella whispered, voice thin and strained. She patted his bicep. Zeph frowned and struggled to make sense of her movements. Her pat turned into a push against his shoulder.

"What—" So tied up in his head, her actions caught him off guard.

"It's okay," she said again, words all mechanical now. He let her push him up onto hands and knees. Under him, she turned to get up.

"Ella." The bleak shift in her aura sucker-punched him.

Damn it. If he'd have kept his attention where it should've been, he would've been able to read how devastating the admission was for her. In that moment, his world shifted. Concerns over self-preservation transformed into a soul-deep need to preserve and protect...her. His gut now demanded, as a man, as a god whose purpose was facilitating the birth and rebirth of spring, to fix it. But a healing of this magnitude was not something that could be offered or achieved without consideration or sacrifice. And his brain cells were too scattered to think on the ramifications clearly.

"Please," she said.

Zephyros's stomach sank. He curled his arm around her shoulders before she could get away, pulled her back against his chest. "Love, wait, talk to me."

She shook her head and clapped her hand over her mouth. Within his grasp, she trembled.

"Are you crying? Ella, talk to me." She shook her head harder and he could literally feel her effort to restrain her emotions. He hiked himself up behind her so he could look over her shoulder. A single silent tear tracked across her cheek. The physical proof of her pain escalated the whole array of these new primal needs within him—to comfort, to protect, to defend.

His kissed the corner of her eye, tasting the salt of her tear on his lips, and slipped into the ancient tongue, whispering a small prayer against her ear. He hated learning that she carried around within her such a deep-seated pain. Of all the traits they might find they had in common, that was one for which he never would've wished.

He kissed her cheek and switched into English. "I'm sorry this hurts you so, Ella. But why do you pull away from me? I would comfort you." *The way you comfort me.*

Her breathing hitched and her eyes cut to him in a sidelong glance. "You…would?"

"Of course. Why would you think otherwise? Good gods, have I given you the impression my only interest here is in having your body?" Zephyros kissed her shoulder. "I want to know you. All of you. If you are in pain, I want to know that. I want to help ease it, if I can." The shadows receded from her face, easing the tension in Zeph's gut. "I understand why this would be upsetting, of course, but is it something more? Did something happen to you, Ella?"

She shrugged the slender shoulder between them. "My husband, or, rather, my *ex*-husband…he left me after we learned I can't have children."

Dark energy whirled through Zephyros. She'd been cast aside and deemed unworthy by someone she'd loved. Just like him.

No. Not like him. Because Ella didn't deserve the way she'd been treated. He shuddered in an effort to restrain an outburst. In the darkness of the rainy night, thunder rumbled.

"What are you thinking?" she asked in a small voice.

"I'm thinking I'd like to hurt him. But then, if he was still here, I couldn't be." His stomach soured. What a horrible thing to say. Had he no common sense? No compassion? He cut his gaze to her eyes, prepared for the recrimination he deserved. "I apologize, Ella. That was truly insensitive of me."

Her muscles relaxed within his grip and she sank back into his chest. "No it wasn't. I liked it. And I agree with you. I hate the idea that I might never have met you."

Zephyros clenched his eyes and absorbed her words into his heart, his soul. By the gods, this woman appealed to parts of him he thought long gone, long buried away, or broken to pieces by ancient betrayals.

"Zeph?"

He opened his eyes and knew how bright they flared from the light that illuminated her face and shoulder. But he couldn't help the release of some of the energy flowing through his veins. "Yes?" he managed after a thick swallow.

"Will you still make love to me?"

"That's not even in question. It would be my honor. And my pleasure." He dragged a finger over her hip, his mind rational enough now to make him want to put her fully at ease. "I know humans must be careful of this, so I want to reassure you that my body is clean and you will be safe, even without protection."

She smiled and bit down on her lip. "Thank you," she said with an expression equal parts shyness and seductiveness. He moved to roll Ella from her side to her back. She grabbed his hip, her touch warm and claiming. "No. Like this. Please?"

Zeph groaned and let himself once again acknowledge the deep, needful ache between his thighs. With his front to her back, his cock lay hard and heavy against the top of her buttocks. "This pleases you?"

She chuckled. "Uh, yeah. And I like the feeling of your arms around me."

"Oh, Ella. I would hold you forever." He shifted his body, loving the satin feel of her skin against his, and gripped himself in one hand. Ella arched her back and they were aligned. He dragged his sensitive head through her folds, coaxing her body. It wasn't long before he thrilled to find the slick evidence of her arousal.

She gasped every time he passed over her entrance. "Don't tease me. I want you."

Zephyros didn't need to be asked twice. He pushed in, inch

by hot, tight inch. Ella gasped and pressed back, encouraging him to go deeper. Wrapping her in his arms, Zeph moved his hips in a slow, steady rhythm. He thought to tell her how exquisite she felt, how much her generosity of spirit meant to him, how scared he was that he was falling so hard, so fast, but the incredible pleasure of physical connection stole his words, and nearly his breath.

And the connection wasn't just physical. As his flesh joined with hers, his soul sung, his psyche eased. When he was seated all the way in her, he paused, savored. He'd had his share of partners, but this felt different, full of some unnamed promise. Perhaps it was his healing energy within her, or her own special calming aura surrounding him. Perhaps it was her honesty and forthrightness—so different from the way his divine brethren behaved. Good gods, he wasn't sure who was claiming who here. But now that he was in her, he couldn't imagine *ever* leaving.

Unbidden, the memory of Eurus's threat slammed into his brain. The challenge to his line was one thing, the implicit threat to Ella—first with Eurus's visit, and then with his command to leave her—was something else altogether. A sharp spike of pain ripped through Zeph's chest. He held Ella tighter. Words in his native tongue spilled from his lips against the soft skin of her neck. Promises. Vows.

Ella gripped his arms, embracing him back in the only way she could, and turned to offer her lips. Zeph groaned and kissed her, so pleased to see the light back in her eyes.

"So good," she panted around his lips.

Oh, gods. "Yes," he breathed, stunned and overwhelmed by the feel of her, and grateful for this experience down to the marrow of his bones. He moved then, easy dragging strokes that stoked the fire burning within him. In his arms, her body was soft and warm, with curves everywhere a woman should have them.

"God, you're amazing," she said. She rocked her hips back into his, arching within his grasp and urging him to move faster.

"Oh, Ella," he rasped, pressing a kiss to her shoulder. "I can't get enough of you." His body demanded that he go harder, faster, deeper, but he wanted her immersed in pleasure, too. Wanted her boneless and sated. And he wanted to be the one to make her feel that way.

One arm still curled under and around her, he explored her body with his free hand. Her breasts filled his palm, the tips both soft and hard against his skin. He teased her there, loving her little gasps and whimpers, before plucking her with his fingers, small squeezes that pulled from her throat more of those sexy utterances.

Caressing over the soft curve of her belly, Zeph played with the curls his fingers encountered below. Ella's body jolted with his first touch there, and he was overcome with an instinctual need to elicit that response again and again. Finally, his fingers found the swollen nerves at the top of her sex just as his cock slid deep into the slick grip of her core.

Her head craned back into his shoulder and she cried out. "Oh, God. Touch me, Zeph. Don't stop touching me. Please."

Masculine satisfaction roared through him. The need in her voice owned him. In that moment, he would've done anything to please her. He swirled his fingers against her clit, firm and fast, wanting her to fall apart in his arms, wanting to know he'd been responsible for sending her heart into a sprint.

Zeph stilled his hips to concentrate on making her come for him. "Yes, love, yes. I'm going to take care of you," he whispered against the shell of her ear. His heart squeezed. What would it be like to do so not just now, but forever? To have someone who depended and counted on you? To have someone who turned to you first above all others to share the joys and sorrows of life?

"Oh, God, oh, Zeph." Ella sucked in a breath, held it.

Around his cock, Ella's body went tight and wet. Zeph groaned in appreciation.

Ella released her breath on a strangled, pleasured shout. Her muscles gripped and milked him until he could hold still no longer. He surged within her, faster and harder than before, as he gave in to the physical need gathering and intensifying deep in his gut.

ജാരു

Ella's head was spinning. And there wasn't much oxygen in the room. And every nerve ending in her body was alive and sensitized.

But yet she was grounded by the strength and caring and attentiveness of this incredible man. He surrounded her with an all-encompassing presence. His body holding and penetrating her was all she could feel. His taste was on her lips. His scent, combined with hers, filled the air. When she reached out, her hands found hard, masculine flesh, smooth skin over cut muscles. It was a maddening combination, all of it, and the most sensual thing she'd ever experienced.

She was torn between wanting to encourage him to go harder, faster, so that he could achieve the kind of earth-shattering release she'd just had, and wanting him to slow down so this could last the night. Forever.

Her mind tried to pull her out of the moment. *Is this a one-time thing? Will I be able to have him again? Why would a god want me when Craig didn't? How can this work out? How can this even be real?*

But Ella shoved it all away. Because all her senses couldn't be wrong. And after so much pain these last months, she deserved this. In the great balancing sheet of the universe, she was due for some good. And Zeph was good. Really good. Great, even. And she wanted him.

Not to mention, sex had never before been like this for her. She enjoyed it because of the closeness and connection it brought. But this…this was so much more. Intense physical pleasure with a soul-deep need for the feeling to go on and on—not for the feeling itself, but because of the person with whom she was sharing it. Everything that drove her wild, he repeated. Against her ear, he uttered a stream of encouragement and affection. His words and touch reached into her chest, and planted within her the incontrovertible belief that she was right where she was supposed to be, and with the man she was supposed to have.

It was a ridiculous feeling, and she knew it. And it was dangerous, too, this slippery slope of falling. She wasn't sure her heart could survive again the kind of betrayal she'd experienced before.

But something in her told her to believe. To risk. To want.

Zeph's arms tightened around her. "Oh, gods, Ella," he groaned. His thrusts quickened. Inside her, his cock swelled, creating more of that delicious fullness and pressure. The drag of his hard length within her was so damn good, and set her body on edge again.

Ella turned her head, wanting to watch him, to see him. His

eyes were brilliant, glowing and serene in his desire, like he couldn't want anything more than her in this moment. Wishful thinking, probably, but even the possibility that a man like this would be so affected by her made her heart flutter and her stomach flip-flop.

Words flew to the tip of Ella's tongue. Intense words. Ridiculous words, given how long they'd known each other. It was her loneliness talking, clearly. But that didn't stop her from feeling the need to release them into the world, into his heart, and hope he returned them.

Before she made a stupid mistake, Ella lifted her head and kissed him. When their tongues met, Ella sucked and stroked, pouring these crazy, bursting emotions into the intimate touch of their mouths.

Zeph groaned. His hips moved faster, less steady in their rhythm. Ella arched her back and broke their kiss, but her new position gave him more access, deeper access. He took full advantage, gripping her and hunching his body around her. Words fell from his mouth in that foreign language, and though she couldn't understand them, they wrapped around her nonetheless.

The desperation in his voice reverberated down her spine and settled into the nerves between her legs. She stroked herself, drawn by her need to share this orgasm with him.

"Oh, yes. Come with me, love. I can't…I have to…*fuck*." Zeph's grip tightened as his orgasm poured into her in pulsing spasms. He moved through it, and it went on and on, pulling incredibly sexy noises from deep in his throat.

Ella sucked in a breath at the masculine power of his body, at the unabashed pleasure of his release. White-hot energy spiraled and built in her belly, traveled lower, then detonated where they were still connected. She cried out, sure she couldn't handle the intensity of it, and then went limp and breathless against the bed.

Awareness came back to her in starts and stops. Zeph's arms still held her. Small kisses rained down on her shoulder and back. His cock moved within her, languid strokes that were infuriatingly arousing and tender at the same time.

He chuckled and his breath puffed against her skin. "You with me?"

Ella laughed softly. "Jesus. I think so." She grinned over her shoulder at him. For a long moment, she soaked in the expression on his face. Even in the dimness of the room, she could only describe what she was seeing as adoration and affection. She'd been loved before, even if it hadn't ended well, and she was sure she was seeing what she thought she was seeing, and not just a figment of her imagination.

Her heart squeezed in her chest. She wanted this, whatever it was or would be, so much. And it was happening so fast. But could she trust it?

CHAPTER SIXTEEN

Ella didn't know the answer to her own question. She only knew how she felt, how Zephyros looked, and what she wanted. She might pay for the leap of faith her heart and soul were telling her to take, but something deep and fundamental insisted this man, this moment, was the beginning of who and what she was supposed to become.

"I want to face you," she whispered.

Instantly, Zeph withdrew, a warm smile playing around his lips.

Ella's gaze raked down his body to the hard length of his cock. She knew he'd come. She'd felt it. Heard him. Maybe his ability to be erect again was a god thing? Well, who was she to argue? Besides, her body needed his, like magnetic forces deep in her chest pulled her to him on some metaphysical level.

Biting her lip, she reached out, inviting him with open arms to come to her, hold her, lie with her. If he was game to go again, no way she was saying no. It had been a lot of months since she'd had sex, and eons since she'd had sex for the pleasure and joy of it and not for the chore of babymaking. At least, that's how it had felt toward the end.

"Are you sure?" he whispered, nuzzling her neck.

"Yes." She raked her fingers through his short hair, earning a satisfied hum from deep in his chest.

He pushed into her and she closed her eyes at the goodness of it. "I don't know how to explain it," she said, eyes still shut, "but this feels so right. Being with you. Like it was meant to be." Her eyelids flashed open.

Zeph's eyes flared as she watched, the blue almost violet in its intensity. "I feel the same way. I can't get enough of you, and I don't want this feeling to stop."

She embraced his shoulders and pulled him down. His shaft slid in and out of her in strokes that were both gentle and powerful. His hips rolled over her pelvic bone, setting her body ablaze.

Again, he whispered those little encouragements in her ear, showering her with acceptance and desire and appreciation. The combination of his words and his cock shattered her control, and she came. Though softer, this release was no less intense for her heart to weather.

When he came moments later, she held him in her arms as he trembled and her name spilled from his lips.

Jesus, being with him felt so intimate. The feeling played tricks with her mind. Made it seem as though, surely, she'd known him for much longer than a calendar or clock would show.

It was exhilarating. Confusing. Exhausting. She covered her mouth with the back of her hand as she yawned. "I'm sorry," she said.

He chuckled. "Don't be." He rolled off her, but didn't let her go. "Ella?"

She turned on her side within his embrace. "Yeah?"

He tucked a lock of hair behind her ear. "I don't know what this is between us, but it's like nothing I've ever felt."

Warmth rolled through Ella's whole body, making her hair stand on end and her toes curl. "I know exactly what you mean."

His big fingers stroked her hair off her face. "You do?"

"I really do."

He smiled and kissed her forehead. "Thank the gods for that. Are you tired?"

"A little."

He grinned. "You're a terrible liar. I wore you out."

She glared at him. "Good to know you don't have an ego to go with that whole god thing."

He threw his head back and laughed. "Well, maybe just a little."

"More than a little." Shaking her head and smiling, she snuggled into his chest and sighed. "I love the sound of rain. So calming. One of the reasons I love March," she said, burrowing in closer.

Zeph's arms tightened around her. "It's like you were made for me."

The words were so quiet, she had to strain to hear them, but she did. And they thrilled her very soul. Uncertain how to respond, she said simply, "Maybe I'll rest a while."

"Yes." He kissed her hair and settled down next to her. The weight of a soft but foreign blanket fell over them out of thin air. Ella gasped and cut her gaze to Zeph's. He shrugged. "I'm too comfortable with you for either of us to move. Think you can get used to it?"

"The poofing?"

The corner of his lip quirked up. "I told you. I don't poof."

"M'kay, well. Whatever you call it, I can try. And it's very handy, so there's that."

He chuffed out a small laugh and pulled her tighter against him. "Sleep, love. I'll be right here."

⊰⊱

"All right, Ben. Thanks for the news." Ella paced the kitchen, phone in hand. "Yeah, I'm doing okay."

Zephyros walked in, fresh from the shower. Ella wondered in passing where he got the new set of clothes. More poofing? She managed a smile as he kissed her cheek.

"Sorry," she mouthed, hand over the receiver.

"It's okay," Zeph whispered.

Ben's voice drew her attention back to the phone. "I'll call ya when the parts are in, but Ella—*True Blue*'s gonna be in dry dock for a while."

"I know." She sighed. "I appreciate your handling this for me."

"I'd say 'any time,' but I hope to goodness never to see you the way you were that day."

Ella's throat went tight. She really liked Ben and had known him for years. He reminded her of the Gorton's fisherman and it always cracked her up. The gruffness in his voice touched her. "I know, Ben. Me neither."

After quick good-byes, she disconnected and tossed the handset to the kitchen counter. "Good morning, er, afternoon," she said, turning to Zephyros.

"Hi. Everything okay?"

"Yeah. Well, no." She rose on tiptoes to kiss his neck. "Got some bad news about my boat, but it wasn't anything I didn't expect."

Zeph stepped back and frowned. "I'm sorry."

Ella shrugged. "Not your fault. And it can be fixed."

He crossed his arms over his broad chest. Cautious, blue eyes bored into her. "But it is my fault."

Her eyes narrowed. "What?"

"Your boat, Ella. Your injuries. All of it."

"I don't…" A voice flashed into her thoughts. His voice. Muffled and distant. "I don't understand. How could it be your fault?"

"I was upset, and not paying attention."

Ella's heart beat faster in her chest. "Still not following you."

"The storm."

"Yeah." She pressed her body into his, reached up and cupped his face. "Whatever you're trying to say, just say it."

"*I* was the storm. I was in my elemental form. I behaved carelessly and recklessly. And you got caught in the middle."

The image of those roiling black clouds flashed within her mind's eye. She shook her head, her brain struggling to process. Finally, she asked, "It *was* you, or you caused it?"

His brow furrowed. "Both."

"Wow," she said. Multiple reactions coursed through her. Remembered fear and new anger competed with awe and wonder. She'd nearly lost *True Blue*, and that would've killed her. She dropped her hands from his skin and stepped back.

"I'm sorry," he said, tracking her retreat with a sharp gaze.

Ella nodded and rubbed her lips, her brain chugging along with this incredible information. But she couldn't make some of the pieces fit together. Her gaze cut to his. "When did we first meet, Zeph?"

His eyes were wary, but still he gave her the respect of meeting her gaze. "When I pulled you out of the water."

Ella gasped. "You?"

"Like I said, it was my fault. So I had to make it right."

Fingers pressed into her eyes, Ella shook her head. "You saved me?" She'd asked it as a question, but the truth of it flowed through her veins. She knew it on a fundamental level. Deep gratitude welled up in her chest. "You saved me."

Zeph shifted feet, like he was uncomfortable with the pronoun-cement.

But then the other part of what he'd said sunk in. *I had to make it right.* Ella's heart dropped into her stomach. Oh no. Was that what this was? "Well, I'd say that evens out for damaging my boat." The words came out more bitter than she'd intended, but learning she was some god's pity project did that to a human. She turned and braced her hands on the counter.

"And I'd disagree." His voice spoke from right behind her. "Your being in jeopardy was my fault. So helping you was my duty."

She sighed and her shoulders sagged. "I'm all better now, so I think you've done your duty."

Fingers gently pulled her hair back, then his lips pressed to her ear. "Duty is why I helped you, but it is no part of why I've stayed. And why I *want* to stay, with you."

Hope expanded within Ella's chest, made it hard to breathe. Ironically, as Zeph's arms wrapped around her, the pressing sensation eased and her whole body relaxed. "Then why?" she whispered.

"Because I am falling for you, Ella, and I'd like nothing

more than to make you fall for me in return."

Oh, God, she'd needed his words like water, like oxygen. She turned her face against his, the short-trimmed whiskers on his jaw rubbing her cheekbone, and met his gaze. "Is that true, Zeph? I know you're a god, and I'm just a human. But please don't toy with me."

"Ella, you're not *just* anything. And I promise you the respect of my honesty, in all things."

Relief rushed through her veins in a torrent and she turned within his arms. Their lips met in a kiss that was full of affection and forgiveness.

Between them, her stomach growled obnoxiously. Zeph pulled away from the kiss with a smile. Ella's face went hot. "I've got great timing."

Zeph cupped her cheeks. "Are we okay?"

Expression earnest, eyes pleading, there was only one answer she could give. "Yes. We're okay."

Relief and happiness colored his expression. "Thank you."

Ella raised on tiptoes to kiss his lips, her heart sprinting as words formed in her mind. She took a deep breath. "And Zeph? I'm glad for why you stayed. And what you hoped to do…it's already working."

One side of his mouth lifted higher in a smile that was both happy and sexy. "Yeah?"

"Yeah."

"Well, I like the sound of that."

She nodded. "So, can I make you something for breakfast, er, I guess lunch, now?"

"That'd be great." With one last squeeze, Zeph released her from his embrace.

"Honestly, I'm not sure what I have. I haven't been to the

store in a while." She turned to the fridge and opened the door. Slim pickings. "I have some leftover pizza. And I have eggs, so I could make omelets or pancakes. Or I could order something. What's your pleasure?" When he didn't answer, she glanced over her shoulder.

Zeph's eyes flashed at her. She arched an eyebrow, and he grinned. She chuckled. "Food first. Now, what do you want?" His eyebrows flew up, his whole face amused now. "You're incorrigible. To eat. What do you want *to eat*?"

"Pancakes?"

"Sure, but I really can order some food. Or we could go out."

"No, pancakes, please," he said with more certainty. "I've just never had them."

Ella halted and looked at him. "Really? Well, then, pancakes it will be." She moved around, pulling out utensils and ingredients. Zeph settled his butt against the counter and crossed his arms. His eyes alighted on her movements like a physical caress. It was nice, this sense of companionship.

An idea came to her and she grinned. "Do you like chocolate?"

"Yeah."

She reached up into her junk food stash and grabbed the bag of plain M&Ms. "How about some M&M pancakes?" She hadn't made them in forever, but Marcus had always loved them.

"I've never had them."

"M&Ms?"

"No."

Ella froze. "So, wait, you've never had pancakes *or* M&Ms? What do they feed you guys up there, or...you know, wherever?"

He shrugged. "Food is bountiful where I live."

"Maybe, but no M&Ms is a huge oversight." She crossed the room to him and fished two out of the bag. Green ones, naturally. "You need to file a complaint with the management. Open."

That odd but utterly sexy light flared up behind his eyes. She grinned when his lips parted. She placed them on his tongue, purposely letting her fingers brush his bottom lip when she pulled away.

He chewed and his eyes went wide.

"More?"

He nodded.

She grabbed a few more and held them out to him. He opened his mouth. Her heart kicked up as she fed him again. "Good, right?"

"They're crunchy, and then they're soft."

"Yeah. Exactly."

He dug his big hand into the bag, then his heated gaze cut to her. "Open."

Ella licked her lips and opened them. He brought the candy to her mouth and she wrapped her lips around his fingers, totally relishing the desire that colored his face.

He pulled his fingers away. She'd barely swallowed before he was on her, his lips pressed against hers, his tongue begging for entrance. She opened and welcomed him in. Oh. God. He tasted of chocolate and spice. The combination pulled the rug out from under her and she had to grip onto his biceps to counter the spinning of the room.

After long moments, he pulled away. "I like M&Ms."

She chuckled. Joy and humor bloomed in her chest,

and her eyes watered. She wiped the tears away and grinned at Zeph, whose face was bright and happy now. "I'm glad," she managed, chuckles still bubbling up. "So, I take it M&M pancakes sound good?"

He nodded and rubbed his hands together. And as it turned out, pancake making had never been more fun. It was sort of a one-M&M-for-Zeph, one-M&M-for-the-pancakes kinda process. But she wouldn't have had it any other way. She glanced up at him as she flipped a cake. "You know, I must really like you to share my M&Ms. I'm kinda addicted."

He leaned down and nuzzled her throat. "Is that so?"

She nodded and tilted her head away, opening her neck to his exploration. "Pancake," she whispered after a moment. Zeph pulled away, a smile on his lips. She scooped it off the griddle and placed it on the growing stack.

A couple more poured, flipped, and stacked, and they settled at the table together and dug in. "Now, since you're a novice here, I'm advising you to just go with a bit of butter and skip the syrup. Let the chocolate do its thing all on its own. But, that's totally up to you." She pointed at the bottle of syrup and shrugged.

Zeph picked up his fork and his eyes darted to the bottle, but he sliced into the sweet breading sans syrup, just like she suggested. He blew on the forkful a few times and then his eyes went wide as he chewed. "It's melty."

Ella had smiled so much this morning, her cheeks ached, but it was wonderful and so needed. "I know," she said. "That's the beauty of it."

They occasionally made small talk as they ate, but even the silence was companionable and pleasant.

It's gonna hurt when he's gone.

The thought broadsided her. Damn. Why couldn't she just trust in what he'd said? She thought she did. She *wanted* to. But clearly a part of her was hanging on to the worst-case scenario. He deserved better than that. He'd been completely honest with her, and hadn't given her a single reason to question him or his motives. She released a deep breath and pushed her empty plate away.

Zeph leaned back and rubbed his stomach over the gray shirt.

She let herself soak in his satisfaction, the way he was looking at her with such appreciation. She had to give herself a break. Craig's damage ran deep, so she was going to get tripped up, but Zeph wasn't Craig.

"Thank you, Ella. I really enjoyed that. And it's been eons since another prepared me a good meal with such care."

His words chased away most of her angst. She ducked her head. "I'm glad."

Fingers tugged at her chin. "Don't hide from me."

Ella felt the heat roar up her face. "I…uh…" She shook her head. "I don't mean to. I'm just out of practice with compliments." She rolled the edge of the napkin to distract herself from the intensity of his gaze.

"Well, we'll have to work on that, because when I look at you, I see quite a bit to praise."

She smiled and fought the urge to squirm. "Okay." Pressing a kiss into his palm, Ella breathed him in, then scooped the plates from the table and rose. As she settled them into the sink, arms surrounded her.

"I'm serious, Ella." He kissed her neck. "No one's treated me like you do for a very long time."

She twisted to face him, and his arms braced against the

sink on either side of her. "Why, Zeph? What happened?" Her hands fell against the warmth of his broad chest.

His eyes searched her face. "It's a very long story."

"Will you tell it to me sometime?" Ella's stomach squeezed. Would they have the time to learn all those stories of personal history that couples learned through weeks and months of dating?

"If you want to hear it, yes," he said, his face resuming the pensive, troubled expression he often wore.

"I'm interested in hearing everything about you. And like you said last night, not just the good stuff."

He closed his eyes for a brief second, then leaned in to kiss her. It was soft and chaste, and just a prelude to a hug that was full of the need for comfort. Ella gladly gave it, her throat now tight at the emotion silently pouring out of him.

She hated whatever it was that weighed so heavily upon him, and wondered what she could do to lift his spirits. When it came, the idea was perfect—providing the friend who owed her a favor was game to help out.

CHAPTER SEVENTEEN

Zephyros couldn't remember the last time someone had attempted to surprise him. That is, surprise him with something good, with a gift, with kindness. He'd many times been caught off-guard by betrayal and hurt. You'd think his godhood would protect him against those moments, but instead, his nature seemed to make him a ripe target.

As Ella bounded down the stairs, she was nearly vibrating with energy. Zephyros was delighted to see her so alive, the flush of enthusiasm and happiness coloring her face.

"You ready?" she asked.

He chuckled. "I don't know. Am I?"

She smoothed her hands over his T-shirt. "You are. Trust me. This is going to be great. But are you sure you don't want a jacket? I've got lots of Marcus's things still around."

But Zeph's mind strayed on *Trust me*. The words put his body at odds—his stomach braced at the idea of fully trusting, while his heart chided the reaction and insisted Ella was trustworthy, perhaps more so than anyone he'd ever known.

Unlike the gods and goddesses he knew, she had no motivation to manipulate and deceive. Or so he hoped.

"No, this is my weather. I'll be fine," he said with a shaky smile. "Now, you lead. I'll follow."

"Ooh, I like the sound of that. Come on."

Soaking in some of that odd, peaceful influence she radiated, he met her smiling eyes and felt his shoulders relax. Having been around her consistently, it didn't impact him as forcefully as it first had, but it was still there. Still powerful. Still something he could dip into when he needed, like ladling a refreshing drink from a cool spring brook. If it hadn't felt so nice, he'd probably have been wary. What was it about her? He was the god and she the human, yet she very clearly affected him physically and psychically.

He followed her out the front door and waited while she locked up, then squeezed himself into the passenger seat of her small car. His knees nearly hit the dashboard, even with the seat pushed back.

She laughed as she started the engine. "Sorry it's such a tight fit. I love my Prius, though. And it was a great car for living in the city." She patted his knee and backed out of her driveway. "Don't worry. It's a short trip."

He grabbed her hand and held it against his leg. "I don't mind." His gaze landed on another vehicle under a tarp at the top of the driveway next to the house. "But I have to ask. What's under there?" He pointed at the covering.

"Oh. It was my brother's car. A Solstice. He left it to me." She shrugged and looked away. "Along with the house and stuff."

Zeph turned his head to her. "You own a car called a Solstice?" Along with the equinoxes, the solstices were two of the most powerful days of the year, when the veil between the human and divine realms was thinnest. The make of car was just a coincidence, surely, but where Ella was concerned, those seemed to be piling up: her powerful aura, her praise of March—the month for which he was surnamed, and now a car named after the day that marked the passing of seasons…

"Yeah," she said, her words pulling him from his thoughts. "It's really fast, too. We can take it out sometime if you like."

He gripped her hand and cursed himself for seeing intrigue where there was none. "Anything, with you."

Her cheeks went pink, and it was lovely. "Glad to hear that. Because I'm hoping you'll like what I've got planned." She pulled onto her street and navigated between the parked cars on both sides, chattering about the neighborhood and pointing out landmarks as they drove. Cool sunshine filtered down through the tree-covered street.

A sign out the passenger side caught Zeph's eye. He froze. "Ella?"

"And over here is my marina. Horn Point. I love that it's walking distance to the boat. That was actually why Marcus bought the house here."

"Ella?"

She turned to him. "Yeah?"

"Please tell me I'm reading the street signs wrong." *And that this one* is *just a coincidence.*

She craned around to see what he was talking about. "What do you mean?" The car slowed as it approached a stop sign at the end of the next block. The crisscrossed green street signs read "2nd Street / Eastern Avenue."

"You live on Eastern Avenue?"

"Yeah."

"In the neighborhood of Eastport." He studied her face as she turned onto 2nd, thinking out loud now. "On the east side of this town."

She frowned and shrugged. "Yeah. Why?"

He shook his head as unease snaked into his gut. Just another coincidence. Had to be. A totally not-meaningful coincidence that the woman he was falling for had this strange, wonderful power over how he felt *and* had all these associations with the East *and* turned out to be infertile just as Eurus was trying to force him into making an heir. Damn, if that didn't have his brother's twisted sense of humor all over it.

A pit of suspicion rooted in his mind. He hated it, but it wouldn't be beyond Eurus. Maybe the whole warning drama had been for show, meant to push Zeph toward what Eurus wanted by telling him to stay away. And then he followed up with this ridiculous ticking-clock ultimatum involving a woman he knew couldn't conceive. If Zeph's fears were true, either way Eurus had boxed him in—to giving up the woman he loved on the one hand, or giving up an heir on the other.

Thunder rumbled low and long in the distance.

"Geez, I hope it doesn't storm again." Ella glanced out window. "Oh, and that is one of my favorite restaurants," she said, continuing the tour without realizing the turmoil roiling within Zeph. "Maybe we can go there." Short minutes later she pulled into a parking lot and announced with a big smile, "We're here."

"Okay," he said, peering out the windshield.

She hopped out of the car, still full of that energy he'd earlier found so remarkable. He got out of the car and surveyed his surroundings, though nothing setting off a particular warning.

She grabbed his hand and tugged. "This way. Come on."

Zeph followed, less enthusiastic than before. He had to be wrong, had to be overreacting. *Give her the benefit of the doubt.* He just wasn't sure how much more of that he had left in him.

They rounded a brick wall and crossed a circular drive leading to a hotel lobby.

"It's just through here," she said.

Zeph's eyes scanned the milling people in the lobby and the old photographs of seamen and sailors. Ella kept them moving forward until they left the building again and stepped out into a gusting spring breeze over the water. The bay lapped against the pilings and rocked the hull of a huge sailboat docked there.

"Surprise!" she called, holding her free hand out toward the boat.

Zeph looked from her to the sailboat and back. "We're going sailing?"

She hopped once, her smile brilliant, even brighter than the sun falling on her face.

"Yes. Just because my boat's out of commission doesn't mean I can't take you out. Plus, if I'm not the one sailing, I get to just relax and be with you. So it's win-win! What d'ya think?"

He felt the smile on his lips despite the unwanted doubt in the back of his mind. Here she was sharing a part of herself with him, and all he could do was look for the other shoe to drop. He cleared his throat. "I love this, Ella. Thank you."

She squeezed his hand. "Oh, good. I was hoping you would say that. Come on." Tugging him to the roped gangway, Ella waved to a man on board. "Kyle!"

A thin man in a baseball hat turned and smiled. "Ella, welcome." He unclasped the ropes on both ends of the boarding plank. "Come aboard. Come aboard."

Ella released Zeph's hand and made her way across, then shook the man's hand. "What luck that you were going out today. Thanks for letting us tag along."

"Well, it was an easy favor to grant. Besides, I can always use an extra set of skilled hands."

"Kyle, I want you to meet my friend, Zeph." She turned her smile on Zeph. "Zeph, this is Captain Kyle. He owns the *Woodwind*. Well, both of them. This is actually the *Woodwind II*. He agreed to take us out on his safety-check run. His season doesn't start for about two weeks, so we got really lucky."

Kyle extended a hand and a kind, open countenance. "Nice to meet you. Welcome aboard."

Zeph nodded. "Likewise. Beautiful boat." Zeph followed Ella and Kyle back toward the boat's cockpit, where a huge silver captain's wheel shined in the cool sunlight. A light crew moved around the deck, and Ella pitched in whenever Kyle asked her to do something. Zeph watched her work, watched her strong body stretch and lift. Her competence was a total turn-on. And before long, they were underway.

"Let's sit here," she said to him after a few moments, a happy flush coloring her cheeks. "I met Kyle through Marcus. The sailing community in Annapolis is both big and way too small." She laughed. "Everyone seems to know each other." Grabbing Zeph's hand again, she asked, "Are you sure you're warm enough? It's still pretty chilly."

Between her touch and her concern, guilt finally replaced doubt as the leading emotion squeezing his chest. She deserved better than what he was giving her. How like him to look for ways to mess up a good thing. "Yes, I'll be fine." He waved a hand at the sky. "This is all a part of me, remember?"

A quizzical expression stole over her face, then she smiled. "Oh, right."

"As long as it's not exceedingly hot or cold, I'm good in any kind of weather," he said, forcing himself to be more open, more talkative. To get out of his damn head.

"Wow, you're really amazing. You know that?" She pressed her cold lips against his cheek.

He wrapped an arm around her shoulders and squeezed. "Not half amazing as you." Tucking his head against her hair, he breathed her in.

She struck up a light conversation that eased his mind and body. He admired how open and free she was, despite her own experience of betrayal and heartbreak. Without question, she could teach him a thing or two. If only he'd have the time to learn from her.

Eurus's warning loomed in the back of his mind. Surely that's why he'd been so edgy all morning. Having claimed her body, received her acknowledgement that there was something special between them, the thought of having to leave her—or of losing her in any way—pained him to the very core of his being. Somehow, in the next eighty hours, he had to disarm his brother's threat, figure a way to truly be with Ella, and settle this heir issue with Aeolus. He couldn't linger in her realm forever, and there had to be a succession plan for the West that didn't involve an eastern god.

"Nice breeze today," Kyle said. "What could be nicer?"

Ella smiled, totally in her element. "Nothing at all. Take us flying, Kyle."

He grinned at her and winked from behind his glasses. "You bet."

A few onlookers waved from shore as the boat passed an

open promenade, then Ella was pointing out the grounds of the Naval Academy, the Severn River, and the old radio towers looming over Greenbury Point. Beyond that, the *Woodwind II* sailed into the open water of the Chesapeake Bay and picked up speed.

At the captain's orders, the crew hoisted the sails, magnificent furls of white going up and up. The wind captured the boat and lifted it, carrying it along the water's surface at a good, strong clip.

Ella tilted her head back, and the wind streamed through the long tendrils of her golden brown hair. "Oh, God, I love this." She leaned against his shoulder. "Isn't it incredible that something seventy-four feet long and weighing 50,000 pounds can move like this?"

"Truly," Zeph said. He closed his eyes and breathed the wind deep into his lungs. He concentrated and let the clean air blow through him. He released his doubts and fears and worries and felt lighter as the stiff breeze carried the dark emotions away.

"In the summertime, you can barely find a free speck of surface, there are so many sailboats out here. The spring and fall are my favorite times to sail because there's less traffic and great winds. Like today."

Zeph couldn't help but smile at her unintentional compliment. What fortune to find a woman who valued and praised the wind. He shook his head. The more she intrigued him, the more vulnerable his heart became to her.

He just had to be sure not to poison the gifts she offered with his self-doubt.

Leaning against him, Ella said, "They used this boat in a movie a few years ago. It was called *Wedding Crashers*. Very funny. Marcus watched the filming. There's a photo album around here somewhere."

Zeph kissed her forehead, enjoying the cadence of her voice mixed in with the breeze. It was like music to him. "Tell me something else," he said, wanting more of the magical notes.

She smiled up at him. "About what?"

"Anything."

Her fingers caressed the curve of bone around his eyes. "Your eyes are bright again."

"Your fault."

Despite the cool air, her cheeks reddened. He liked that his words, his look, could do that to her. "Okay, well…" She looked away, out over the ship's bow. "Um, that bridge there." She pointed to the massive dual-span bridge that crossed the bay just ahead. "That's the Chesapeake Bay Bridge. It connects the Western and Eastern Shores of Maryland."

Zeph froze and eyed the impressive suspension cables arcing out over the bridge. The thing was a literal portal between East and West.

Ella continued on in that same warm lilt of her voice. "The views from the highway are phenomenal. You can see all the spires of Annapolis. Just beyond the bridge is where all the international ships anchor to wait for pilots to take them into the port at Baltimore. They're fun to sail near—you can see flags from all over the world. Sometimes Navy ships anchor here, too, even naval ships from other countries. They often come for events at the Academy."

The sound of her words continued to intrigue him, but he remained stuck by that one thing she'd said. "So, what you're saying is that you live on the divide between the eastern and western parts of your state."

"It's the east thing, right? That's what's bothering you?" The tone of her voice completely different now, Ella's words pulled him from his thoughts. She turned her whole body toward him.

Zeph felt his mouth drop open. "I…"

"In the car, too? I didn't put it together right away. But I'm right, aren't I?"

"It's just a coincidence," he said, willing belief into his voice.

"Do you really believe that? Because, honestly, you looked kinda freaked out in the car, and you just had that same expression on your face again."

He sighed and dropped his head. So much for not ruining what was between them.

"Hey." The warmth of her palm curled around his jaw and tugged his eyes back to hers. "I met your brother, remember? I was on the receiving end of his freaking curse. So I understand why anything to do with him would make you suspicious." Her gaze was all rich brown and open concern. "But how can I prove to you it *is* all coincidence?"

"You don't need to," he said, hearing the gruffness in his voice and feeling like shit. Here she was meeting his insecurities with understanding, when she would've been in her rights to be hurt or indignant, especially given the incredible hospitality and affection she'd gifted him.

"Are you sure about that?"

He nodded. "I'm sorry, Ella."

She shook her head. "Don't be sorry, Zeph. Just help me understand. What happened between you and Eurus? What happened that so damaged your trust? You know my story. Will you please tell me yours?"

CHAPTER EIGHTEEN

The *Woodwind II* returned to dock an hour later, and anxiety flooded Zeph at the thought of his promise to Ella. But she deserved the truth, and her reaction to his suspicions gave him hope that, just maybe, she would respond to the wreckage of his past relationships with equal grace and acceptance.

It wasn't a story he wanted to tell in public, though, so until they returned to her house, he was putting thoughts of the looming conversation aside.

Zeph followed Ella into the hotel lobby through which they'd earlier passed. Amazing the difference a few hours made. Having shared in her foremost passion, Zeph was more enamored with Ella than ever before. Here was a woman who prized the outdoors, who valued the natural environment and understood its functioning, who came to life the more the wind blew through her hair.

As they passed the maître d' stand, Ella whirled on him. "Are you hungry?" She rubbed her hands together and blew her warm breath over them.

His eyes fixed on her open lips. "Very."

She chuckled. "You're so bad. I'm talking about food, mister. I'm starving."

Zeph's gaze flew up to meet her laughing eyes. He loved seeing her so lighthearted. Amazingly, he felt his own cheeks heat up. How curious! But wonderful, too. Especially as the rapid beat of his heart accompanied the sensation. "I could eat."

She grasped his hand and squeezed. "Great. They have good food here. Wanna try it?"

"Love to."

A short wait later, they were seated at a table with a view of the water they'd just sailed.

"In warmer weather, you can sit out on the dock," Ella said, "and watch the boats sail up and down Ego Alley." Zeph frowned and Ella chuckled. "That's what they call the city dock inlet that runs along the front of these restaurants. Boaters drive in and out to see and be seen."

"Did you ever do that with *True Blue*?"

Smiling, Ella looked down at her menu. "Well, yeah. It's like a boaters' rite of passage or something. It was Marcus's idea, though. I don't think I would've done it without him pushing me. He was such a freaking showboater." She laughed, a sound full of good memories.

"Tell me about him," Zeph said, eager to keep that look in her eyes, on her face.

Just then, the waiter approached the table. He was tall, young, and without an apparent iota of self-preservation, given the way he was staring at Ella. "Welcome to Pusser's," he said, awaiting Ella to look up from her menu. "I'll be your server tonight. What can I do for you?"

Zeph raised an eyebrow as he glared at the man. He glanced

at Ella, who looked oblivious to the other man's interest. She seemed unaware in general of her effect on men, but he'd seen it in the way the younger crewmen on the *Woodwind* had watched her, and now the waiter.

She smiled at Zeph, eyes alight. "Their crab dip is incredible. You have to try some."

"Sounds great." He reached across the table and grasped her hand as Ella ordered. At first he'd done it to stake his claim—a ridiculous, foreign desire, especially given the awesome power differential between him and the human male—but then he'd felt how cold she was. He stroked his thumb over the back of her hand. "Why don't we have some wine, as well. It'll warm us."

Ella's smile grew. They selected a bottle and the waiter thankfully departed.

"So, Marcus?" he asked.

She stroked soft fingertips over his knuckles, a thoughtful expression on her face. "It's really hard to reduce my relationship with him to words. He was my other half, my entire life. He was born four minutes before me, and he never let me forget it." She smiled and her gaze flickered to his.

He sucked in a breath at the pain behind the smile. "You don't have to talk about him if it's too hard, love."

Shaking her head, she straightened in her chair and shrugged. "I don't have anyone else to talk about him with. I'd like to, if that's okay."

His heart squeezed in his chest. "It's more than okay. I want to know you, and with brothers of my own, I know how important they are."

Her grip tightened on his hand. "Yeah. We grew up on the bay and were into sailing by the time we were nine. My dad was retired Navy and loved it, totally encouraged it, which was great, especially since it's not the cheapest hobby a kid can be into." She smiled again, a small, sad expression. "Then we joined a junior sailing club and spent every possible second we could on the water. We started racing, and then we started teaching at the camps ourselves. I can't even talk about Marcus without talking about sailing. It's who we were. Where we thrived. We could fight about how he'd destroyed the bathroom we shared in one breath and be bonding over an upcoming race in the next."

The waiter placed the crab dip onto the table and poured the wine, then took their dinner order with a more professional demeanor. Hopefully, that meant he'd gotten the message.

"You have to try this," Ella said, spooning some of the creamy dip onto a piece of crusty baguette. "Some of the best crab dip in town." She handed the bread to him.

Zeph's tongue tripped over competing emotions. Gratitude that she wanted to serve him with her own hands warred with the conviction that she have her fill before he took from her plate. "You first, please," he said.

"Don't be silly. I'm dying to see if you'll like it. Growing up on the bay, eating crabs is almost in the blood. Go on, now, try it."

Unable to resist her enthusiasm, Zeph leaned forward and took a bite out of the heaping morsel in her hand. As he closed his lips around the food and chewed, a conflagration ignited within his mouth. The dip was molten hot. Totally surprised by the pain, Zeph choked the food down and the burn slid into his gut and stole his breath.

"Zeph? Oh, my God. Are you okay?" Ella flew out of her chair and rounded the table. "Your face is bright red. It's too hot, isn't it? Oh, God. I'm so sorry."

He heard Ella's concerned words and felt her hand on his back, but he couldn't respond. Sweat dampened the skin under his hair and ran down his spine. Zeph closed his eyes and attempted to focus his special healing energy inward. It didn't work, though. It never did. He'd just have to wait for the normal powers of his godhood to address the injury.

"Here, Zeph. Drink." Cold glass touched his lip and he recoiled. Without looking, he sensed the ice water, and knew that would increase his distress. But he couldn't talk. His tongue lay fat and swollen in his mouth and rawness coated the tender flesh of his throat. "Zeph. It's water. It'll help." Her hand caressed his hair. "Oh, God. You're sweating. Tell me what to do."

But there was only one thing that would help. He opened his eyes, met hers, and prayed she would understand.

☙〇❧

Zeph disappeared. Right out from under her hands. Stunned, Ella gasped and the water glass slipped from her fingers. It fell against the padding of Zeph's empty seat, splashing water and ice cubes everywhere but at least not shattering the goblet.

Ella's head whipped right and left, looking to see who was watching and how they were reacting to Zeph's invisible man routine. But no one was sitting right next to them, and those nearest were wrapped up in their own conversations.

Dazed and trembling, Ella sank into her own seat.

Zephyros.

Guilt ripped through her. Her eyes landed on the appetizer, thin curls of steam rising from the dip. What the hell was she thinking? He'd specifically told her he couldn't tolerate temperature extremes. The sharp angles of his face, the mottling of his skin, the way he shook beneath her hand—she'd never forget those pained, glassy eyes looking up at her as he endured what she could only guess had been agonizing, shocking, and totally foreign.

Where had he gone? Would he come back? And, oh God, would he think she'd done it on purpose?

The memory of their earlier conversation surfaced then, and she recalled how he'd tried to hide his fear and suspicion. Her heart had gone out to him, because she knew what it was not to trust. She'd been sad to learn he was doubting her, doubting them, but mostly because she knew that must stem from some big hurt in the past. At least that was her rationale for questioning what was going on between them. As she'd dressed to take him sailing this morning, all she could think was how she could ever be interesting enough to hold a god. He could apparently travel the world in the blink of an eye, and she was offering him an hour on a boat. Woo-hoo. It was everything to her, but how it could it possibly be enough for an immortal?

She reached for her wine, her hand shaking, and took a long gulp. The alcohol trailed warmth down her chest into her belly, and she could only imagine how much more intense that sensation had been for Zeph. The merlot went right to her head, and the room went hot and spinny around her.

The waiter delivered their meals, chatting and asking her questions she could barely understand through the roar of noise between her ears. She nodded in what must've been the right places, because he finally left. Her stomach rolled at the smell of her shrimp and she shoved the plate away and slumped back in her chair.

Minutes passed, and dread joined guilt. She sucked down

deep breaths, pushing back the threatening nausea and alleviating the tightness in her chest. The waiter came to ask if something was wrong with the food. Then he returned to ask if she wanted it boxed. Some time later, he offered dessert and coffee. Finally, he cleared the table, left the billfold, and stopped asking questions. Ella paid, but was at a loss for what to do. Should she wait? Should she go? Zeph obviously knew where she lived, but would he come here or go there?

She dropped her head into her hands and fought through the gathering panic to formulate a plan. Home. He'd come there twice before. He'd go there again.

Assuming he returned at all…

Ella shoved out of her seat so hard it tipped onto two legs. She grabbed the armrest and righted it before she made a scene of herself and tugged on her coat. The pity on the cute waiter's face didn't help. Great. He clearly assumed she'd been ditched by her date. Well, maybe she had—you know, right after she'd scorched the flesh off his insides.

Her knees felt weak, like they couldn't possibly carry her weight, but before she knew it, she was back at her Prius, remembering how adorable Zeph had looked all squished into the passenger seat. And not a single gripe.

A gasping sob tore up her throat and she slapped a hand over her mouth. She dropped her head against the cold metal of the car's roof and let it ease the headache blooming behind her eyes.

A heavy palm fell upon her shoulder.

Hope exploded in her chest. *A hand that big could only be…*She whirled around.

And found Eurus looming over her, less than an arm's reach away. Her arm, not his.

Her back against the car, Ella was trapped. And though the lot was lit and people walked the sidewalk along the street not thirty feet away, Eurus seemed to deaden and suck into himself every bit of surrounding light, like a black hole from which there was no return.

Ella's heart tripped and sprinted against her breastbone, and her earlier nausea worsened until she was swallowing repeated mouthfuls of sour saliva. "What do you want?"

"You hurt my brother." He cocked his head as if studying her, and even with the sunglasses she could feel his gaze slither over her face.

"I didn't mean it," she said in a rush of words, an ache settling in her neck from looking up at him.

He smiled, and despite the objective beauty of his mouth, her skin broke out in frightened gooseflesh. "Well, don't worry. I didn't mind. I was rather impressed, actually. Death by crab dip. I'll have to remember that one."

His low chuckle was like ice water down her spine. Then his words hit home, and she gasped. "Death?" *No, nonono.* She shook her head.

Eurus tilted his to the other side, still holding her in place with his hidden gaze. He reached out and fingered a length of her hair. "I heard how you praised the winds of fall. I think I misjudged you."

"What? No. I didn't…" She shivered as a cold breeze snaked around her. At the edge of the parking lot, the new spring growth on the trees stood perfectly still.

He braced his hands against the car on either side of her. "Yes, definitely misjudged you." His nose grazed her temple and she reared back as much as she could, which wasn't nearly enough. He leaned in closer. "Mmm, there is something so interesting about your scent. I think I'm going to need a taste of you, Miss Ella."

Ella's throat went dry, which was good because the sudden shock of it cut off the rolling nausea. The momentary relief unleashed a new sensation—anger. She shoved against him. When her hands made little progress, she turned and crashed a shoulder into his rib cage, sending him back a good step.

But it didn't have the desired effect.

He grabbed at her hands, lashed them to his chest in one gloved hand. His touch set her skin to crawling. "Yes. Hit me. Touch me. No one ever touches me. They're too afraid. But not you, right? Show me what you've got."

The taunting fueled her anger into rage, white-hot and explosive. She fisted her hands in his coat and wrenched her knee up between them, hoping, praying.

He shifted his thigh and turned his hips, chuckling darkly as he sandwiched her body against the car's frame. "Really, *love*," he sneered in an all-too-knowing voice. "Like I wasn't totally expecting that. Points for playing dirty, though."

Ella shuddered, from his tone, from their proximity, from the repulsive ridge of flesh grounding into her stomach. Jesus. He was getting off on this. The reality of her situation pressed in on her, literally. He had a good eight inches and eighty pounds on her, not to mention the powers of his evil godhood. She had no defense here, no recourse.

Still pressed against her, he nuzzled her cheek. "There it is. Nothing like human fear in the evening."

Ella huffed out a breath, her teeth chattering from the adrenaline rush. She hated the reaction, but couldn't control it. "I'm not afraid of you, Eurus," she spat.

"Is that so? Then what's responsible for these delicious

pheromones, Ella? I might come just from smelling your terror and feeling your body shake." He thrust his hips against her.

She clenched her teeth together to control the gag squeezing her throat. "You're just a big fucking bully. You might hurt me, but I expect that. It's predictable. I'm scared for Zephyros. You said he was dead. I don't believe you, but he is hurt, and that scares me."

From head to foot, a wave of ice cold shot right through her body. Her muscles went tight at the frigid shock of it.

Eurus sighed. "Zephyros. What a fucking bore. You're right, he's not dead. But he's not returning for you. Think he'd really let me do this if he was coming back? If he wanted you?" A wet, open-mouthed kiss fell against her ear. "He doesn't want you. Just like your husband didn't want you. Just like your brother wanted to get away from you. And your parents." He outlined her ear with his tongue, his heavy breath sounding right against her face. "Besides, Zephyros doesn't have the luxury of accepting your little defect. He requires an heir, and you can't really give that to him, can you?"

Ella sucked in a gasp and wrenched her head to the side. Tears pooled in her eyes and the bottom dropped out of her stomach as Eurus gave voice to her worst fear.

He stroked her hair, fisted at the back of it. "Nobody wants you, Ella. Except me. And you know what I want most? Do you? I want you to fear me." He bit her ear. Hard enough to make her want to cry out, but she resisted and bit her tongue. Blood spilled into her throat, a good distraction from his mouth all over her neck.

His words lit off a firestorm in her brain. Loneliness. Grief. Abandonment. Humiliation. Guilt. Shame. It was like he reached inside her head and plucked every hurtful moment from her memories. He stroked them, worried at them, twisted them around until she was drowning in them. Until she didn't know which way was up or down.

"Oh, don't believe me, Ella? I feel you resisting the truth of my words. What I say might not be pretty, but it'll always be true. How 'bout a test? Hmm? Would that help?"

Ella didn't respond, couldn't. She was literally trapped in the mental box he'd painted her into with his words, with his touch. Some part of her was conscious that her turmoil was likely the result of the chaos Zeph had said Eurus enjoyed creating. But she could only hold onto that piece of information for mere seconds before she was flung once more into the dark maelstrom of her worst fears.

"Just a little insurance," he rasped, his nose brushing hers. "Then, I'm going to call our boy, and you're going to see how he reacts. Moan for him, Ella. He comes."

Outside the mindfuck he'd trapped her in, agony shot through Ella's hand as it crumpled inside his crushing grip. Eurus's mouth devoured hers, smothering her screams, his hand pulling the back of her hair. Ella could neither resist nor participate. Her mind had closed in on itself. Her body had numbed out against the pain. Protective measures that left her an unwitting actor in Eurus's little show, of which she was suddenly aware because, there, in the middle of her box of fears, she saw Zeph standing on the edge of the parking lot.

Watching them kiss.

Hearing her moan.

Seeing her give herself so freely to the brother he hated.

With a roar and a crash of what sounded like thunder, Zeph disappeared.

And so did Eurus.

The car held her upright for a long moment, enough to hear evil laughter ring through her skull. Her knees buckled like soft butter on a hot day, and she went down, hard, onto the gritty pavement. And blessed nothingness overcame her.

CHAPTER NINETEEN

Owen Winters barreled off Interstate 50 onto Rowe Boulevard, and it was the first time the speedometer had dropped below 90 miles an hour. Two hours before, the closest thing he had to a father appeared on his doorstep, agitated and concerned. Boreas, the Supreme God of the North Wind and Winter, rarely asked for help. So when he did, Owen gave it, freely.

And thus he found himself driving into Annapolis, Maryland, looking for…he wasn't sure what.

Boreas feared that something bad was brewing between Owen's uncles Zephyros and Eurus, and it seemed to center on a human woman in whom Zeph had taken an interest. That news was shocking enough, but to learn that this person was important enough to tip the simmering feud between the two brothers into outright fighting was downright baffling, not to mention the harbinger of even worse things to come.

As he hit a traffic circle surrounding an old church, the skies opened up. Rain slashed down and pounded on his new

Porsche Panamera. Thunder and lightning exploded in the sky overhead. Damn it all to Hades, this was no natural storm. In it suddenness and ferocity, it had Zephyros written all over it.

Regret squeezed Owen's stomach. Earlier, he'd debated flashing here in his elemental form. It would've been a hell of a lot faster. But as a demigod now, that mode of movement exhausted his power in a way that would've been dangerous if some sort of preternatural battle was going down here.

He didn't like this. He didn't like it at all. He had more to lose than ever before in his eons-long existence. Megan, Teddy, the baby on the way. But he had another family, an older one, who apparently needed him now. He couldn't very well turn his back on them. And, at over seven feet tall, with swirling fur robes, and a long-ingrained habit of floating above the ground, it wasn't like Boreas could pop into the little town to assess the situation on his own.

At the next light, Owen checked the GPS and headed down the hill. Midway, something niggled at his consciousness, pricked to get his attention. He frowned and surveyed the dark, quiet street through the rain-streaked windows. At the stop sign, he debated. Right over the drawbridge or left into town? His senses flared, demanded he turn left.

Owen swung the car toward Annapolis's downtown. Extending his mind, he summoned that sensation, almost a signal—though weak—and followed the oddly powerful scent of it. Suddenly, it spiked. He hit the brakes hard as he passed a parking lot on his right. Throwing the car into reverse, Owen tore backwards into the lot, the heightened alert of his body reflected back at him through the glow of his eyes in the rearview mirror.

He turned up the first aisle, and the car's headlights swept over a hand lying limp on the ground. Unease swept through him, followed by certainty. This was what had unsettled Boreas. This was why he was here.

Owen drove past the body and parked the car. Ignition off, he blinked into his elemental wind form and soared up over the parking lot, sensing, surveying. That odd, powerful energy was concentrated here, though he couldn't identify the source. Beyond that, neither human nor god hid here. The heartbeat radiating from the prone body was the only life force besides his own in the immediate vicinity. Before the crumpled form of the injured human, Owen resumed his physicality. His sojourn into the wind had been short, so it hadn't cost him—much— though just enough to convince him he'd made the right decision in driving.

Crouched beside her, Owen stroked the rain-soaked tendrils of hair off the woman's face. Out cold. In the dark, with the storm raging around him, he couldn't make out her injuries, but her shallow breaths and elevated heart rate told him enough.

If this was the woman Zephyros cared for, why the hell would he leave her here? Why wouldn't he have come for her?

With a gentle hand under her shoulders and knees, Owen lifted the woman from the ground. Shoulders bent over her, trying to shield her from the cold needles of rain, he jogged across the lot to the Porsche. Megan's Jeep might've been a better idea, after all, but without question the Porsche got him here faster.

Door unlocked, he tucked the woman into the passenger seat. Her head lolled to the side. Owen bit out a curse. What looked like teeth marks marred the soft cartilage of her ear, and an angry bruise—good gods, was that a hickey?—

formed a big circle on her neck. He imagined this was Megan. Lost. Alone. Abandoned and injured in the middle of a night-darkened parking lot during a raging thunderstorm.

His mind rejected the image out of hand, and an unbidden, fear-laced rage spiked through his chest. Around him, the rain turned to sleet and snicked against the car. Where the hell was Zephyros?

Owen closed the door, careful that she was clear of it, and sent the summons. Once. Twice. He growled his frustration and called out, "Zephyros!"

Nothing. No sensation of acknowledgement. No ripple of approaching energy.

Soaked through, Owen ducked into the car and debated. Something told him not to take her to a hospital, but it was a ninety-minute ride back to his house, assuming he didn't hit traffic or an accident.

His gaze cut to the woman. Maybe she had some sort of identification, a driver's license, that would tell him where to go. Cursing Zeph, Owen reached across the center console and searched a coat pocket. Then another. He unzipped the coat and victory flared through him when his hand brushed something hard and rectangular lodged in an interior pocket. The small neoprene wallet contained cash, a credit card, and a driver's license. Perfect.

"I'll take care of you, Marcella," he said to the unconscious woman. At least he knew her name now. "Don't worry."

He typed the address into the GPS and took solace in the fact his destination was less than two miles away. Short minutes later, he pulled curbside in front of a small yellow house on a quiet, narrow street.

Owen lifted her from the car, trying to ignore the puddles

they'd both left all over his pristine interior—Zephyros was *so*
getting the car detailed for him—and dashed up the driveway
to the porch.

No key. Man if he hadn't had this problem before. He
refused to let his brain linger on the unhelpful memory and
scanned for hiding places. He found the key on his second
attempt, resting on the molding above a window.

Getting the key in the lock was a bit of a juggling act, but
soon they were in the embracing warmth of the house. Owen
marshaled the wind to close the door behind them. And damn
if Zeph's energy and scent wasn't all over the interior of the
place.

He shook his head, beyond mystified and getting more
pissed at his uncle by the minute.

There wasn't much to the main floor, so he took the stairs
in search of a place to let Marcella rest.

The first room he passed was a large office, the second a
bathroom. He found the bedroom at the back of the hall.

Good gods, not only was Zeph's presence palpable, it was
crystal fucking clear he'd been with the woman. The scent of
sex and divine energy clung to the sheets he settled her weight
upon.

Lighting the lamp on the nightstand allowed Owen to
get his first clear view of the woman. Very pretty. Almost
wholesome. He frowned and peered closer. Her left hand was
purple, swollen, and misshapen. A crush injury, if he wasn't
mistaken.

What the hell?

Careful of her hand, Owen tugged layers of covers over
her body. Her clothes were saturating the bedding beneath her,
but no way he would even think about changing her. He pulled

the folded throw off the footboard and added it on top.

Ducking out of the room, he was already dialing.

Boreas picked up on the first ring. "What did you find?" came the gruff, serious voice.

"A woman named Marcella. Injured and unconscious in the middle of a parking lot in town. I found her address on her license. We're at her place now."

"Marcella? Zephyros called her Ella. Nickname, I suppose."

"Probably. Would make sense. How's Megan?" Hand tugging the wet hair off his face, he paced the living room.

"She is fine, Owen, worry not."

"Can't be helped," he said firmly, which was why the only thing he'd asked Boreas in return for performing this favor was that he stay with Megan until Owen got back. He didn't fully understand the situation he'd walked into, but he didn't like it. And Boreas's presence with his family was the only thing that made his separation from Megan remotely tolerable. "Things don't add up here, Boreas."

"How do you mean?"

"Zephyros's scent is all over the woman's house. He's been with her. Recently. And"—he shook his head—"repeatedly, I'd guess. Good gods, I can't begin to imagine the scenario in which he'd leave her hurt and unprotected in a dark parking lot."

"Damn it. I better summon Chrys. Given what Zephyros said when I last saw him, he would not have done that. This has Eurus written all over it. Something has happened to Zeph."

"Well, the sky's damn near falling over here, so he's around somewhere." He lifted a curtain and glanced out at the street. Save for the pounding rain and streams running along the curbs, it was as quiet and still as when they'd arrived. "The woman's hand is crushed and she never even stirred as I moved her, but my gut's saying to keep her here, not to take her to the hospital. There's something about her, Boreas. There's an energy around her. Maybe it's Zeph's. I don't know." Owen fingered the iron amulet resting against his chest, an ancient piece that had belonged to his birth father millennia ago. "Damn mess."

"Go with your gut. And stay on the alert. I'll send Chrys your way as soon as I can find him."

"Okay. Is Megan still awake?"

"No. Fell asleep about a half hour ago."

"Hmm. Did she eat dinner?" he said, regretting not being there to take care of her.

Boreas chuckled. "Yes, Owen."

"What? I need to know she's okay."

"I understand, son. And she is. They all are. You have my word."

He sighed. "I know. Thanks. I'll keep you posted." Owen exchanged good-byes with Boreas and slipped the cell into his pocket.

At a loss for what to do, Owen returned to Marcella's room. If it was his woman, he'd hope his brethren wouldn't let her out of their sight. So he'd do the same for Zephyros and give him the benefit of the doubt. An oversized armchair drew him to a dark corner of her room, and he sank down into the embracing cushions.

He waited and kept watch as darkest night eased in to early morning gray.

∞✕∟

Brilliant pain roared through Zephyros's consciousness and

poured out of him in the form of driving rain and buffeting winds. But the intensity was unsustainable. Exhaustion swamped the shocking agony and sucker-punching betrayal until he felt gutted, hollow, hardly there at all.

So damn hungry for affection and connection, he'd ignored every fucking warning sign. The odd influence she held over him. The repeated associations with the East. The too goddamned many ways she seemed absolutely perfect. Made for him. As if.

And he'd fallen so hard and so fast, he'd never suspected, when and if an attack came, it would come from her. Why he'd gone back to the human realm, he didn't know. On some pathetic level, he'd held out blind hope his injury had been just a stupid accident. He'd seen the panic on her face, heard the concern in her voice. Or a close facsimile, anyway.

Now all he could see was the harsh truth staring him in the face. Eurus, all over Ella. Her, pliant and willing against him, passionate moans ringing out into the night.

That he was even surprised showed he never learned.

For the love of the gods, knowing what he knew now, no way her infertility was a coincidence given Eurus's threats. They were clearly in cahoots.

Zeph howled into the night wind.

His exasperation at himself did absolutely nothing to dull the agony squeezing the center of his being.

Fuck it. He was done.

Allowing the wind to carry him home, Zeph blanked out his mind and rode the flow. His subconscious achieved awareness as he approached the Realm of the Gods, and he willed himself to his private chamber.

Blood and flesh returned around him, adding physical pain

to the psychic agony already tormenting him. But it was good. Needed. It drove the fucking lesson home, in spades.

He was better off alone.

Soul-deep weariness crushed his insides, and he collapsed onto his bed so hard the giant wooden headboard crashed against the wall. Yanking covers over his hips, the fifty-pound weights covering his eyes slammed shut. The movie playing on the inside, well, he was going to ignore that fucker like there was no tomorrow.

A jag of warm energy shot through the room. "Comfy, Z? Can I get you anything? Another pillow? An eye mask? An Ambien? A fucking clue?"

Zeph groaned. No way he could handle his little brother right now. "Leave, Chrys. I'm serious. I don't want to hurt you, but I have only the slightest hold on myself right now. So I can't make any fucking promises."

"Try me. I'd love the chance to beat some sense into your thick skull, even if it meant I got my ass kicked in the process."

Zephyros cut his gaze to the younger god, the picture of rest and repose reclining alongside him on the bed. Bracing back on long arms, ankles crossed, golden waves tousled carelessly around his face, currently wearing an uncharacteristic expression of anger. "Why are you here?"

"Oh, maybe because B was worried enough about your ass to summon me from halfway 'round the world. He seems convinced some shit went down tonight, and you got hurt. But as you seem to have all your parts, I'd like to know what was worth interrupting my holiday."

"Yeah, because it's all about you."

"Don't give me that bullshit attitude—"

"If Boreas is so damned worried about me, why'd he

send you?" Usually Mr. Fucking Sunshine, deep power and aggression resided under the surface of the Supreme God of the South Wind and Summer. Zeph had changed the topic so he didn't have to deal with his brother's temper.

"Because B's a little busy hanging with Owen's family while Owen takes care of your woman. Which makes me wonder why *you're* not doing that your damn self." Golden light burst out of Chrys's eyes and cut a trail of heat over Zeph's face.

Zephyros narrowed his gaze, the words a jumbled mess in his brain. "What the fuck are you talking about?"

Chrys switched into the ancient language. "What part didn't you understand, brother, because I thought I was rocking the English pretty damn clearly."

Hiking himself up to sit against the mammoth headboard, Zeph glared at Chrys and fired words right back in their native tongue. "She's not my woman, and Owen needs to clear the hell out of there. Now."

Scrubbing his hands over his face, Chrys shook his head. "Wow. I thought the love 'em and leave 'em bit was my schtick. But at least I leave them happy, not injured and unconscious in the middle of a fucking parking lot."

"What?" A damp wind whipped through the room.

"Owen found her maybe two hours ago. Took her back to her house. When I left there, she was still out cold."

What in gods' hell was going on here? He almost felt he and Chrys were having two different and mutually unintelligible conversations. "You were at Ella's house?"

Chrys frowned. "Who's Ella?"

Zeph clunked his head back against the heavy wood. Once. Twice. "Try to keep up, Chrysander. Who the hell were we just talking about?"

"Marcella."

Zeph's head flew forward and he stared, disbelieving, at his brother. "I don't…that's not…"

Tugging a hand through his curls, Chrys sprang off the bed. "That's what Owen told me her name was. Maybe I misunderstood. At any rate, doesn't matter. I know she's the right woman, since your marking scent and erotic energy are all over that fucking house, and her."

Marcella. Her name is Marcella? He ground the heels of his palms into his eyes. Could it really be a coincidence that she, too, bore the name of Mars? The god of war and agriculture was his namesake and benefactor. Mars gave his name to the month of March, in ancient times known as Martius, during which Zephyros ascended to power each year.

No, doesn't matter. She's with Eurus.

Except…"I'm so fucking confused right now." His shoulders sagging, he looked up at Chrys.

"Well, that's pretty damn clear." Chrys braced his hands on his hips. "There's a kinda obvious way to get unconfused, you dig?"

Zeph pushed out of bed and materialized jeans to cover himself. "She's with Eurus, Chrys," he said, voicing his thoughts. "I saw them."

"I don't know what you saw, brother, but Eurus was nowhere to be seen. And Marcella was alone, hurt, and unconscious when Owen found her. Besides, since when has Eurus been with anyone? That shit stinks."

The truth of Chrys's words curdled in Zeph's gut.

Mother of gods, was it possible he'd misunderstood? But how? He'd been sure of what he saw, but then again, how many times had he made an errant assumption? He turned the scene of Ella and Eurus around in his head—what if what he'd seen hadn't been consensual at all? The new version of what had happened sucked the air from the room. Dread snaked up his spine. If Chrys was right, he'd just made the biggest mistake of his life.

CHAPTER TWENTY

Ella gasped awake, her mind resurfacing into consciousness all at once, as if she'd been frozen in time, not asleep. Her eyes expected the dark, Eurus, the rain. Her brain expected the psychic and physical violation of Eurus's little game. Her stomach rolled in remembered turmoil. At the end of her left arm, her hand felt like it had been put through a meat grinder.

For long minutes, she was totally confused and couldn't make out what surrounded her. As if her eyes were divorced from her brain.

"Are you okay?" came a deep, quiet voice.

A man appeared in her peripheral vision. Tall, dark hair… her pulse pounded through her veins. Eurus, he was—Wait, no glasses. Not Eurus. Another god, then, given the odd reflective quality of the eyes, visible even in the soft light of morning.

She shook her head. "Who are you?"

"My name is Owen. Owen Winters. Um…" He tugged a hand through the long layers of black that hung over his eyes. "I'm, uh, well…"

"A god." Hysterical laughter threatened to erupt, but Ella managed to batten down the reaction.

Owen narrowed his gaze. "He told you?"

Ella moved to sit up, but only had one hand to readjust her position. Owen rushed to help and piled pillows behind her back. "He who?" she asked, her brain struggling to shake the disorientation, and the pain from her hand adding another layer of haziness.

Kind eyes met hers. They were different colors. So interesting. "Zephyros," he said.

Zephyros. The very sound of the name set her body to trembling. Her fear for him. Her longing for him. How his expression shifted from disbelief to devastation as he watched Eurus kiss her. Her own despairing hurt as he abandoned her to the god from whom he'd promised to protect her.

She glanced up at Owen. "Yes, he did," she whispered.

He shook his head. "Well, okay, then."

A hundred questions raced through Ella's mind, but the main thing demanding her attention was the blasting throb of her hand. Her fingers extended like fat raw sausages off the softball that used to be her palm. The memory of how it happened shuddered through her. "I need a hospital, Owen," she said, her voice shaky even to her own ears. No way this didn't require surgery.

Owen sat at the foot of the bed and sighed. "I know it's necessary, Marcella, but I don't think it's a good idea."

"Uh…" She stuttered, unused to hearing her given name. She so rarely used it. "It's…actually, it's Ella. And why the hell not?"

"Sorry. Ella. Something bad went down here last night, and more might be on the way. Keeping all this private is better."

She scoffed. "For who? For all you god-types? Certainly not for me." She gestured to her hand, and immediately regretted the movement.

"I know. You're right. But I think I can help with that, at least temporarily."

Ella frowned, but the earnest look on the man's face sucked her in, made her believe him. "You have the ability to heal, too?"

Owen's mouth dropped open. "Good gods, he told you that, too?"

"Well, yeah, right before he healed me."

Owen sprang off the bed and paced the room. "I don't understand this. I don't understand any of this. No way he would reveal all this about himself if he didn't trust you and care about you. I know Zeph"—he paused to face her—"he hasn't had the best luck, so he doesn't trust easily. But when he does, it's everything. What happened between the two of you?"

Ella's breath hitched in response to Owen's impassioned defense. It just made her miss all the more that she couldn't have the man she wanted—shouldn't have him, at the very least. She let out a shaky sigh. "Eurus. Eurus is what happened. Well, mostly."

Owen held out his hands, silently asking her to continue.

She blew out a halting breath. "Look, I'd be happy to catch you up, but can we get back to how you're going to help my hand first?"

He bit out a curse under his breath and returned to her bedside. "Sorry. Of course." He settled by her knees, where he could reach her hand easier. "I'm a snow god," he said with a shrug. "I should be able to offer you some pain relief and get this swelling down until we can get you more help."

"A snow god."

Looking up from her hand, he nodded. "You ready?"

"I have no idea, but give it a try."

Owen cupped both hands around her injury. Even with the swelling, his big hands engulfed hers. A cold chill bloomed around her skin, only where they touched. The colder it got, the more relief poured through her. The throbbing eased, the ache dulled. She wasn't fooled into thinking it was all better, but with every passing moment, it became more and more tolerable until she felt she could take an easy, deep breath.

"So, if you're a snow god, does that mean you're not one of the Anemoi?"

Owen cocked his head and lifted his mismatched gaze from their joined hands to her eyes. "I am the adopted son of the Anemoi Boreas." He gave a wry laugh. "Is there anything you don't know about Zeph?"

"Yeah. Where he is. If he's okay. And why the hell he let Eurus assault me last night."

Shock molding his expression into hard angles, Owen sucked in a breath to respond—

"Well, if you'll let me, perhaps I could shed some light on those questions," came a voice from the doorway.

Ella craned to see around Owen's broad shoulders. Her ears must be playing tricks on her.

Belated knuckles wrapped against the wood. "I've brought company, Owen," another voice said.

"Yeah. I hear that," he murmured under his breath.

"Hey, you look better, Marcella. I'm Chrys." Whoever he was, the man possessed a star-fallen beauty: wavy, tousled blond hair, bright green eyes, sun-kissed skin, and muscles his shirt did nothing to hide.

"It's Ella," she whispered in response, unable to take her eyes off the man standing quietly next to Chrys.

Zephyros. With a haggard face and ancient eyes, he was still the most incredible man she'd ever seen. His gaze moved with calculating intensity between Ella's face and where her hand was joined with Owen's.

"Well, okay. See, Z? Clears up that whole name thing."

From across the room, Ella could tell Zeph was struggling to say something. Though he stood still, she could feel the tension rolling off him, sense his muscles screaming to move. Emotions she didn't understand played out across his face. "Owen," he finally said. "What are you doing?"

Ella shook her head at Owen and nailed Zephyros with a direct gaze. "He's giving me a little relief for this broken hand Eurus gave me last night."

"E broke your hand? What the hell?" Chrys whirled on Zeph-yros. "He broke her hand?"

Dark light flashed from Zeph's eyes. "Let me…I mean, may I heal it, Ella? Owen can help you temporarily, but I can fix it," he said, his voice nearly trembling. He clenched his fists.

"Can you, Zeph?" She glanced to Owen, who dropped his gaze. "Seems you could've done that last night, but didn't. So, why now?"

Chrys shifted feet, jammed his hands into his jeans pockets, and looked to the floor. Clearly, Owen and Chrys would've preferred to be anywhere else, but she was glad they were there. If she had to face Zeph on her own, she might give in to the soul-deep urge to fling herself at him, crawl up against his chest, and never let go. But that would be wrong on so many levels.

Zeph's gaze flickered over the other men in the room, but

he didn't back down from her challenge. "I made a mistake last night, Ella. A monumental mistake. I know that now. And 'I'm sorry' doesn't begin to describe the depth of remorse and regret I feel. But, still, I am sorry. And if you'll let me, I'd like to explain. Or try to."

Ella pressed her lips together, clamping down on the naïve, knee-jerk "yes" her heart wanted her to utter. But even if his words tempted her to forgive him, even if she could put aside the memory of Eurus's hands and body and mouth all over her, there was still the problem of her infertility. If what Eurus said was true and Zephyros was in need of an heir, she would never be able to provide that for him. As much as she already felt for this man, she knew her heart would never survive if she became more attached to something biology would prevent from ever really being hers. No matter how much they both might want it.

Better to not get in any deeper, then have to give him up later.

"You know, seems like we were just here," she said, remembering Zeph's troubled form sitting on the edge of her bed and asking for five minutes to explain. "Maybe it's not supposed to be this hard." She tucked her hair behind her ear and peered up at Zeph.

"Ella—"

Chrys cleared his throat. "I think I'll just…" He thumbed over his shoulder and turned for the door.

Owen tracked his retreat with a sidelong glance.

Ella took pity on him. Touching his arm with her good hand, she caught his attention. "You don't have to stay. It's feeling better. So, thank you."

"I don't mind," he said, frowning. "I should've taken you to the hospital."

She shrugged. "It's okay. Thank you for helping me. Zeph can take it from here," she added, letting Owen off the hook.

The younger man glanced over his shoulder and nodded. "All right." He gently released her hand into her lap. Where it wasn't bruised purple, her skin was bright red from the cold, but the swelling seemed to have gone down some. "I'm not leaving though. I'll just be down there with Chrys."

"Chrys, as in…"

"You've met them all now except my father. Chrys is the summer guy," he said smiling. It was a warm, genuine expression.

"I might've guessed that. Wait. Can you, you know, be down there…with him?"

"I don't—"

"You're a snow god, he's a summer god?"

Owen chuckled. "Yeah, as long as he doesn't try to kiss me or anything, I'll be okay."

"In your dreams," came a voice from downstairs.

Ella grinned, but the smile slid off her face. They would've been a really cool family to get to know. Hollowness filled her chest. Not gonna happen now. She wondered if she would even be allowed to remember them. Could they remove memories? Her stomach dropped at the thought.

Shaking his head, Owen said, "I'll be downstairs." As he passed Zeph, still standing by the door, he clapped him on the shoulder. It appeared a typical male greeting, but the way Owen's hand lingered for a moment communicated silent support.

Zeph watched him leave then turned to her. "Ella—"

She put her hands up, and the movement made her suck in a breath. Not smart. The pain in her lefty was only dulled, not gone.

Zephyros stepped to the center of the room, then stopped. "Can I please heal you? I know I've fucked this all up between us, but that...that I can fix."

Letting out a shaky breath, Ella nodded.

He appeared at her bedside. She hadn't even seen him move. This time, she knew he probably hadn't. Or, at least not in the usual way. His urgency warmed her heart and made it ache. "Do you want to lie down?"

She dragged her knees up and braced her elbow against them. "No. Just do it."

Zeph nodded. He held her gaze for a long moment, then reached down and placed his hands where Owen's had been. This time, instead of cold, there was light. That warm glow she remembered from...God, how many days ago had that been? Reverent words in that language she didn't understand spilled from Zeph's lips as the buzz of energy seeped into the structure of her hand.

Avoiding his eyes, which were too laden with emotion for her heart to resist, Ella dragged her gaze over Zeph from short hair to jeans. Memorizing every detail. The spot of gray at the temple. The way his brown hair just turned into a curl at the ends. The hard angles of his face and jaw, and the way a smile could make him look so much younger and freer. The broad shoulders, visible under the tight fit of his T-shirt. And, Jesus, no one wore a pair of jeans like Zephyros.

Her gaze trailed to his hands. No chance she'd ever forget them. How they healed her. How they touched her. How they made her hope again.

The scowl on Zeph's face drew Ella's attention. "What's the matter?" she asked.

He released a troubled sigh. "I'd say that's pretty obvious, love. This is an incredibly serious injury."

She barely heard the end of what he'd said for his use of the term of endearment. She just…couldn't. "But you can fix it, right?"

Zeph shifted feet and nodded.

"You can sit down, you know." She swung her legs to the side.

Eyes trained on their hands, he sat. Heat radiated off his body, and it took everything Ella had not to lean into it, especially since moving made it clear that her clothes were damp all down her backside. She couldn't wait to get them off and take a shower.

She sucked in a breath. "Oh, God. Did he mark me again? Are you gonna have to—"

"No," he rasped. "He didn't. I'd be able to feel it now." He nodded to their hands. "You're okay. Or at least you will be."

She nodded rapidly, her eyes blinking back threatening tears. "Okay. Okay."

"Gods, Ella, I am so fucking sorry."

The tight rein she'd held on her emotions slipped. Her breathing hitched. She clapped her good hand over her mouth and shook her head.

He swallowed thickly, the sound loud in the room. "Can you hold your hand out straight? I want to do a pass from the elbow down, just to be sure."

Ella extended her arm, grateful for something clinical on which to focus.

Gentle fingers bathed her in that preternatural light, starting at her elbow, trailing down her forearm, pausing over her wrist. He focused the light over the center of her palm for a long moment, and it was the oddest sensation—the bones seemed to tumble over one another and click into place, like the pieces of a 3-D jigsaw coming together. He moved on, then, and stroked each of her fingers from knuckle to tip in succession. The pain relief was so complete, her body began to react to his sensual, caring touch. Ridiculous. Dangerous.

Impossible.

With a tender squeeze, the light faded away within Zeph's grip. He looked up at her, eyes on fire. "It is done."

Yes, and so are we. Done and over. Or, at least, given what he needed and she couldn't provide, it should be. Ella bit her tongue and nodded, heart in a million pieces in her chest.

CHAPTER TWENTY-ONE

The look in Ella's eyes had Zeph's heart racing. He was losing her, or was about to. Or maybe he already had.

She drew in a long breath. "Look, Zeph—"

He laced his fingers with hers. "Wait, Ella, don't say anything," he blurted out. "Can I please explain? Yesterday, I promised to tell you my story. Will you hear it? It won't excuse what I did, but it might help you understand."

Her eyes flickered around the room, anywhere but at him. Thoughts and emotions played out in her changing expressions. That odd calming aura he'd felt from her before was still there, though greatly diminished at the moment. He didn't allow himself to take any of the feeling from her, though. Not now. Not when he'd failed her so spectacularly. He deserved to feel the full brunt of that. Time seemed to stop while Zeph waited for her to speak. Her head dropped on her neck and her shoulders sagged. When she looked back up, her expression was resigned. "I need to shower first."

Hope and gratitude exploded in Zephyros's chest. "Of

course."

Ella stared at him. "So, uh, can you…" Her gaze went to the door over his shoulder.

The request tempered his happiness. "Oh, right. Yes." He rose and walked backward toward the door. "I'll just be…" He nodded his head sideways.

"Okay. I won't take long."

"Take whatever you need, Ella." Zeph meant that in any and every way she might interpret it. For her, he would give anything, do anything. He turned and left the room, though it made his chest ache to separate himself from her. For a long moment, he held his hand flat against the wood of the closed door, willing her to understand, to accept, to forgive. If it would make up for the horrible mistake his blind mistrust and self-loathing had led him to make, he would spend the rest of his life earning those things from her, showing her he deserved them.

Zeph braced for the shitstorm that was awaiting him downstairs. He took the steps slowly, like a man on his way to the gallows.

Expressions filled with a whole lot of what-the-fuck, Chrys and Owen both stood in the center of the living room, his brother with his hands on his hips, Owen with his arms crossed over his chest.

Owen cocked an eyebrow, waiting.

"What do you want me to say?" Zeph asked, his ears picking up the whine of the plumbing as Ella turned on the water upstairs.

"Gods, Z, he broke her hand," Chrys said. "Where were you?"

"And that's not all," Owen said, voice quiet. Chrys's gaze cut to Owen. "When she said she was assaulted, she didn't just mean her hand."

A burst of wind whirled through Ella's living room, lifting the curtains in waves of fabric, scattering magazines. "I swear to the gods, Owen. What. The fuck. Are you saying?"

The younger man heaved a breath. "She's got marks on her ear and throat, Zeph. Um, bite marks."

Zeph went elemental. It was the only way he could cope. He remained in the living room, and knew his brethren would be able to sense his presence. But he needed an infusion of metaphysical energy to deal with the mounting pile of evidence of his massive fucking failure. As a man. As a lover. As a protector.

Owen's words forced him to face the truth of it: he watched Eurus assault Ella, the woman he loved—yeah, he knew that shit now, without question—and did abso-fucking-lutely nothing about it. Worse. He left her to it.

How could she ever forgive him? How could he expect her to? He knew, right down to the bottom of his soul, he didn't deserve her, but that didn't keep his selfish heart from wanting.

Chrys sighed, his voice softer now. "So, I gotta ask again, Z. Where were you? How did E get his hands on Ella?"

Returning to corporeality, he sagged onto the couch, arms braced on his knees, head hanging. "Ella and I...we were at dinner. I didn't pay enough attention, and let her feed me something that turned out to be scalding. I went elemental to heal the injury, back to the Realm of the Gods." He sighed, his voice going more and more monotone in his own ears as he spoke. "Earlier in the day, I'd learned she had all these associations with the East, there were all these coincidences piling up, so I was already suspicious."

"So you thought she'd done it on purpose," Chrys stated. It

wasn't a question—he knew Zephyros well.

Zeph nodded, finally looking up. The combination of pity and understanding from the pair of gods was a real kick in the ass. "When I returned, hoping I was wrong, I found them kissing. She appeared a willing participant. I'd found exactly what I'd been looking for all along—proof she was too good to be true."

"So you left," the blond said.

"So I left."

Owen cleared his throat. "Do you love her, Zephyros?"

"Yes." He spoke without thinking. He knew it to the very marrow of his bones.

The men exchanged glances. "You realize there's another thing you're going to have to deal with here, right?" Chrys asked, tugging a hand through all that hair.

Zeph frowned and nodded. He'd been wondering when Chrysander would pounce on him for this healing. He hadn't required a sacrifice from her—because it wasn't her sacrifice to make. But, in so doing, he'd violated a major tenant of the use of divine magic in the human realm. "It was worth it."

"You're going to have to see Father, Z. No doubt he already knows."

"I know. I have something else I need to discuss with him anyway. But right now, I just need to talk to Ella. Father can wait."

Chrys groaned. "The longer you wait—"

Zeph flew off the couch, appeared right in Chrysander's face. "I'm not leaving her! What part of that don't you understand? I did that once, and look what happened."

Owen put an arm, then a shoulder, between them, proving he was madly brave or just plain mad. He'd never been as strong as the Cardinal Anemoi, and as a demigod, was even less so.

But what he lacked in power, he made up for in character and integrity. Zephyros nodded to him and stepped back.

Chrys squeezed Zeph's shoulder. "When you're ready to go, I'll go with you."

Zeph stared out the front window for a long moment, then turned back to Chrys's serious gaze. He nodded "Thank you, brother."

Upstairs, the water shut off. Zeph's eyes tracked the sound.

Owen got right in his line of sight. "Fight for her, Zephyros. It's worth it. I'm telling you. You have to put all the shit aside and fight." Wisdom and compassion flashed out of those strange mismatched eyes.

"I will. I have to." Zeph sighed. "You guys don't have to stay for this."

"We'll stay," Chrys said, plunking into an armchair and picking up the remote.

Owen stretched out on the couch. "We'll stay. Just"—he grinned at Chrys—"go get us a snack."

Zeph glared, but headed to the kitchen. Ella's fridge and cabinets were alarmingly sparse. What did the woman eat? Bingo. He'd found what could only be called a stash. Candy. Cookies. Something called Nutella. He grabbed the Oreos for the guys. He looked wistfully at the bag of M&Ms. What he wouldn't give to go back in time to yesterday afternoon when she made him pancakes full of the candies. The list of things he'd do differently was a mile long.

Back in the living room, Zeph chucked the package of cookies onto Owen's chest. He caught them with a curse, then his face went all kid-in-a-candy-store.

"Aw, man, these are awesome." He took three and passed the container to Chrys. Zeph shook his head and paced.

Light footsteps descended the stairs. Zeph froze. Waited. Behind him, he could feel the other gods trying to act normal, affect some casual nonchalance. He appreciated the effort, for Ella's sake.

When she cleared where the staircase met the wall, she paused. "I'm done."

Zeph could hardly breathe for the fresh, magnetic scent of her. Cheeks still pink from the warmth of the shower, hair damp over her shoulders, she looked lovely to him. "Okay. Should I…"

She glanced at Owen and Chrys, gave them a small smile that made Zeph's heart hurt. "Yeah, let's go back upstairs."

Zeph followed her up and frowned when she led them into the office, not her bedroom. He had no context for her here. Even with the light on, the room felt formal, stiff. He didn't know what to do with himself.

She sat on the far end of the futon. He followed her lead, choosing the middle—not as close as he wanted to be, but not as far as he could be.

Zeph dropped his head. "Ella?" When she didn't answer, he turned toward her. Exhaustion and heartache painted her expression. He hated that he'd put those there. "Do you have marks on your neck?"

She gasped. Her hand tugged more hair over her shoulder. Though she normally tucked it behind her ears, he noticed she hadn't. His stomach dropped.

"Can I get rid of those? Please?" he rasped, almost unable to talk for the rage and guilt bubbling up his throat.

"It's fine," she said, looking down.

"For the love of the gods, it is not even in the same realm as fine. The sheer number of ways I failed you…" He balled his fists and closed his eyes, reining himself in. No use scaring her by losing control. And he was hanging way out over the edge. "Please, Ella, I can't begin to imagine—" He heaved a breath. "Please."

It was a single nod, but it was all he needed.

He scooted right next to her, relieved to be closer. She smelled of vanilla and woman, that light, calming aura shimmering around her. "Can you pull your hair back?"

Her eyes flicked to his, then away. She pulled her hair into a ponytail and held it there.

Zeph ground his teeth to restrain the curses poised on the tip of his tongue. But mother of gods, his brother's teeth had actually penetrated the top of her ear at one point, and otherwise left a semi-circular trail of angry bruises. As horrific, an enormous red-purple monster of a hickey dominated the tendon on the side of her neck.

Hand shaking, Zeph focused the healing energy over that round mark first. There would be more hell to pay with Aeolus for this, but it couldn't be avoided. In this moment, undoing what he had caused was the only important thing in the world.

⛤

Ella's eyes traced the weaving in the futon cover, humiliation rolling her stomach, heating her face, and making it impossible to look at Zephyros.

This was a mistake. She should never have—

"When I was young," he began in a sad, quiet voice, "I had what you would understand as a wife. Her name was Chloris, and she was one of the goddesses of spring, of flowers, and of new growth."

Jealousy flared in Ella's belly, but then she'd been married before, hadn't she? Though, not to a god.

"We weren't together long, because of Eurus. I didn't know it, but he loved her. His hatred for me, it started all these long millennia ago, because he believes I stole her from him. She didn't love him, she didn't even really notice him. But that didn't matter to my brother. To get even, he told everyone in the Realm of the Gods that I'd kidnapped Chloris, held her hostage, and raped her until she acquiesced. He even lodged a formal complaint with our father, demanded an investigation."

Ella gasped, and outrage for him stole her breath.

His hand cupped her neck. "We were young and impulsive. We essentially eloped. But I didn't do those things, Ella. I promise."

Her heart squeezed in her chest. "Oh, Zeph, I never would've thought you did, or that you ever could."

He nodded. "The gods live and breathe on one another's misfortune, and rumors spread about me and Chloris. We couldn't go anywhere without murmurings we were meant to hear and blatantly disapproving looks we were meant to see. It wore on her. She cried all the time. Word finally made it to her father. He exploded. Beat me to a pulp, and I let him, because I hated that she'd been hurt. She finally left me, which gave credence to the rumors in some people's minds."

Zeph's hand slid up to her ear, the warmth she recognized as his healing power spreading over her skin. She didn't know what to say, so she just let him speak, let him purge some of the weight he'd been carrying. "I was alone for a long time after that." His chuckle was without humor. "You can imagine that few were interested in me, given my reputation. Sometime later, I met another goddess of spring, Maia. We courted for a long time and planned to join our godhoods—what you would call marrying—but the week before the ceremony, she was found dead. Poisoned. No evidence could be found to identify the guilty."

"Jesus, Zeph." Ella's sympathy was a heavy weight on her chest.

He shook his head. "Through all this, I had a close friend who believed me, supported me, and after Maia's death, we became lovers. For a long time, we were together. Hyacinthus made me believe again, in love, in family, but then I learned that he had cheated on me—"

Ella gasped, and her stomach dropped through the floor. Her heart demanded empathy for the fact that he, too, had experienced the betrayal of unfaithfulness, but her brain, conditioned by Craig's lies, reacted to the other thing he'd said—that this Hyacinthus person was a *he*.

Zeph's eyes narrowed. "What are you thinking?" He caressed her cheek. "Your expression worries me."

"I…um…nothing."

"Please, Ella. Please tell me. I need your honesty as much as you've said you need mine."

Well, when he put it that way… "Okay. So, uh, this Hyacinthus person, he was a…*he*?"

Zeph tilted his head. "Yes. Does that bother you?"

"Not for the reason you might think. I mean, I guess it's a bit surprising, but I don't have a moral objection or anything to homosexuality. It's just, um, my husband, when he left me, he told me that he was gay. So it was better that we hadn't been able to have children, because he wanted to leave. And I was… God, Zeph…I was so mad at him, not because he was gay, but because how could he not know it, you know? But then… then I found him in bed with my best friend—a woman, by the way—who was four months pregnant. He'd started sleeping with her before he broke up with me. When I confronted him, he said he thought thinking he was gay would be an easier let-down than knowing the truth."

Zeph scowled, dark light flashing from his eyes. "Your husband was a coward and a fool, Ella, and you deserve so much better." He scoffed. "Better than me, too. Last night proved that."

"Zeph—"

"No, don't. Though, I feel you should know that, where I'm from, becoming intimate with someone of the same sex is accepted, somewhat common even. We don't distinguish or moralize the way humans do. But are you sure it's something you could accept? Because Hy wasn't the only man."

Conflicting emotions stole Ella's voice. Not because she had a problem with his sexuality, which was surprisingly intriguing, if she was honest, but because in answering him truthfully, she'd be giving him hope that they could be together. And given her wasted womb, they couldn't. Not really. Finally, she murmured, "Your bisexuality is not a problem for me, Zeph. Honestly." She chose her words carefully, aiming for honesty and neutrality, too. "So, I'm sorry, I interrupted. You said he'd cheated on you."

He nodded and released a breath. "Yeah. Does the name Apollo mean anything to you?"

She shrugged. "Um, one of the gods who was supposed to have lived at Olympus?"

"Yes. One of the twelve Olympic gods. Zeus's son. Very complicated, and very powerful. That's who Hy was cheating with. In the end, guess who he picked?"

Ella didn't need to ask. It was clear from the way his shoulders sagged and his eyes went downcast, he'd lost Hy not only as a lover, but as a friend. "I'm sorry that happened to you."

"These stories, Ella, they go on and on. Every time I put myself out there again, put my heart on the line, I was betrayed or abandoned. I began to suspect Eurus was behind some of my bad luck, but at first I wrote that off as paranoia and scapegoating. But then someone I'd been with told me he broke off the relationship after Eurus had planted some concerns about me in his ear that he just couldn't shake, just couldn't risk. And my suspicions gained more and more credence in my mind. I can't prove it, but everything in me tells me he murdered Maia, which is why what I did last night is so damn unforgiveable. Even I see that. I should've known. Because I've been through this with him in the past."

Before he looked up, Ella fisted the dampness that spilled from one eye away. Apparently she didn't get it all, though, because Zeph swiped a gentle thumb under her eye. "That you cry for me breaks my heart. I don't deserve it."

"Stop that, Zephyros. Stop it right now. You have been through hell. And you certainly didn't deserve that. I've only been betrayed and left once, and I still struggle with trust. I question myself, my own judgment, the motives of the people around me. I get it."

Zeph leaned in, and Ella nearly groaned as she breathed in his clean masculine scent. Part of her wanted to close the gap between, to taste that scent off his skin. "I know I failed you, and I will regret that for the rest of my life. But I have to ask— can you see your way to forgiving me? To trying again?"

CHAPTER TWENTY-TWO

Ella's head was swimming. His heat, his scent, his hand on her throat—her body knew what it wanted. Him, in her, with her, now and always.

But no matter how gorgeous he was, how phenomenal in bed, how sweet he could be, and how appealing his words, Ella was still hung up on two things. "I think…I think I can forgive you, Zeph. Because on some level, I share your fears. I do understand. The problem is"—she leaned against the back of the futon and drew her knees up in front of her, forcing some space between them—"I'm not sure I can forget." She closed her eyes. "I can feel him on me. I smell his breath. It takes no effort at all to recall how he'd made me feel trapped in my own mind, with every worst fear come to life. I don't know how to forget that."

Zephyros winced and reached out to her, grasped her hand.

The words rushed out. "And, Zeph, I needed you. I needed you to find me, to help me, and you left. You left. And I thought…I thought…" She fisted her hand against her mouth.

"Oh, gods, Ella. I know. I wasn't there for you. I let you down on so many levels. And I'm so goddamned sorry. All I can do now is vow to you that I will always be there for you in the future, and hope you'll give me a chance to prove it. To prove I'd do anything to earn your trust, your belief, your love."

Ella closed her eyes and shook her head, willing her emotions under control. If she fell apart now, she'd fall right into him, and then what her body wanted would take over with no regard for what her mind knew was right. She blew out a breath. Once. Twice.

"Just tell me," he whispered. "Tell me what I have to do to win you back."

"It's not that easy. I wish it was. And, anyway, it's not the only thing."

"What do you mean?"

Despite the sweatshirt she wore, she shivered and wrapped her arms around herself. "Eurus said something—"

He groaned. "Ella, please do not listen to what he told you. Do not act on the lies he spreads. This is his M.O., over and over."

She heaved a breath, expecting just that reaction after what he'd shared with her. And while she had no doubt that Eurus had twisted the truth and lied and manipulated in those other situations, here, it was the truth. Plain and simple. "I can't have children, Zephyros."

His brow furrowed. "I know that. We spoke of that. I don't—"

"And you…you need an heir. Right? You need—"

Zeph flew off the couch, paced. "Damn it all to Hades, he's doing it again." He whirled to face her. "Don't you see, Ella? He found your greatest fear, your greatest insecurity, and he played it, planted doubt within your mind. Don't let him, Ella. Don't let him pull us apart."

Ella's breathing hitched. Haltingly, she said, "You didn't say he lied."

"What?"

"He didn't lie, did he? You need an heir. And if you're with me, you could never have one. And then…what? I know nothing of your world, Zephyros. What would that mean for you?"

He shifted feet, clenched and unclenched his hands. After a long moment, he finally said, "It means nothing we'd have to worry about now."

Ella narrowed her gaze at him. "That's not the same as saying it would mean nothing."

He held out his hands. "We would figure it out."

"What if we couldn't? Where would that leave you?"

Zeph came to her then, sank down onto his knees before her. Big hands rested gently on her shins. "It would leave me with you, Marcella Raines. You, who have opened my heart again to love, brought warmth and light into my existence once more, who have believed in me in ways I haven't known in eons. I would be with you. And it would be enough. It would be everything."

Ella gasped as a new obstacle reared up in her mind. "Until I got old and died." Oh, God, why had she not thought of that sooner? Them, together, twenty years from now, thirty, forty— him appearing just as he did now, and her…She shook her head.

"Be well. It wouldn't have to be like that. Owen's wife is human, but shares his immortality. We have ways."

"Oh," she said dumbly, relief flooding and confusing her at the same time. And that was part of the problem. The intensity of his speech, the desire in his eyes—it was impossible to think when he was touching her, pleading with her, weaving a future with his words so wonderful she wanted nothing more than to believe.

"I love you, Ella. If you feel the same for me, that's all I need to know. Everything else will fall in around that, just the way it should."

"I don't know, Zephyros. I just don't know."

"Do you love me?" he asked, blue light playing behind his eyes, giving them a backlit effect that was so mesmerizing.

Ella's heart hammered within her chest. She could say nothing but the truth. "I do. I love you. And I think I did from the moment you appeared in my hallway that night, soaking wet and asking for a chance."

"Praise the gods," Zeph groaned. And then he was on her, parting her knees and climbing into the cradle of her thighs. His hands found her neck and guided their mouths together for an urgent, searing kiss. They swallowed one another's small needful moans. Clutched at one another with too-tight grips they couldn't help. The reconnection was pure bliss and full of heat and warmth and belonging and acceptance.

A war erupted inside Ella. Her body was already gone, already his. Her heart wanted, oh it wanted, so desperately to give itself freely and completely. But her mind kept tripping on the questions, on the doubts, on the concerns she wouldn't be everything he needed.

She broke the kiss and turned her head away. "I can't," she said, panting.

"Love?" he rasped.

"I can't just fall into you, Zephyros. I can't think. I need to think."

"What are you saying?"

She released a shuddering breath. "I need some time, some space."

"How much?" he pressed.

She hated the change that had come over his expression, his eyes. She'd done that. She'd deflated the joy he'd so beautifully worn just moments before. But she couldn't help herself. She had to be sure. And she just couldn't think through what was in all their best interests with him here, loving her, wanting her.

"I need the day, Zephyros. At least."

Zeph's head dropped back on his shoulders, and Ella had to resist combing her fingers through his short hair, had to resist soothing the hurt she knew she was causing.

"Whatever you need." He pushed up from the floor. "I need to see my father, so I'll be departing for a while anyway. But I'll return just as soon as I can, tonight or tomorrow morning at the latest."

"What for?"

He dragged a hand through his hair. "Just touching base on some family business."

"Oh, well, then, good. Tonight or tomorrow morning would be…yeah, that would be fine," she said, her chest pinching at the thought of being separated from him. Didn't matter that she was the one who asked for it.

"I would like Owen to stay with you, though. Would you permit that? I couldn't stand the idea of you being here alone, not with Eurus lurking out there somewhere."

Ella's answer was immediate. "He can stay. I'd like him to." She didn't want to be alone anymore than he wanted her to. Anyway, she liked Owen.

"Thank you." He shuffled his stance. Tension and unease

rolled off him, but Ella didn't know how to make that better. Finally, Zeph crossed the room to the door, opened it, and stepped through. He paused and leaned back in. "I love you, Ella. Please don't forget it."

And then he was gone.

∞⟶∞

Zephyros hadn't stepped foot on Aeolia in eons.

He and Chrysander materialized on the beach, the Aegean Sea lapping at the white sand. In the distance, the skeletal remains of ancient shipwrecks rocked in the surf, a physical reminder of their storm god father's power—and temper.

Zephyros turned to his brother. "You don't have to be here for this."

Chrys grunted, fidgeting with the traditional tunic and cloak their father still favored. "I don't mind."

"I mean it, Chrys. This is not going to be good."

"Which is why I'm staying. Doesn't the 'I'm-an-island-I'm-a-rock' routine get old after awhile?"

Zeph bit out an ancient curse. Chrys might look too damn pretty for brains, but he was one of the most observant—and loyal—gods Zeph knew. And he was right. Going it alone did get old, it really fucking did. The wave of gratitude had Zeph fidgeting with his own itchy as hell wool tunic. "Come on," he finally said.

Their father spent half of each year ruling over the winds and causing storms in the human realm from the ancestral citadel built into the bluffs above them. The architecture of the compound reflected its age, having been reconstructed and expanded multiple times over the millennia. A large section of it was situated underground, concealing its true size and strength.

They could've materialized in the courtyard outside the main entrance, but Zeph wasn't in any rush. Instead, they climbed the hidden path that twisted through dense stands of swaying palm trees. All the while, Zeph planned what he wanted to say. It wasn't a defense, really, because he didn't believe what he'd done was wrong. But he knew Aeolus wouldn't see it that way.

The path widened and the trees thinned, allowing more of the intense Mediterranean sunlight to filter through to the ground. Topside, they stepped into a clearing at an iron gate that looked deceptively antiquated. But everything about the compound was high-end, modern, and damn near fool-proof. No question their father knew of their arrival, not to mention their precise location.

Because of their lineage, the gate retracted automatically, sliding along itself to create a five-foot gap that allowed their passage into the side of the main courtyard. Full of well-tended gardens and extensive sculpture, the space was meant to impress. But Zeph barely noticed. The front door opened the same way, reading their genetic connection to the master of the house.

As was expected, they walked to the reception room and waited.

And waited.

"Shit," Chrys said after a long while.

"That about sums it up," Zeph agreed. The longer they were made to wait, the more pissed it meant their father was. At this rate, it would definitely be tomorrow morning before he could return to Ella. If he was lucky.

The doors swung open. Two guards in full-out classical military dress flanked the opening. "You are received," one of them said.

Zeph and Chrys exchanged glances and made for the door.

The guard held up a hand. "Only Zephyros Martius. You are to wait here, Chrysander Notos."

Dark golden light flared from Chrys's eyes. "What the hell?"

Zeph squeezed his shoulder. "Probably for the best. Why don't you just go? I can summon you," he added, when Chrys started to protest. "I don't want you getting caught in the crossfire."

Chrysander crossed his arms over his chest. "I said I'm staying. I'm staying."

Zeph nodded and left through the doors. They banged shut behind him, the heavy clinking of the locking mechanism echoing in the cavernous hallway. He tracked his father's presence immediately and cursed. He'd been hoping Aeolus would receive him in his study, but the passing hours should've disabused him of that idea already.

Instead, Aeolus's unique energy signature was located in the Hall of the Winds, the ceremonial center of the compound. So, no warm-and-fuzzy family reunion, then. Not that the Anemoi really did warm or fuzzy.

At the far end of the marble corridor, another larger set of doors opened as he approached. In resplendent color on every wall, massive murals depicting the mythology of the Anemoi covered the walls. Along the sides of the windowless, fortified room, minor wind and storm gods—including some who worked for Zeph himself—lounged and talked in low tones that turned to murmurs, then curious silence, as Zephyros proceeded up the center aisle of the great hall.

Pretending not to notice his approach, Aeolus sat at the head of the room on what could only be called a throne. He was a mountain of a god. Deep red robes wrapped around him in the traditional way, leaving one massive shoulder and a large swath of his broad chest bare. Wavy brown hair alive with golden and bronze highlights hung to his shoulders. Barefooted, his only other adornment was a massive firestone ring with gold carved wings.

At the appointed place, Zephyros dropped to one knee and bowed his head. Ella's image came to mind then. Deep brown eyes alive with passion. That beautiful open smile. The guileless joy as she'd tilted her head back and let the wind blow through her hair. The sad hesitancy from this morning was there, too—he didn't allow himself to forget that.

By the time his father acknowledged him, Zeph's back screamed and his neck had nearly atrophied into the downcast position.

"Zephyros," Aeolus finally said, his voice booming through the hall and hushing all other conversation. "How fare thee?" His typical greeting.

"Well, my lord. Thank you."

"And how fares the emergence of spring?"

"The West Wind is fair and powerful, my lord. All is well."

"Hmm. If that were true, you wouldn't be here." He stepped down off the dais, a soft breeze circulating around the hall. "Clear the room," he commanded.

Zeph held his position as the other gods obeyed. Those who could dematerialize did. Those who couldn't left with haste. When the doors thundered closed, shutting the two of them in together, Zeph's heart tripped over itself and set into a sprint.

It wasn't fear, exactly, but his body was already bracing for whatever was coming. The surge of adrenaline was uncontrollable.

"Your brother is here." It wasn't a question.

"Yes," Zeph replied, head still bowed.

"He demanded to come?" Aeolus circled around him.

"He did."

Aeolus sighed. "Chrysander, come."

Zephyros felt rather than saw Chrys's energy enter the room. The rustle of fabric meant Chrys had taken a knee. "My lord," he said in an uncharacteristically solemn voice.

"Rise, Chrysander," Aeolus said, skipping the greeting this time. "Why are you here?"

Hold your tongue, Chrys, for the love of the gods. Zeph clenched his teeth, waiting.

"Because he will need me," Chrys finally said.

Relief coursed through Zeph. No one could be more irreverent than his little brother. But these words ignited a pride and gratitude that made it a bit easier to straighten his back and hold his position.

"I didn't want this," Aeolus said in a tired voice. Chrysander was his favorite, the golden boy, the one to whom he had shown the most paternal affection. Surely, he didn't want him to witness the pain and horror that were about to unfold here. Zeph had no illusions about that. "But as you are here, so be it. You will stand witness." Aeolus's feet appeared directly in Zeph's line of sight. "Rise and hear the charges against you."

Ignoring his muscles' protest, Zeph rose to his feet with as much fluidity as he could muster. Legs spread and arms folded behind his back, he faced his father. "My lord, may I first beg your indulgence?" Afterward, he would be in no position to discuss Eurus with their father, so this needed to be done now, even if the unorthodox interruption further soured Aeolus's mood.

Bright green eyes bored into him, challenged him to look away. Zeph straightened his shoulders and held the older god's gaze. Aeolus narrowed his eyes. "You really want to discuss whatever this is now?"

"Only because it's apparently time-sensitive."

His father gave a tight nod. "Proceed."

"Eurus intends to propose his son Alastor as the heir to my line if I don't conceive one by New Year's end, which is in less than three days. He intends to submit his petition then and is under the belief you'll approve it." Zeph felt and ignored Chrys's surprise as he stared at his father.

Aeolus's jaw ticked. "I am aware of his petition."

The words were a kick in the gut. "And you plan to entertain it? A son of his has no place in the service of the West Wind."

"It's not ideal—"

"*Ideal*? A son of the East wouldn't possess the power of the West." Not unless what Eurus said about the god's parentage was true.

Aeolus heaved a sigh. "Normally, that would be the case."

Zeph growled, "So it's true then. And you knew. For how long?"

"Zephyros—"

"How long?" The booming shout of his voice echoed against the colored murals.

"Since her father brought the child to Eurus. It's why you've never met him. You would've felt the power of spring within him."

The room spun. Gods, would the betrayals never stop piling up at his feet?

Chrys huffed a breath. "Look, I know I'm supposed to keep my trap shut, but if you're seriously entertaining a proposal to foist an unwanted heir on Zephyros, that affects me, too. Why the big rush with this?"

Zeph dragged his gaze back to their father, who spoke to Chrys but kept his eyes on Zeph. "Given your proclivities, you likely have a dozen heirs already."

"That's not—"

Aeolus's blazing green eyes cut to Chrys and halted his protest. "The same is not true for Zephyros. Nor does that seem likely to change, particularly as I've already been apprised that the woman with whom he now consorts cannot even bear a child."

Zeph broke position and braced his hands on his hips. "And I have no say in the matter? Several of the Ordinal Anemoi would make superior candidates. As the god of the Northwest, Skiron especially could—"

Aeolus held up a hand and commanded Zeph to cease. "I will take all viable possibilities into consideration."

Rage seethed under Zeph's skin until it became difficult to remain still. But not once did any part of him even consider choosing another woman, one whose fertility would solve this dilemma. What he'd said to Ella earlier had been the truth. The possibility of being with her far overshadowed these issues of succession. Besides, Zeph had no plans to go anywhere. He'd stick around just to spite all their asses.

Not to mention he wanted every second he could have with Ella.

Assuming she agreed to give him another chance.

His stomach plummeted. The thought she might say no was far more devastating than Aeolus's pronouncements about…all of this. And didn't that tell him everything he needed to know about what was important in the world.

Zephyros resumed his position, feet spread and arms behind his back, and glared at his father.

With a troubled sigh, Aeolus opened his palm and a rolled parchment appeared out of thin air. He unrolled the scroll and read. "Zephyros Martius, Supreme God of the West Wind, son of Aeolus, God of Storms and Ruler of the Winds, you are charged with three counts of unlawful use of divine magic in the form of healings, unlawful revelation of your divinity, and endangering the Realm of the Gods with reckless use of divine magic in the human realm."

Chrys cursed under his breath. "Why is Zephyros here alone when Eurus's infractions were the same or worse?"

Zeph ground his teeth and hoped Chrys would say no more. While he appreciated the thought, Zeph didn't need his father thinking of Eurus while administering his punishment. And, honestly, after the previous conversation, he wasn't nearly as surprised or troubled by the charges, although the last one seemed a bit kitchen sink to him. He wasn't certain what it referred to. Maybe dematerializing in a public place? Who knew.

Aeolus glared at Chrys. "I *will* deal with Eurus." His eyes were blazing when they cut back to Zeph. "Now, what say you?"

"Guilty on the face of it, my lord. But my actions were just."

"Is that so? Continue."

"The injuries I healed were the result of my own actions, thus I deemed no sacrifice necessary."

"*You* deemed it so?" Aeolus nodded, his face the picture

of skepticism. "So, what you're saying is there were multiple counts of reckless use of divine magic."

Chrys spat an ancient expletive into the ringing silence between them.

Zeph recognized his mistake, but in point of fact it was a more accurate charge. "Yes, my lord."

Aeolus sighed. "You acquiesce too easily, Zephyros."

"If a sacrifice is required, I am prepared to make it. That is all." He had no more debate left in him.

"So be it. The additional charges are added." Two things happened—the room went pitch black, then candles flared in sconces only used for high ceremonies. The punishment of a god apparently counted. "Your sentence is seven lashes, one for each charge, on the bare back well laid. Additionally, you will not take the healing waters of the Acheron."

"Father—" Chrys interrupted.

"Silence!" A warm wind, charged with latent electrical energy, whipped through the room, telling Zeph of things to come. "You will watch in silence or not at all. Which is it?"

"I will stand witness," came Chrys's embittered voice.

Aeolus nodded, turned his fierce green gaze to Zeph. "Disrobe and receive your punishment."

Never dropping his eyes, Zeph removed the cloak, let it fall to the floor. He unclipped the pins at his shoulder. They pinged against the marble. The wool tunic fell loose, and he unwound it from his body until he stood as his god had made him.

Without waiting to be told, Zephyros turned. Chrys's eyes burned such an intense gold they were hard to meet, but Zeph tried to communicate strength and thanks in a look. Then he offered Aeolus his back and dropped to his knees.

Zephyros embraced Ella's image in his mind. Closed his

eyes and blocked everything else out. In just a few short days, she'd given him more happy memories than he'd accumulated in years, decades, more. She could get him through this if anything could.

Energy rippled through the room and accumulated behind him, accompanied by a great flickering yellow glow he could still perceive through closed eyes. As a storm god, Aeolus had command over rain, wind, thunder…and lightning. Zeph had seen this before, long ago. His father meting out punishment at the end of a lash of harnessed electricity.

"It pains me to do this, Zephyros," came his father's quiet voice. "But balance must be restored." Zeph didn't respond, he braced. And rightly so.

The lightning landed diagonally across his back and flayed his skin, the scent of charred flesh filling the air. Zeph's muscles seized and strained as his body absorbed the impact. Blood flowed in his mouth from where teeth tore into tongue, cheek. As was his nature, his power, his body set to restoring the wounded tissue.

And the second stroke fell, igniting the conflagration all over again.

CHAPTER TWENTY-THREE

"Where are you?" Ella murmured to herself as she sat at the kitchen table, staring down the clock and willing the hands to go faster. The morning was almost over. Eleven-fifteen had the day knocking on afternoon. And Zephyros still wasn't back.

Brilliant sun dappled through the tree behind the house and brightened the kitchen. Absolutely gorgeous outside, it was the first spring day where warmth truly infused the air. Birds sang. Flowers bloomed. People emerged from winter's hibernation.

But without Zephyros, she could find enjoyment in none of it.

Yesterday had been a total roller coaster. The heartache at watching Zeph leave. The knee-jerk reaction that she wasn't enough. The loneliness of the house—even with Owen here, doing his darnedest to keep her good company. Even after Marcus died, the house hadn't felt so empty, and that was saying something. By midnight, she'd crawled into bed, disappointment that he hadn't returned a rock in her stomach.

She sat propped up against the pillows trying not to fall asleep, just in case he might yet arrive. At three, she woke up with drool down her cheek and a kink in her neck. She ditched the pillows and turned over. It took her a long time to fall back asleep.

At seven, she instantly came wide awake. Still in her pajamas, she ran downstairs. When she entered the living room, Owen's eyes eased open and he shook his head. Her heart plummeted to her stomach. Right then, Ella knew.

She loved Zephyros.

She wanted him.

She should've never sent him away.

Amazing how fear and panic and want made things that had seemed so complicated so very plain and clear. True, what happened the night before last had scared the shit out of her. Not just…Eurus—she could barely say his name—but the depth of Zeph's mistrust. Though, really, wasn't she doing the same thing to him?

Her biggest hang-up was her infertility, and whether the lack of an heir would harm Zeph in some way she didn't understand. He said it wouldn't, or that something could be worked out. But she hadn't believed him, had she? That was the crux of it.

She'd sent him away because she didn't trust him to tell her the truth.

And, now, *oh God*, now, what if he didn't return?

She pushed up from the table and debated another cup of coffee, but she'd already had four. Wandering into the living room, she paused to make sure Owen wasn't on the phone with his wife again. He wasn't. But she'd walked in on him earlier, and it had been hard to listen to the depth of devotion in his voice. Would she ever have that? *Oh, Zeph, where are you?*

"You need anything, Owen? I feel bad keeping you here

away from your family."

"I'm glad to be here, it's not a problem," he said with a genuine smile. "But, uh, any chance you have some ice cream? I have the munchies."

Ella smiled. "I think I have ice cream sandwiches. Want one?"

"Aw, yeah."

She pulled two from the freezer and plunked down in the armchair next to the sofa. "Here you go." Ella opened hers and let it rest on the wrapper.

Owen moaned as he took a big bite. He frowned at her ice cream. After he swallowed, he asked, "Aren't you going to eat that?"

"Yeah, but I'm letting it melt."

"Why?"

"Because it's really good when the ice cream's soft." She grinned, feeling lighter than she had all day. "Does the snow god disapprove?"

Owen smiled around another big bite. "Seems to defeat the purpose."

Ella chuckled. "Maybe." She glanced sideways at the television. He had a movie on, but the volume was so low he couldn't have really been watching it. The colorful bouquet on the coffee table drew her gaze. Still pristine the last time she'd noticed them, out of nowhere they'd started to wilt. The full blooms sagged on their stems and the edges of the petals browned and curled.

And all at once, Ella knew. How she hadn't put it together earlier, she couldn't imagine. But they were clearly from Zeph, *of* Zeph. And they were wilting. Her heart lodged in her throat. "Owen?"

"Yeah?"

"Do you know what's going on?" she asked, wondering what kind of "touching base on family business" required twenty-four hours. Maybe she was reading too much into the flowers, but something just felt...wrong to her. She couldn't explain it any other way.

He glanced at the television and shook his head, long strands of black falling over those interesting eyes. "I can't say."

"You can't, or you won't?"

Owen released a deep breath. "I can't."

Her stomach dropped and her scalp prickled. "So you do know?"

He stared at her a long minute, then nodded.

"Is he okay?" She wasn't sure why she asked, except her intuition demanded it.

"He will be."

"God, Owen. Please?"

He shook his head. "I'm sorry, Ella. But he shouldn't be long."

"He's late."

"He'll come." He tugged a hand through his hair. "I am sorry."

Fidgety, she reached out for her ice cream, but pushed it away. "You can have it if you want," she said.

His eyebrows shot up. "Really?" She nodded, so he grabbed the sandwich and took a bite. "Hey, that is kinda good."

She gave a small smile. "Told ya."

"You should eat something, you know," Owen said, frowning.

"I will. Later."

Owen's frown deepened, but she couldn't have eaten if she

wanted to. Her stomach was all knotted up. She sank back into the cushion on a long sigh.

A thump sounded upstairs. Another.

Ella flew out of the chair and across the room.

Arms lashed around her waist before she hit the bottom of the steps. "Wait, Ella. Just wait," Owen whispered.

"He's here," she said. "I heard—"

Owen put his fingers to Ella's lips. "*Someone's* here. You don't know who. Let me check it out."

She gasped and her already racing heart went thunderous. Eurus. She never even considered…

"Oh honey, we're home," came Chrysander's voice.

Ella about sank to her knees in relief. And, honestly, it appeared Owen was on the same wavelength. Well, maybe not the falling-to-the-knees part, but relief washed off him in palpable waves.

The men—the gods—appeared at the top of the steps.

Adrenaline left Ella shaky, and she could barely stand still as Zeph and Chrys came down the steps. Then, after what seemed an eternity, he was standing in front of her again.

She gave in to the days'-old urge to bury herself in his chest. Up against him, she breathed in his clean, male scent, felt the reassuring pound of his heart under her hand, and about melted when his arms came around her. "Hi," she whispered.

"Hi," he said, voice gravelly.

"I was worried about you."

His breathing hitched. "Thank you."

Zeph squeezed her again, then tucked her under his arm. The other he extended to Owen. "Thank you for being here, for taking time away from your family. Straight up, I owe you."

They shook, and Owen gave Zeph a stare she didn't

understand. "You or Ella need me again, just ask."

Zeph nodded.

"Well, I don't know about you, Owen, but I need some chow," Chrys said.

Owen's eyebrows shot up. "I could definitely eat."

Ella chuckled, laughter coming easier now that Zeph was in her arms. "You just had two ice cream sandwiches."

He scoffed. "They were small."

Chrys clapped him on the shoulder. "Besides, this boy can eat ice cream like nobody's business."

Owen frowned at Chrys then shrugged. "Actually, that's true."

She and Zeph walked them to the door. The round of good-byes was noisy and full of commotion, mostly due to Chrysander's antics. She wondered if she would get to see these guys again. How she hoped.

But when they were gone and the quiet returned, she was glad down to the bottom of her toes to be alone with Zeph.

As the front door closed behind the two gods, she and Zeph both spoke at once.

"Zephyros—"

"Ella—"

They chuckled, the sound dissolving into a bit of awkwardness Ella hated. Grasping his thick biceps for support, she pushed up on tiptoes and paused just a breath away from his lips. He closed the gap with a groan.

Oh, God, the taste of him in her mouth. The kiss wasn't aggressive, but it wasn't gentle, either. Their tongues curled and stroked, lips pulled and sucked. Zeph buried his hands in her hair and guided the kiss until she was dizzy. It might've gone on for minutes or hours. She had no way of knowing, she was so completely lost in him. And it was exactly where she was supposed to be.

The truth of that rang out of every cell of her being. Abruptly, she pulled away from the kiss. Zeph frowned, his brow furrowing over flaring eyes that made dark promises she yearned to make good on. But now, in this moment, there was something more important.

"So, I did some thinking," she said, panting.

He released a deep breath. "And?"

She nodded, tears blooming across her vision but not falling. "I love you and I want this, Zeph."

"And your concerns?"

"They're not completely gone. But I trust you to help me work through them. I trust us to be able to work it out."

Expression solemn, he gave a single nod. "So do I." His hands cupped her face as a smile brightened his face. "Thank the gods. I love you so fucking much it hurts."

Her heart swelled in her chest until it was hard to breathe, but it was the most miraculous feeling she'd ever experienced. And the look on his face told her he felt it, too.

He leaned down as she stretched up. His arms anchored around her lower back, hauling her up against him. She held tight to his neck as their lips and tongues explored one another anew. As close as it was, it wasn't enough. Ella writhed against him, rocked her hips into him, loving how hard he was, wanting to feel that skin-to-skin.

Her body went hot and wet as she readied for him. She whimpered into his mouth, needing him like she'd never needed—or wanted—any man before.

Jesus, she might come just from kissing him, feeling his need, sharing his desire. Her hands slid up, grasping his head and pulling him in tighter to the kiss.

He groaned low in his throat, his mouth turning against hers, kissing, licking, sucking until they were both breathless.

Ella stumbled, pushing them back, and they both laughed around a kiss. She snaked her hands between them and yanked up his shirt. Zeph sucked in a breath, then moaned as her fingers traced over the ridges of muscle covering his abdomen. Tugging the shirt up higher, Ella teased his nipples until his one hand fisted in her hair.

Drunk on lust, Ella pushed him back and brought her mouth to his nipple. In great, flat strokes of her tongue, she tasted him, teased him. He never let go of her hair, and his hand made sure she didn't stop. She switched nipples and they stumbled again. Zeph backed into the foyer wall.

He gasped and his whole body flexed.

Ella glanced up to find his face a mask of pain.

CHAPTER TWENTY-FOUR

Zeph bowed off the wall, his teeth aching from how hard he clenched them. Staying in the Realm of the Gods longer than he'd intended sped his recovery, and his back was better, but not fully healed. In his want for her, he'd momentarily forgotten. Just being in her presence made everything better.

Ella cupped his face. "What's wrong?"

He hated that alarm had replaced pleasure as the dominant expression on her beautiful face. Not yet able to speak without knowing he wouldn't whimper, Zeph simply shook his head and tried to breathe through it.

"Zeph, what's the matter? You're scaring me." Her hand swept over his forehead, and the gesture was so tender a groan escaped before he could stop it. "Jesus, are you sick?"

He gave in to the urge to draw off some of her unique calming energy. Would he ever understand the source of it? It was more than he could think on in that moment. His shoulders sagged as her aura wrapped around him, warmed and relaxed him to the center of his being. "No," he finally bit out. "But, I'll be okay. Just gimme a minute." He attempted a smile.

Ella narrowed her gaze at him as her hand stroked over his hair. "Something happened to you while you were gone, didn't it?" she asked gently.

He released a tired breath as the sharpest edge of the pain dulled. There was no way to avoid telling her, showing her, especially if he wanted her to trust him. And he did, with everything he had, everything he was. He wouldn't do anything to sully the words they'd exchanged moments before. He vowed to handle her heart and her faith with kid gloves, like it was the most fragile spring blossom, and attend it with all the light and nourishment it would need to bloom again and again.

He grasped her hand and pulled it to his mouth, pressed a lingering kiss against her palm. The scent and taste of her against his lips felt like home. "Yes, something happened, but it had to happen, and it's over now."

"Tell me."

"I will, but I don't want to upset you."

"Too late. But I'll feel better when you tell me what's wrong, and how I can make it better."

"Gods, Ella, you do. Just by wanting me."

"How could I not, Zeph?" She leaned in and extended her arms as if to embrace him.

He grabbed her by the elbows and stepped back. "Sorry. That's, uh, that's what I need to tell you."

He slipped his hands into both of hers. "Just as humans do, the gods have rules and laws. And, in the past several days, I broke a couple. Because our very existence is based on magic, maintaining that supernatural power balance is critical to keeping harmony and protecting the world we all share."

She shook her head. "So..."

Dropping her hands, Zeph reached for the hem of his shirt. Carefully, he lifted it over his head and tossed it to the back of the armchair. "When a god uses magic illegally, balance can be restored through physical sacrifice and, frankly, that is usually required before magic is used in the first place."

Ella shivered. "Physical sacrifice. You mean..." She gasped and her eyes went wide, understanding rolling over her expression. Clutching and tugging his arm so he turned, she peered around to his back and let out a small moan. "What is this?" she said, her voice shaking. "You're bleeding."

Zeph winced. "It's coming through?" he asked, wondering if the layering of gauze Chrys had taped over nearly his whole back had been sufficient. Apparently not.

"Yes. In, like, three places. What the hell, Zeph? Who did this to you?"

"My father," he said, "but he really had no choice," he rushed to add. Someday, she might meet the god. Best she didn't start out hating him.

"Oh, my God. Ohmigod. What can I do? What do you need me to do?" Her hands stroked softly over his obliques, just beyond the edge of the tape.

Zeph let his head hang on his neck and enjoyed the light touch. It eased him, as everything about her did. "I love that you want to help me, but I heal. Another day or two, I'll be good as new."

"A day or two? That's sounds like forever right now. How much pain are you in?"

"It's manageable, I promise. And being with you, I can almost forget."

"God, I really want to hug you right now, but I don't want

to hurt you."

He turned around within her arms. "I would love a hug," he said, nearly melting inside as her arms curled warmth and belonging around him. That she wished to offer him comfort was the sweetest pleasure. He grinned against her hair when her hands settled on his ass. In her defense, nowhere was safe on his back. And, anyway, he wasn't complaining. Not at all.

Against his chest, her breathing hitched. Something wet dripped onto his bare flesh. The muscles of Ella's back when tight within his grasp. "It was because of me, wasn't it? Because you healed me," she finally said in a tear-strained voice.

"No, love, it wasn't. It was because of me. You got hurt because of things I did. Was only right I fixed what I wrought. And now it's over, and we can be together."

Her face was wet when she glanced up at him. "You promise?"

"Always," he said.

"I'm still so sorry."

His heart expanded at her expression of care and concern. "Thank you, but don't be."

"And what about Eurus? I can't imagine his opinion has changed."

He thumbed the tears off her face. "My father planned to summon him next. All should be well."

"That's good to hear." She leaned her forehead against his chest. He pressed a kiss to the crown of her head. "I just want to be with you."

The need and love in her voice sent blood pooling to the thickening organ between his thighs. "Say that again," he rasped.

Deep brown eyes cut up to his. "I want to be with you."

"Yes." Holding her gaze, he licked his lips and rocked his

hips forward. Just enough to cue her in on where his mind was heading. Understanding dawned across her lovely face.

Between their bodies, his erection was already rock solid.

"But Zeph," she breathed, "we can't. You're hurt."

Hands on her shoulders, he pushed her back one step, then another. "But you're not." Her back hit the hallway wall. Bending his knees, his thrust his pelvis into hers. His body screamed to get in her.

"Oh, God," she rasped asked his neck. "Please tell me you're not up to acting human again."

Zeph frowned and peered down at her. Eyes hooded, mouth open, cheeks flushed—the lust and love radiating off her knocked the air from his lungs. He heaved a breath, then her words sank in. He grinned and willed their clothes away, reveling in every bit of the appealing beauty of her body.

Her smile was radiant and he devoured it like a starving man at a feast. His kissed her breathless, adoring the sound of her pleasured whimpers. He tasted her neck with openmouthed kisses and long strokes of tongue. She was sweet and salty, clean and feminine. His hands cupped the weight of her breasts and teased her nipples with flicks of his thumbs. As the peaks went rigid under his touch, he salivated for a taste. One breast, then the other. In between, he paused to press lingering kisses over the racing organ in her chest, the one that owned him completely and forever.

But his exploration had only just begun. He dropped to his knees, careful not to pull the bandages on his back, but frankly willing to risk it to taste the core of her, drink her down, make her fall apart with his mouth alone. He'd dreamed of this for days, ever since the freight train of his desire the other night had made it impossible to slow down and savor. Now, he could, and he intended to do so to the fullest.

He nuzzled her hip bone, ran his teeth over what must've been a sensitive patch by the way she squirmed. He tucked that away for later and grinned up at her. Chest heaving, she smiled down at him and one hand rose to stroke his hair. He held her gaze as he pressed a kiss to the dark triangle of curls above her sex. Breathing her in made his cock twitch with need, but there was no rush.

Hands splayed over her lower abdomen, he used his thumbs to open her most secret place. Her scent made his mouth water, and he gave in to the intense urge to have her. Burying himself right against her, he laved his tongue through her slick folds. Mother of gods, she was sweet nectar and irresistible temptation. He flicked and sucked at her clit and reveled in every throaty moan and breathy gasp of his name. As much as it was, it wasn't enough.

Lifting her leg over his shoulder opened her to his deeper exploration. His tongue found her entrance and penetrated again and again until she rode his face, her desperation and need a living thing. He growled his appreciation and a scream tore out of her as her muscles convulsed around him. Gripping her hips, he pulled her tighter against his tongue and never stopped moving, licking, sucking, until her body went limp in his grasp and he was all that held her up.

Gently, he returned her foot to the ground and rose to his full height. Her lidded gaze followed his movement and she pulled his face down. She kissed his cheeks and lips until he could taste a hint of her honey from her own tongue. It was intoxicating. His cock jerked against her belly.

"I need you, Ella." He shook his head. "Like I've never needed anyone before."

"Me too, Zeph, so much." Warm hands engulfed his throbbing flesh, stroked and pulled. He loved her hands on his body, but in that moment, he desired more than the physical pleasure of her touch. His soul cried out for the fundamental sense of belonging only joining their bodies would create.

He lifted her leg again over his hip, and crouched down until the head of his cock aligned with her feminine slit. Heat radiated from the core of her and drew him in. He entered her, savoring the wet heat as it surrounded him. Closing his eyes, he became sensation, smelling her scent on his mouth, feeling her slick grip on his shaft and her short fingernails dig into his neck, hearing the long, satisfied sigh that escaped from her swollen lips.

When he was all the way in her, he paused and breathed through the tight urgency in his balls that demanded he race to the finish.

"Zeph?" Ella rasped. His gaze lifted from where they were joined. She raised her hands above her head. "You better hold them out of the way so I don't forget. I don't want to hurt you…"

He groaned, all his calming effort undone. But he fucking loved her idea. "This pleases you, love? My restraining you?"

Her cheeks went red but she nodded. "Yeah."

Caressing the flushed skin with his knuckles, he kissed her. "Don't ever be embarrassed about what you need, Ella, what you like. I will give you anything you ever want." He gripped her crossed wrists in his left hand. "Gods, I have to move in you."

He pulled out, pushed back in. She was so wet and hot and tight he thought he might lose his mind. The pleasure was so intense, the remaining rawness on his back faded to nothing.

All he knew was her, being in her. His chest swelled around the crashing beats of his heart.

This feeling, this love, this woman—it was all such an amazing revelation to him. Down deep, in a dark part of himself he didn't like to visit, he'd totally surrendered to the idea he'd never share in the joy of loving partnership. That he'd found it in such an unexpected place with a woman who might as well have been made for him was beyond miraculous. It felt like destiny.

Ella moaned as he picked up the pace, driving faster, harder into the core of her. Above the grip of his hand, her fingers clenched into fists. The image of it slayed him, and blood and energy raced from his extremities into his groin, creating an erotic pressure that had him groaning from deep in his chest.

"Oh, God. Ohgodohgod," she whimpered. She thrashed against the wall and her thigh trembled until he feared for her.

"Leave. Them. Up," he commanded against her ear before he released her hands and cupped the soft skin of her ass, lifting her entirely off the floor.

The change in position allowed him to go deeper, faster, as he used the leverage of the wall to bring them together. With each stroke, he rolled his hips against her pubic bone, loving the gasping moans the contact drew out of her. Ella's hands slid down to the top of her head. Her fingers tangled in long strands of golden brown. Around his cock, her body constricted and triumph flared through his veins.

"Yes, Ella, yes." He tugged her hips down as he thrust up. "Let go, love. I've got you."

Her mouth dropped open, eyes rolled back, and her body detonated around him. The high-pitched scream that tore from her lips set him to soaring. His pace quickened and concentrated against her clit, drawing out her ecstasy until he could hold back no more.

The walls of her sex still milking him, Zephyros's orgasm erupted within her. Body, heart, and soul, he was hers. In every way he could be, in every way he would ever want.

"I love you, I love you," she panted over and over as his body still shook. And he knew he would be able to live on this moment for the rest of his life. But thank the gods he wouldn't have to.

Because, as he pulled her off the wall and into the tight hold of his arms, still buried deep within her, he had everything he wanted and more than he'd ever hoped for in his grasp.

And the miracle of it all—she was his to have and to hold, forever.

CHAPTER TWENTY-FIVE

Ella woke up first from the midday nap neither of them had been able to resist. Zeph was on her like a blanket, one leg over hers, his head and chest draped across her abdomen, arm tucked under her. As her eyes adjusted to the sunlight streaming through the window, she drank in the picture of him. Truly, he was the most beautiful man she'd ever seen.

And he was hers. And she was his.

She didn't know where they went from here, but it was so goddamned freeing not to worry about it. Whatever arrangements they needed to make, whatever obstacles they encountered—they'd work through it all together. She trusted in that now, down to the very depths of her.

Unable to keep from touching him, she stroked her hand over his short hair. He always seemed to enjoy that simple touch, and she liked the way it relaxed and calmed him. She hoped to always be able to do that for him.

The thought had her frowning at the enormous blood-streaked bandage covering his back. What she wouldn't give to have his power, to take away his pain. She would make any sacrifice. For his health and happiness, anything at all.

"Feels good," Zeph murmured in a sleep-deepened voice.

"Didn't mean to wake you," Ella said.

He propped his chin on her chest and smiled up at her. "I don't mind." He stared at her a long minute. "You are my miracle."

She gave him a small smile. "I know just what you mean."

Her stomach growled. Then again. Zeph's eyebrows flew up and he grinned. Ducking his face against her bare belly, he blew a loud kiss against her skin. Ella screamed and writhed, trying to get away as he did it again.

"Stop," she said, laughing and squirming, her heart and mind alight with the wonder that was playful Zeph. He dove for her stomach again. "Uncle, uncle!"

He cocked his head at her, one eyebrow raised. "Uncle?"

"Yeah, you know, uncle. Stop."

"You humans say the weirdest things."

"Oh, it's 'us humans' now, is it? At least we don't poof."

She didn't even see him move. His whole length covered her and his mouth devoured her. "I told you," he said in a breathy voice.

"Yeah, yeah," Ella said rolling her eyes while parting her legs. "I know. You don't poof."

"I don't poof. But I *do* do this." He pushed into her. His hands found hers and pressed them to the bed by her shoulders, fingers entangled and holding tight.

It was sweetness and love. Face to face, trading soft kisses and affectionate encouragement, it was the most intimate moment of Ella's life.

Afterward, they lay holding one another for a long time.

Quiet and still, as if they were the only ones in the universe.

Head resting on her chest, Zeph said, "I have an idea. Will you give me a minute?"

"Sure," Ella said, going into a full-body stretch as Zeph lifted off her. "Do you need some help?"

He pushed off the bed, the sunlight playing across the taut planes and cut muscles of his big body. Jesus, he was so fucking gorgeous. "No, and I won't be long. Get dressed?"

She swung her legs off the bed. "Do I have time for a shower?"

His eyes narrowed. "Yes, just be quick, or I'll be tempted to join you and then we'll never get to my surprise."

"And"—she rose and sauntered across to the door, putting an extra swing in her hips—"that would be bad because…?"

Dark blue light flared behind Zeph's eyes. "You better go now." Between his legs, the thick length of his cock twitched and grew.

Ella grinned and left. Curious and excited, she rushed through the shower and threw on the first clothes her hands could find—a pair of worn jeans and a Georgetown Sailing sweatshirt.

She flew downstairs and nearly crashed into him coming out of the kitchen.

"Whoa. That was fast," he said, catching her. "Which is good, because I'm ready for you."

"Mmm, that sounds nice." On tiptoes, she pushed up and kissed him. She almost regretted that he'd materialized clothes from somewhere, but then again, she really did want to know what he had up his sleeve for her.

Smiling, Zeph broke the kiss first. He grabbed her shoulders and pointed her whole body toward the kitchen. Now that she wasn't totally distracted by him, she felt a cool breeze blowing through the archway separating the rooms. His big hands covered her eyes.

"Er, whatcha doing?"

"Surprise, remember?"

Grinning, she nodded, well, as much as she could with his hands around her face. "Okay."

They laughed and stumbled as he led her forward. The drop in temperature and outdoor sounds indicated they'd stepped onto the back porch. She was nearly giddy with excitement and anticipation.

"Step down twice," he said, and she did, familiar enough with the house now that she could picture where they were in her mind. He walked her a few steps further then stopped. "Ready?"

"Yes!"

"Surprise." He released his hands and stepped to her side. On the ground, spread under a just-budding cherry tree, was a blanket laden with colorful fruits, crusty breads, a half-dozen types of cheese, and a platter of carved ham and turkey. In the center of it all was a bowl of green M&Ms.

She sucked in a breath. "How in the world did you do all this?"

Cheeks adorably pink, he shrugged one big shoulder. "I can poof stuff, remember?"

Free, joyous laughter bubbled up out of her chest. "It's very handy." She pulled him into her arms, careful to avoid where she knew the bandage lay on his back. "Thank you. This is lovely. And I'm starved."

He returned her hug and pressed a kiss to the top of her head. "Me too. Come on."

Ella's eyes didn't know where to go first, it was all so beautiful. She picked up the bowl of M&Ms. "How did you know?" she asked, popping two candies in her mouth.

"You only ever ate the green ones." He set out a plate and linen napkin in front of each of them.

"I can't believe you noticed that."

"I notice everything about you, love. You mean the world to me."

Her cheeks warmed at the intensity of his words, his gaze. "I love you, Zephyros. Thank you for all this."

"It's my pleasure. Now, let's eat."

They made small talk as they filled their plates to heaping. Ella suddenly couldn't remember the last time she'd eaten and somehow one of everything appeared on her plate. Red, ripe strawberries, succulent pineapple, sweet mango, and juicy nectarines were among her favorite fruits. She spread creamy brie on fresh-baked French bread and added a slice of roasted turkey.

Zeph swallowed a bite and pointed at her shirt. "Did you go to school there?"

Ella had to glance down to remember what she was even wearing. "Oh, yeah. I went to Georgetown for college. Marcus and I both did. Typical twins, we stuck together even when we went away for school. Plus, they have a nationally ranked sailing team, so we could still pursue the sport, and in waters we generally knew. My parents lived here in Annapolis then, so Georgetown was just far enough away to feel independent, but close enough to come home for some of my mom's famous French toast or to do some free laundry." She smiled. God, those days seemed so far away.

Zeph listened attentively while he ate, like he was memorizing every detail of her history. "And, your parents, they died?"

"Yeah, but how did you—"

"Oh. Right. Uh, I was with you in the hospital. I heard the nurses say you had no known family. Apparently, someone at the marina told the paramedics your immediate family was gone."

"I thought I'd dreamed you," Ella said, remembering her first hazy images of him. She met his gaze, his eyes a brighter blue in the late-day sun. "I'm so glad you weren't a dream."

"I'm not, Ella. I'm real. And this is real, what we have."

She smiled and her stomach flip-flopped. "I know." Sighing, she added, "My parents died in a car accident toward the end of our sophomore year. The anniversary is actually in a couple weeks. Anyway, a tractor-trailer ran them off a highway just before an overpass. They didn't have anywhere to go but into the concrete supports. At least that's what Marcus managed to learn from the police reports. I couldn't read them."

"That's horrible. And you were so damn young. I'm sorry."

"I wouldn't have gotten through it without Marcus. Legally, we were adults when it happened. But we'd just turned twenty, and in that moment, I sure didn't feel like a grown-up. As if we hadn't already been close, their deaths really brought us together. Marcus bought the *True Blue* with money we'd inherited. It was our twenty-first birthday present, and we spent a lot of time on that boat together. Out on the water, fighting the wind"—she gave him a small smile—"it was easier not to think about it."

"I would've liked to meet Marcus," Zeph said.

The idea of it was bittersweet. "I would've loved for you to meet him. He was a great person, strong and generous and kind."

"You had a lot in common, then."

Ella smiled and glanced around the yard. Every green thing seemed so much brighter and fuller than she remembered from the other day. She sighed. "I don't know. He was much stronger than me."

"I don't know how that could be. You're one of the strongest, most courageous people I've ever met."

Ella rolled her eyes but smiled despite herself. She pushed her plate away. "I'm stuffed."

Together, they moved the plates and platters and baskets of leftover picnic food to the edge of the blanket. They'd be eating well for the next few days.

Zeph stretched out on his side and it took him a minute to get settled.

"You still hurting?"

"It's getting better."

"M&Ms will help. Here." She handed him the bowl and stretched out on her side facing him.

He smiled and threw a few candies in his mouth. "Mmm, I think you might be right. Better have a few more to be sure." He grabbed a handful and picked at them. Ella adored the way his eyebrows went up each time he ate one. It was possible he rivaled her in his enjoyment of the candies. They might want to take stock in the company.

"So, when is your birthday, anyway?"

"Oh." Ella couldn't hold in a small groan. With everything else going on, she'd pretty much forgotten. It wasn't like she'd been expecting to celebrate it anyway. "If I tell you, you have to promise not to do anything."

"I don't want to promise that."

"Come on, Zeph." She rubbed his arm. "Just having you,

I already have everything I want. And you just arranged this beautiful picnic for us."

"When is your birthday, Ella?"

"Can I distract you with a kiss?"

He grinned. "You can always distract me with a kiss, but I'm still going to want to know when your birthday is."

She sighed and grabbed more M&Ms. Her stomach was going to burst soon, but the sensation of satiation was so gratifying for once. "Fine. It's tomorrow." She picked at her candies.

He leaned into her line of sight. "Your birthday is tomorrow?"

"Mmm-hmm. March 31st."

His eyes were alive with wonder. "That's extraordinary."

"Why?"

"Not only were you born in the month for which I was named, but by the old calendar, you'd be a new year's baby. March 31st was the last day of the new year's celebration back when March 25th was the start of the year."

"Really? That's kinda cool." She shrugged. "Well, I've always liked March because it was my birthday. And because I like the rain. And now I guess I have another reason." She grinned at him and held up an M&M. "Open."

Obeying, the light in his eyes went molten. He accepted the candy and pulled her in against him. Ella savored the combination of Zeph's natural masculinity with the chocolate. It was divine. She smiled at the thought as they kissed, but then his tongue stole her ability to think.

She reclined against the blanket and he followed. The kiss was sweet with a whole lot of promise of more to come. But, for just that moment, neither rushed, neither pushed. She was entirely content to lay there outside on a blanket enjoying Zeph and the late afternoon spring air. And she could tell from the satisfied sounds he made, he felt the same way.

Something tickled her hand where it held the back of Zeph's head. She was so deep into him, she didn't think anything of it until it happened again. And then something brushed her cheek.

She pulled away. "I felt something."

"What?"

"I don't kn—" The words died in her throat. She gasped and pushed out from underneath Zeph. "Oh, my god." Perfectly formed cherry blossoms fluttered from the tree.

The rose bush that had bloomed out of turn a few days before now had a whole lot of company. The entire garden was in full bloom.

The huge canopy of the cherry tree above them was cotton-candy pink. All along the rear fence, the hyacinths stood like sentinels in a row, their white, pink, and purple buds releasing the most fragrant perfume. Ancient azalea bushes dotted the yard in reds and whites. Lilies and crocuses and bluebells and tulips and larkspurs and pansies, not to mention all the other flowers she couldn't name, filled every corner of the garden with color.

"How…?" was all she could manage. She rose to her feet and turned in a three-sixty, right there standing on the blanket. Not only had the whole garden bloomed, apparently spontaneously, it seemed more vibrant and full of life than ever before.

And then she knew.

Zeph sat reclined on the blanket, braced against his arms, watching her. His eyes were as bright as she'd ever seen them, so alive with that magical light. "You overwhelm me." He shrugged and looked up at the brilliant pink above them. "It's hard to restrain myself when I'm with you. This time, I didn't bother to try."

"You did this?" He nodded. "Don't you dare get me a birthday present, Zephyros. Nothing could top this."

She walked around the garden, inhaling the heady floral scents down deep and brushing her hand over the full, heavy blossoms, each one more beautiful than the next. As she took it all in, she felt his gaze on her and didn't mind in the least. She wanted him to know how much she appreciated the incredible gift of his magic.

After she made a circuit around the garden, she stretched back out on the blanket. They laid on their sides, hands joined and his knee tucked between her thighs. "Thank you. You've given me the most wonderful day."

"It pleases me to make you happy."

Ella shivered.

"Are you getting too cold?"

The sun had dropped in the sky, drawing down the temperature and leaving more shadows than light across the verdant gardens. But Ella's body had more been reacting to the miraculous turn her life had taken these past few days. "I'm fine. And I don't want to give this up yet."

"You don't have to, we're in no rush."

She dozed off for a while, so comfortable in his arms, and only awoke as he lifted her off the blanket. "Your back," she whispered, groggy.

"I'm being careful."

"'kay." Her eyes were so heavy. She pressed her face against his chest. "Love the flowers."

He chuckled. "I'm glad."

Upstairs, she forced herself to wake up enough to use the bathroom, brush her teeth, and change clothes. She was almost asleep again when she fell into bed. Zeph opened his arm to her and pulled her back against his chest. As she drifted, she swore she could smell the perfume of the garden. "Did you open the window?" she mumbled.

"Yeah. I thought you might like it. Is it okay?"

"Love it. Love you," she managed, and she fell into the most peaceful sleep and hopeful dreams she'd had in years.

CHAPTER TWENTY-SIX

Arms wrapped around her, softly at first, then tighter. Still mostly asleep, Ella smiled and let herself be moved where he wanted her.

And then she was wrenched from the bed.

She snapped awake. The pitch-dark room spun around her. There was a grunt and a curse, the creak of what sounded like leather.

Terror shot down her spine, brought tears immediately to her eyes. She sucked in a breath and a huge hand slapped across her mouth.

"Won't do you any good," a voice snarled in her ear. "Best hold on now."

Eurus.

Ella had no time to react, and didn't understand what happened next. She could hear, she could see, but she didn't feel like herself, in herself. Stranger, she was flying. It was the only way she could describe it. Through the window, out over the dark garden, and across the neck of land on which the neighborhood of Eastport stood.

Zephyros! Oh, God, Zephyros!

She heard the scream inside herself, but hadn't actually vocalized. Because…*oh, no, oh, God*…she had no body.

Mmm, yes, scream for him. He'll like that, came Eurus's voice in her mind.

All at once, she remembered the first night she'd made love with Zeph. Him flashing them from the hallway into the bed. Her mind whirled. Eurus had…taken her. Clearly. And she was…

What's happening? Where am I?

His chuckle echoed through her consciousness, and she hated the violation of his presence there. *Just look around, Ella. You're an avid sailor, are you not? You'll recognize the landmarks.*

She focused, concentrated, looked down at the landscape over which they soared. Red lights flashed along the length of a grouping of towers. They looked so familiar…the radio towers at Greenbury Point! Directly beneath them, the bay was a black surface in motion.

Oh, Jesus, the tops of those towers were really fucking far beneath them. A panicked shudder rippled through Ella's soul.

Eurus, please take me back. Please.

The begging's a nice touch. Do keep that up.

She tried to struggle, but had no idea how to manipulate her body, her existence, whatever, in this state. But no way she was giving him the satisfaction of her begging for her life or crying out for Zeph.

Besides, the reality of the situation was sinking in down to her marrow. Begging wouldn't make any difference. Nothing would.

They rode the air currents over the bay, near the bridge that bore its name, and shot upward unexpectedly.

She slammed back into her physical body so hard, she choked and gagged.

"Careful now, wouldn't want to fall," Eurus said with dark delight.

Ella sucked in a breath, still feeling fragmented and confused. Cold, damp wind whipped her hair around her face. Orientation returned in starts and stops, but exhaustion swamped her, made her muscles heavy and sluggish.

"Why?" she groaned.

"Don't look for meaning where there is none, you fucking human piece of trash. I do it because I can. And because you should've died the first time. I'm just setting things straight."

Ella groaned and her head went slack on her neck. She forced her eyes open, and...*No. Nononono.* "Oh, God, no." Adrenaline shot awareness through her system. A moan ripped from her throat. They'd come out of the wind and materialized on top of the tallest suspension tower of the Bay Bridge. Below, westbound traffic appeared tiny, like toy cars, as it headed toward Annapolis and D.C., completely unaware of the disaster unfolding above them.

From where she stood, swayed, it had to be pushing four hundred feet to the water's surface.

Another realization exploded into her brain. No way Zeph would've allowed this to happen. She fought and pushed until she whirled in Eurus's arms. "What did you do to Zephyros?" She ripped her hands free and pummeled his chest, clawed at his face, newly disfigured in some way she couldn't fully make out in the darkness. "What did you do to him?"

He trapped her wrists in an iron grip. She winced as a

gaudy winged ring bit into her skin. "Now, Ella, why would I have done anything to Zephyros? I would never want him to miss this."

Ella frowned, tugged at her hands. "What are you talking about?"

"Just this." He released her hands. The preternatural weight of his stare boring into her through those dark glasses, a blast of cold wind hit her square in the chest.

She shot backward out into open space.

Her body, her life, went into a freefall.

∞❁∞

Zephyros Martius was gone. In his place was a growling, roaring, feral beast strapped down against a bed like an animal tethered in a cage.

The supernatural restraints held him still and powerless as seconds passed, minutes, eternity. Eurus had gotten the jump on him that one other time because Zeph had been drained from the intensity of the healing. But this…he couldn't understand, couldn't fathom…it shouldn't have been fucking possible.

All at once, he was free. He bolted off the bed and whipped into the elements, already flying, already tracking.

Ella!

His soul screamed to the heavens, thunder rumbling across the night sky in a low, eerie lament. Some part of his consciousness sensed Chrysander's summons, but he couldn't stop, couldn't think about anything other than his beloved.

She was dying.

Her life force cried out, fought, denied, each emotion crashing into Zeph's soul.

Up, up, into the air he went. Searching, calling out, hunting down that unique aura that was all hers.

There! Ahead. Oh, gods, he'd found her. He dug deep into his godhood and threw everything he had into getting to her. An unending chant sounded in his mind, a prayer, a litany.

Her special signature flared in a fantastic, brilliant explosion of energy.

Zeph's psyche froze, suspended in time and space.

That special peaceful aura crackled and sparked. He poured out every last molecule of his godhood, racing, driving. He could still get to her. He had to get to her. It wasn't too late. It *couldn't* be too late.

Not again not again not again. Not Ella.

His heart, his life, his whole fucking world balanced on a knife's edge. He couldn't breathe, couldn't think, he was just energy in motion, energy in pursuit of life.

Then her energy, her life, was gone.

He strained to pick up even the smallest thread of her unique force, but it was no use.

There was nothing but devastatingly dead, white silence. The loudest thing he had ever heard, it shattered his ears and his heart.

Grief and rage flashed out of Zephyros, manifested in an instantaneous killer storm over the bay. Winds tore at the sky, rain and hail pummeled the earth. Waterspouts spiraled up from the surface, dancing, stalking, sucking up everything in their paths.

By one of the bridge's concrete footings, something bobbed on the surface.

Zeph plunged from the sky. He knew what he would find before he got to her.

The freezing temperature might've harmed him if grief hadn't already sucked the life and energy from his very existence. He grabbed Ella, turned her face up, felt the unnatural way her head flopped on her neck. "Oh love, oh love, oh love," he keened, hugging her face into his throat. She was warm against him, and it was a horrible lie. A horrible fucking facsimile of life.

Zeph flashed them to the debris-strewn surface of the bridge footing and fell back against the concrete with Ella in his lap. Since she'd been gone for a few minutes, he didn't possess the level of power required to bring her back. The worthlessness and uselessness might've been soul-piercing if every part of him wasn't already obliterated. Around him, the sea, the air, the sky mirrored the catastrophic turmoil in his heart and soul.

Head to the heavens, Zephyros screamed and screamed.

Hands pulled and tugged at Zeph, but he barely felt it, couldn't decipher the meaning of it.

"Z, come on, buddy. Z? Zephyros! I can't get through to him. Damn it all to Hades, B, we gotta roll in more fog."

A cold hand fell on his forehead. "Zephyros. I summon thee. Brother mine, maybe there is hope," came a deep voice.

Chrys cursed under his breath. "B, what are you—"

"Zephyros, the Acheron."

"Oh, fuck, Boreas. A human can't—"

Zeph groaned and his head lolled on his neck, but slowly he regained control of his muscles, his faculties. He blinked, surprised to find Chrysander and Boreas hovering over him— he thought he'd dreamed them. He almost couldn't make them out through the white blanket of some of the thickest fog he'd ever seen in his life. In the near distance, booming horns sounded from multiple locations.

"Gone," he croaked, his vocal chords destroyed.

Huge hands grasped his face, tilted it upwards. "What would you be willing to sacrifice?" Boreas asked.

Zephyros sucked in a shuddering breath. "Anything."

"Then take her to the Underworld. And make haste."

"Fuck," Chrys bit out again, blinding gold light blazing from his eyes. "This is such fucking shit!" He whirled on Zeph. "You go. You save her, Zephyros. You fucking save her. I'm going after Eurus."

"Chrysander, no!" Boreas shouted.

But it was too late. A searing hot wind flashed through the fog and disappeared.

"Damn it." Boreas' head sagged, then his silver gaze cut to Zeph. "All right, Zephyros, give Ella to me. Come now, we must go."

Zeph clutched her against him, heart thundering in his chest.

"Let me carry her for you. Your godhood is dangerously depleted. Concentrate on yourself, and I will take care of Ella as if she were mine own."

"Please," Zeph said, not recognizing the thin, shaky voice that came out of his mouth.

"You have my word." Boreas slid his arms under Ella and lifted her from his brother's lap.

Zephyros rose with her, as if they were attached. And they were. His heart, his soul, everything that was good and worthy about him, she owned every bit of it.

They shifted into their elemental form, rose up through dense fog that seemed to go on forever. Up, into the starless night sky. Away, toward the Realm of the Gods. Zephyros struggled to keep up with Boreas, but no way he was letting himself be separated from Ella, no way he was letting Boreas slow down. As they passed through the divine realm, Zeph imbibed the smallest amount of additional power. Drained as he was, it made a huge difference.

Down they soared, through the Styx and into the ancient Underworld. Zephyros went on full alert, every sense heightened and anticipating attack or interference from every direction. As they approached the Acheron, one of the five infernal rivers of Hades, they returned into corporeality.

Feeling a gratitude he might never be able to express, Zephyros quickly took Ella back into his arms. So pale now, so terrifyingly pale.

Ahead in the distance, Charon's red eyes watched them, beckoned. But Zeph had no intentions of turning Ella's soul over to the demonic ferryman to shepherd across to the Isles of the Blessed.

It wasn't her time.

Zephyros turned to the water. As with all things divine, the Acheron worked on a give-and-take. The water possessed miraculous healing abilities, but it came at the cost of pouring your sorrows into its cold, dark currents. Over a year ago, Owen had found himself in need of the river, and said of the experience it was like living through every sadness and tragedy of your life as if they'd happened all at once and would never end.

Zeph would gladly open himself up for the soul-letting so she could partake of the healing.

Aeolus appeared out of thin air, right in his path.

"You cannot do this, Zephyros," he said in a gentle, pitying voice.

Before Zeph even opened his mouth, Boreas stepped up

next to him. "My lord, surely you can—"

Aeolus held up a bandaged hand, dark green eyes flaring. "This is not your concern, Boreas."

Zeph narrowed in on the injury. "What happened to your hand?"

Aeolus glared. "It matters not."

In that moment, Zeph agreed. Ella was what mattered now. Only Ella. Zeph nodded to his brother. "He's right. You've done enough. I'll take it from here."

Boreas's eyes flashed a sharp silver and his displeasure cut deep creases into his face. He shifted that intense gaze to their father. "I am going to say something that needs to be said, and you can strike me down for it if you want. But none of this would be happening if you had dealt with Eurus earlier, or dealt with him at all. Her death lies at *your* feet as much as Eurus's."

From behind them, a deep voice boomed. "I have to say, I rather agree."

CHAPTER TWENTY-SEVEN

The wind gods pivoted, Aeolus and Boreas falling to a knee immediately. Zeph sank down slower, careful of the precious cargo he carried in his arms, and gaped up at one of the most powerful deities in the entire fucking pantheon.

Mars.

Breathing hitching within his chest, Zephyros met the god's gaze head-on. Hope—deadly, dangerous hope—flared in his heart. While Mars and his brother Ares shared a legendary masculine aggression, Ares directed his toward war-making, while Mars focused on peace-making. Moreover, because Mars's power extended to guardian of the earth's cultivated plant life, he possessed enormous life-giving abilities—abilities so potent they made what Zephyros could do look like a child playing at magician. He was male enough to admit the disparity.

Dressed in his traditional military regalia, Mars stood in front of Zeph, his dark gaze tracing over Ella's face. Lost in thought, he tugged at his curly dark beard.

"My lord," Aeolus said from behind Zephyros.

"Silence," Mars said quietly. He knelt in front of Zeph, who drew Ella further into the shelter of his body. Muscles so tightly wound they might pull loose from his joints, Zeph saw the warning his body issued the stronger god reflected in the blue light that colored Mars's face. "Fear not, Zephyros." Gingerly, he reached a hand out and stroked Ella's forehead and hair. Zeph relaxed, minutely. "She is one of mine."

Zephyros gasped, his gaze lifting from Ella to Mars—no, from *Marcella* to Mars. The pieces clicked into place just as an intense wave of calm and peacefulness poured through Zeph. By the gods, what flowed from Mars's energy was a thousand times stronger, but it was the same calming influence he'd wondered at over and over in Ella's presence. Still, he had to hear the god spell it out. "Are you saying—"

"My blood runs through her veins. It is a generations-old familial connection, but I felt the call of it as soon as you entered the divine realm." Mars cocked an eyebrow. "You bear the name of Martius. You come to power in the traditional month of my dominion. Why would this surprise you so?"

Zeph shook his head, at a loss, his brain struggling to keep up with each new input of information the situation threw at him.

"Do you love her?" Mars asked.

"With everything I am," Zeph said.

Mars nodded, then stood and moved to Aeolus. "Rise, all of you, so we can sort this mess out. Boreas, your father was correct in one respect. What is to be discussed here does not involve you. And, at any rate, I suspect your youngest brother needs your assistance."

"Thank you, my lord." Boreas nodded, cut a supportive glance to Zephyros, and dematerialized.

"Now," he began. "Aeolus, your son, Eurus, is unworthy of his godhood. He has wreaked havoc on the human realm for years, without provocation, without retribution. For gods' sake, he killed one of his own sons—another god. He has been out of control for years, but the ruling pantheon has not interceded because it was largely your family's affair."

Zeph took a certain satisfaction in his father being confronted with the fact his treatment of Eurus was half the problem, had been for eons.

Aeolus bowed his head. "Everything you say is true, my lord. I—"

"The only thing I want to know is how you're going to help make this right. She. Is. My. Blood," he thundered.

Zephyros glanced around the dark, bleak landscape bordering the river, wondering what kind of attention they were attracting. At some point, this wouldn't go unnoticed. But you didn't rush a god of Mars's standing.

"Restoring a life would require major sacrifice," Aeolus said, voice respectful but firm. "The balance of nature must be preserved at all cost."

Mars nodded. "I don't disagree with you there. But your son killed my daughter—makes no difference to me she's several long generations removed. So, between the three of us, we will make a bargain big enough to pay that cost."

Aeolus's eyes went wide. Zephyros almost fell back to his knees in relief.

Mars whirled on Zeph and narrowed his gaze. "How much are you willing to sacrifice to have her live?"

"Anything."

The god arched an eyebrow. "So be it. Ella will have no memories of you *unless* her love for you was true and strong enough to bind them to her soul."

A weight fell over Zeph's heart and he stumbled back a step. The cavernous space of the Underworld closed in on him until he couldn't breathe, couldn't think. What if she didn't remember him? What if she hadn't loved him enough to meet the god's requirement? He'd failed her in ways too numerous to list, and they'd been together so few days…

But, still, she'd live. Even if she never remembered him, never loved him again, he would take solace from knowing her beauty and strength still walked the world. In a voice so strained it hurt to speak, he said, "I accept and agree, my lord."

"On the chance the gods smile upon you and she remembers, you need also to agree to allow Aeolus to appoint Alastor as your heir, or else you will have made no sacrifice at all."

Zeph ground his teeth until his jaw ached. The thought of losing even more to the god responsible for taking so much of what was rightfully his sat like a white-hot rock in his gut.

"The blood of spring flows in his veins, Zephyros. Alastor is not his father."

Zeph's gaze fell to Ella, skin porcelain white, lips a bruised blue. She'd remember him. She had to. Nothing else mattered. Cutting his eyes to Mars, Zeph nodded once. He said he'd give anything, and he meant it. "So be it."

Mars nodded, turned back to Aeolus. "You will sacrifice your third son's life."

Zephyros barely restrained the growl of approval that clawed up his throat. Death was the least of what Eurus deserved. Frankly, it was *more* than he deserved. After all, dying was easy, freeing. It was living—in want, in need, in solitude—that was so goddamned hard.

Aeolus's eyes flashed green and his mouth dropped open. Outside of occasional bursts of rage, it was more emotion than Zeph had ever seen his father express where Eurus was concerned. So blinded by his grief over their mother's childbed death, Aeolus couldn't see what he was doing to Eurus, to all of them.

As Zeph stood there holding the love of his life in his arms, her body cooling with each passing moment, he found himself understanding his father in a way he never could before.

Mars continued, "At my behest, the ruling pantheon has already met and drawn up a list of charges so long they had no choice but to find for the death penalty. Do it yourself or deliver him to me, I care not, but it must be done as soon as possible."

Aeolus looked shell-shocked. His gaze slid to Zephyros, then to the woman in his arms. "I…I agree and accept," he whispered, his voice cracking.

"My sacrifice will make both of yours worthwhile. I will remain here in the Underworld and meet whatever demands Hades requires to release her soul to my care." Zephyros opened his mouth to protest, but Mars cut him off. "Understand me, Zephyros. She can be your consort, if she remembers you and so chooses. But her human life force is gone. When we restore her, her godly lineage will come to the fore. She will be a goddess. And she will work for me."

೮೧೦೪

She was disconnected, adrift, floating. A soul without a corporeal home.

Time passed without meaning, without context.

All she knew was the fundamental urge to search. For what

or for whom was just beyond the reach of her consciousness. But she knew she must find…whatever it was. When she did, everything would be better, would make sense again, would have meaning once more.

Indeed, deep yearning was all that defined her. She must not give up, lest she fade to nothingness altogether.

Out of nowhere, pain, like the sensation of pins and needles, only a thousand times stronger and with actual pins and needles, wracked her whole existence. The torturous assault concentrated at the very center of her being, sent her heart pounding at such a rate it must surely give out. But even in the pain, there was relief. Because the torment gripping her heart meant she must be corporeal again.

Time stretched on indistinguishably as the phenomenon spread out from her heart in concentric circles of agony. It was like someone was taking her apart and putting her back together again, none of the pieces fitting the right way because the very shape of her had somehow changed.

As the pain roared out her extremities, something miraculous happened. Incredible relief flowed in behind the pain, a wave of peace so sublime she could've cried, would've begged for more. But she couldn't, because while she now felt a physical presence in herself, she was still disconnected, still searching, still yearning.

Her hearing came back online first. She couldn't make sense of the words, but there was something about the voice that made her want to listen and decipher. Feeling returned next. Warm hands surrounded hers, caressed her face, brushed her hair. Her soul sang out at each and every stroke. The sound of it was so loud in her head, she didn't know why whoever showed such tenderness didn't hear it.

Sight, speech, and smell came back at the same time.

For long moments, she didn't realize her eyes had opened. Her optic nerve seemed disconnected from her brain. Then a world in brilliant Technicolor slid into focus. There were colors even for which she had no name. Details she never before noticed. A depth of perception that swamped her in vertigo. A loud moan sounded, and she finally realized it poured from her own throat, but that didn't mean the voice was familiar to her.

Pounding steps rushed toward her. "Oh, thank the gods. Ella, you returned to me."

Under soft covers, Ella scrabbled back against...her eyes skittered around, surveying, assessing...she was on a bed, crouched, back against an enormous wooden headboard. As she moved, she didn't recognize the feel of her own body. Stronger muscles, faster responses. Within her, intense pressure built up, and she had the oddest sense she could release some of it if she wanted.

"Ella?"

Her gaze swung on the male standing at the edge of the bed. Recognition flickered in her mind's eye, but she couldn't hold onto it. Power radiated from him, setting off her body's defensiveness. Worse, looming in the doorway across the room, two other beings stood. Huge males, both of them, and powerful.

"We first met in a hospital, Ella, after the *True Blue* was damaged in a storm I caused. Remember?" His eyes were a beautiful blue and terribly sad. She could barely look away. "And then I came to your house and healed you. We made love. You made me pancakes. And we went sailing on the Chesapeake Bay. Gods, please remember."

He ducked his head and heaved a breath, looked over his shoulder to the others.

"Keep it up, Zephyros. She is in there. We'll leave you." The men at the door turned and left.

The blond one leaned back in wearing a big smile. He waved. "Welcome back, Ella." Then he was gone and the door clicked shut behind him.

Ella frowned. Fragments of words and images flashed through her brain, but nothing would stick.

"I'm going to sit right here on the corner. Okay?" the man with the sad blue eyes said in a heartrending tone.

She had the oddest urge to crawl to him and stroke his hair. "O-kay," she said, trying out her voice again. It sounded almost musical to her own ears, and loud.

He sank to the mattress, his body angled toward her. "Your name is Marcella Raines, but you prefer Ella. You had a twin brother named Marcus whom you loved dearly." He closed his eyes and shook his head.

Ella climbed across the bed, just partway, but felt as if he'd reached into her chest and pulled her to him. "I know you," she said.

His eyes flashed open and flared an incredible dark blue light. "Gods, yes. You do, Ella. Because I love you. And you love me. We are together. Please remember."

Warm pressure filled her chest and dragged her forward until her knees touched his thigh. He froze and she lifted her hand between them.

"Go ahead, touch me."

Lightly, she pressed her palm to his cheek. The skin at his jaw was prickly, and it tickled her hand. She stroked up to his temple and her fingertips pushed into his short hair. She gave into the urge and petted him, softly, slowly. The intense joy and desire reshaping his face nearly knocked the breath out of her.

In that moment, she would've done anything to draw out his pleasure.

Her heart kicked into a sprint and her mouth dropped open. "I want to kiss you," she breathed, shocking herself.

"I would adore it if you would." He tilted his head and gave her a small smile that tugged at her brain.

She leaned in, anticipation and something else—something new, foreign, powerful—trembled within her. He released a shaky breath just as her lips met his.

Skin against skin. Tongue against tongue. Physical contact exploded the locked chest of memories in her brain and rearranged the pieces like a broken mirror reassembling itself.

She was Ella.

And he was Zephyros.

And they were meant to be together forever.

A great moan ripped up her throat, but she couldn't, wouldn't, break the kiss. She climbed up him, unable to get close enough, and wound her legs and arms around him so tightly she worried for his safety. But she couldn't fight these urges—to have, to claim, to protect.

Victorious growls rumbled in his chest, against which strong arms strapped her body. She pushed him back against the bed, tore at his clothes, unable to make her vocal chords catch up to her body's needs and her brain's plans.

The clothing disappeared from her grasp. She grinned at the delightful surprise, and memories piqued at her consciousness, but she couldn't slow down to think on them. All she knew was that she wouldn't be whole, couldn't be complete until he was in her.

Between them, she found him hard as steel. Her gaze shot to his as she sank down on his cock.

"Thank you, thank you for coming back, for loving me enough," he groaned. "I have missed you so goddamned much I thought I'd die waiting for you to return. Ride me, Ella, just have me."

She was already moving, pulled forward by urges more intense than any she'd ever experienced. Rolling her hips, she'd take him all the way inside, an incredible fullness that sucked energy from the rest of her body and congregated low in her belly. She'd lifted off him, until just his tip remained. The shifting expressions on his face guided her. He wore a mask of love and desire, need and contentment. Faster, harder, she went, racing them toward a finish line that might shatter her to pieces.

But it felt so damn right.

His hands grasped her hips. Guiding fingers dug into her flesh and threw her body over the edge. A scream ripped up her throat as her muscles convulsed around him. Relentlessly, he moved her through it and ground himself up into her until his own body went rigid. Head digging back into the covers, neck taut, mouth open, her beloved Zephyros shouted her name in release.

She crashed into his chest. Arms embraced her. Oh, he held her so very tight.

Emotion gathered into a rushing current, built into a tidal wave, and swamped her where she lay. Sobs she didn't understand poured from her mouth and wracked her body.

"Oh, love." Zeph rolled them so they lay side by side. His big hand cupped her face and his thumbs swiped beneath her eyes.

"Ov-er-whel-med," she hitched, unable to control her breathing. Tears streamed from her eyes, dripped over her nose and into her hair. It was like the physical symptoms of a panic attack, without the panic. As she lay there, struggling to pull herself together, the analogy drew a darker memory from her brain. Her eyes went wide, allowing more wetness to spill. "Eu-eu-eur—"

"I know. I know. Sshh. It will be okay." He stroked her hair. "He's not here, and a death sentence has been placed on his head. It's only a matter of time. He will pay, Ella, for what he did to you."

"Was so…so…worried." She sucked in a deep breath, frustrated with the overload of emotion.

"Oh, gods, love. So was I."

She shook her head. "No. No. About…you."

He groaned and his mouth pressed to hers. The gentle slide of lips and tongue was soft, slow, reconnecting. And it proved she was alive. Surely she had been hurt in the fall from the bridge—seconds of her life that were so terrifying she couldn't let herself linger on the memory in her current state—but once again, Zeph had come to her rescue.

Leaning her forehead against his, she asked. "How bad was it this time?" His eyebrows drew down and he searched her gaze. "The healing," she offered.

"Ella, so much has happened."

She pushed onto an elbow and leaned into him, the curtain of her hair dropping around her face. His back! Oh no! She wrenched off of him. "I'm sorry. I totally forgot. Why didn't you say something?"

He sat up. "Why do you apologize? Forgot about what?"

She waved her hands at him. "Your back. How sore are you?"

Sighing, he leveled a serious gaze at her and reached out for her hand. "That's what I was saying. You've been unconscious for nearly two weeks. My back is long healed."

"What?" Glancing down at herself, she took inventory. No apparent injuries, no pain.

He pulled her into his arms, smoothed his hand over her cheek. Their faces tucked together, Zeph released a breath. "I don't know how to say this other than to just say it."

"Please. I'm starting to freak out here."

"No, don't, because everything has worked out. But you have to know. You died, Ella. From the fall. I couldn't get to you fast enough. I…I tried…" He struggled to swallow. "But I couldn't let you go. Boreas helped me bring you to the Underworld. There's a river there, with waters powerful enough to heal even the gods, to restore life. But your human life force was already gone."

"What are you saying?"

"Your name is Marcella. Your brother's name was Marcus. Yes?"

"Of course. You know this."

He nodded. "What were your parents' names?"

"How is that relevant—"

"Please, you'll understand in a moment."

"Okay. My dad's name was Henry and my mom's was Margaret."

One side of his lips curved into a smile. "And your mother's parents—what were their names?"

"Joseph and Marlene."

"Sounds as though it mostly ran in the female line, then. Do you know Marlene's mother's name?"

Ella frowned. "Yes. I was named for her."

"Those names aren't a coincidence, Ella. A long, long time

ago, a very important god had a child with a human woman, and she had a daughter. And that daughter had a daughter. And so on. Down to you."

The hair rose on the back of her neck, all down her arms. "I, uh, I'm—"

"Yeah. You have the divine blood of Mars in you, one of the ruling gods of the whole pantheon. And that's how we were able to bring you back. But not as a human."

She froze, and that odd energy she noticed before stirred within her. "If I'm not human, then...what am I?"

Zeph's smile grew slowly, until joy and pride brightened his whole face. "You, my love, are a goddess."

EPILOGUE

Two weeks later

"What if he doesn't like me?" Ella asked checking herself in the mirror for the tenth time. Zephyros had helped her don the traditional dress of the gods. The cloak and tunic were comfortable enough, and her hair looked pretty styled in big loose curls that fell over her shoulders, but this whole situation was just so surreal.

She still couldn't believe she was a freaking goddess. Jesus.

Zeph came up behind her, wearing the male version of the traditional costume, and circled his arms around her waist. Meeting her eyes in the looking glass, he chuckled. "Not possible. First of all, he technically has already met you when he helped save you in the Underworld. Second, you are so fucking lovable my heart can barely stand it." He winked. "And third, if he doesn't like you, then fuck 'im."

She chuckled and dissolved into full-out laughter. God, she loved this man—this god.

"What do you think he's going to want me to do?" Ella was more excited about this part of the meeting with Mars. That she was related—even really, really distantly—to a mythological god who turned out to be real after all had the power to make her dizzy if she thought on it long enough.

"I don't know, but I'm sure whatever it is, you'll do great. Just remember, it will take time before you possess the full power of your godhood."

"I know." Her situation was so unusual, no one knew how long to expect it might take. The children of the gods were born with their abilities, but they honed them over a great many years. The thought of kids made her shoulders drop. She turned in Zeph's arms and rested her head against his chest. The sound of his heartbeat calmed and reassured. She no longer harbored an insecurity over her infertility—it seemed like ancient history now—but she was no less astounded by the sacrifice Zephyros had been willing to make for her. That he'd allowed his father to approve Alastor as the heir of the West after Eurus's betrayal had to have been a major blow.

Admittedly, she was less impressed by Aeolus's sacrifice, which maybe was horribly insensitive and vengeful. But she couldn't help it. If Eurus taught her anything, it was that there really was such a thing as too evil to live.

The topic of sacrifices had her obsessing about Mars again. "Okay," she said. "What I mean is, what if after he meets me, he decides I'm not worth whatever horrible sacrifice he had to make…down there. Geez, Zeph, it's been a whole month."

Fingers on her chin, Zeph lifted her face and kissed her. "Mars is a big boy. Just about the biggest. Whatever Hades threw at him, he could take it. Trust me."

"I do. You know I do."

She heaved a deep breath that just about calmed her. *What would Marcus think of all this?* The thought had her smiling against Zeph's chest, but it was also bittersweet. Marcus's death had placed her in Zephyros's path that day. Had he not died, they likely would've never known about Mars, the existence of gods, any of it.

"I wish Marcus could've shared in all this," she said softly, tilting her head back to meet Zeph's gaze. Because his human life force had departed peacefully and his physical body no longer remained, no similar feat was possible for him. She understood that, she really did. But, still, sometimes she wished.

"I do, too. I would've loved that for you."

Zeph changed their position and started to sway. He tucked their joined hands against his chest. He led, she followed, and they danced in front of her dressing room mirror, just off his—now *their*—private chamber within his estate in the Realm of the Gods. She smiled up at him. "There's no music."

His expression was the picture of contentment, and it made him so unbelievably gorgeous. "Maybe not, but I don't need music to feel moved to dance with you."

"I love you," she said, resting her head against his chest again. "Even if you are just trying to distract me."

His chuckle rumbled against her ear. "Is it working?"

"Wonderfully."

"Good."

For long moments, she simply reveled in the feel of the man she loved and enjoyed his arms around her, his body against her. Oh, for the day her godhood would be strong enough to be joined with his, formalizing the love and commitment they already felt and had privately pledged.

"When things calm down and you're stronger, we can return to the human realm."

"I think I would like that," she said. There were things she already missed—spring rains, the sun on her face, the *True Blue*, M&Ms. Sad that there were no people included in that list, but that made all this so much easier to enjoy and appreciate.

"We could—" Zeph froze. "Oh. We've got company. Come. Mars will be here any minute."

Ella nodded, picking up the energy signature that announced another god's arrival. The only one she recognized immediately so far—besides Zeph's—was Chrysander's. He dropped in all the time. She secretly loved it, but he was so good at playful banter she couldn't help but give him shit.

Hand in hand, they left their suite of rooms and threaded through the great house. It was large, almost a villa in its style, and had a beautiful western exposure, but it was so sparsely furnished and decorated it was clear Zeph did little more than sleep here.

Together, they would change that, and make his house their home.

Zeph led her to the ceremonial center of his world, his godhood, a domed circular room with an intricate and stunning tiled compass rose laid into the floor. All the Anemoi had rooms of this sort, apparently, though they differed in one fundamental way—they were oriented around each god's cardinal direction. In Zephyros's world, the arrow pointed west, toward an enormous ornate 'W'.

They'd no more entered the room than Mars appeared. Ella gasped. Zephyros sank to one knee and bowed his head. His hand tugged hers. She shook the surprise away and mimicked Zeph.

Mars chuckled. "Well, aren't you lovely, and the absolute picture of health? Rise, rise, both of you." The men exchanged greetings. "She retained her memories after all?" he asked Zeph.

"Yes, my lord. Praise the gods."

The other god nodded. "Indeed."

Heart in her throat, Ella stood, Zeph's support radiating through her, and faced the man who had not only helped save her, but who turned out to be a distant relative. "My lord," she said, trying to remember the protocol Zeph had gone over earlier. "I am so thankful to you." She met his good-humored gaze and released the breath it seemed she'd been holding all day. He was a hulking man of a god with warm brown curly hair and beard, wearing a much finer version of the same costume Zeph had on.

He bowed his head once. "Your thanks are not necessary, but they are appreciated. Are you well? Happy here? Is there anything you need?"

Her mouth opened and closed. She was stunned by his caring and generosity. "I…no, I don't think so. I'm still just trying to adjust."

"That's as it should be," he said.

"Zephyros told me I will work for you, but I fear I will be of no use for a long time."

He crossed the room and smiled down at her. "Be well, Marcella. I had no illusions you would come into your full power from the start. Therefore, I am giving you a job with which you already have some familiarity and interest, and where you can learn and practice your powers before we expand your purview."

Her stomach flip-flopped in anticipation. "Okay, that

sounds wonderful." She glanced over her shoulder at Zeph, who wore the most self-satisfied smile.

Mars's deep voice continued. "I have many natures, and they play different roles. One of them is guardian of all those things cultivated and harvested for food. Given your love and knowledge of the Chesapeake Bay, and its dire state of health, you will be the goddess of that waterway, working to restore its sea grasses and oyster beds, increase the oxygen levels of the sea and, with that, the crab and fish populations. All these provide enormous foodstuffs, so it would be a small, manageable locale in which you could develop and hone your powers within my realm of responsibilities."

"That would be…" She clasped her hands to her heart. "That's just…it's perfect and amazing and exactly the kind of thing I'd hoped for." Stepping forward, she closed the gap between them and grasped Mars's hand.

Zephyros sucked in a breath and tugged her back. "She means no offense, my lord."

Ella's head spun as she belatedly remembered the rule that a lesser god should never touch a major one first, lest they invite provocation.

"Both of you, calm down," Mars chuckled. "In case you haven't already figured it out, I consider Marcella as family now and, by extension, you, Zephyros, also. I cannot claim the role or function of father here, but I hope you will call on me, seek my guidance and assistance when needed, and meet the other members of our quite large family." He smiled.

Relief coursed through Ella and she straightened and smiled. "I would like that."

"Good. Then it is settled. Your first task is to familiarize yourself with that over which you will have dominion, and then we can teach you how to put your power to work." Ella nodded, another smile making her cheeks ache. Mars tugged at his beard. "Oh, yes, one other thing." He grinned so broadly it made him look almost jovial.

Ella glanced at Zeph, whose expression was as mystified as she felt.

Mars stepped in front of Ella and held out a hand. "May I?"

Bewildered, Ella nodded. "Yes?"

For just a moment, Mars pressed his hand to her abdomen. That grin grew impossibly bigger. "It's as I thought." His gaze went from hers to Zeph's and back. "You will be able to conceive, Marcella. When you have gained the full power of your godhood, you will be fit to carry a god in your womb."

Ella gasped and felt her jaw go slack. She reached a hand out and Zeph's was right there, grasping hers, providing strength. And, oh God, his hand shook and she didn't have to look at him to know what he was feeling. But she did, and the utter joy lighting his eyes and shaping his face was as brilliant as Mars's news.

"I…I'm beyond…just, thank you."

Mars nodded. "My pleasure. Now, I would love to have a longer visit, but given the length of my absence, I have things I should check on, people who will have missed me." He winked. "I hope they did, anyway."

"Of course," Ella said in a shaky voice, not fearing to take his hand again and offer a gentle thanks. The good-byes were quick and then Mars was gone. Ella's heart was so full it might burst.

Zeph stepped in front of her and pulled her into his arms. Reverent words spilled from his lips against her neck in that foreign language. "I'm so happy about this, Ella. Happy you'll get the chance to have something you didn't think you would. I didn't either, for that matter. And now we not only get each other, but, someday, a family."

She stroked his hair and held him. Tears and joy made her throat go tight. She nodded and whispered, "I'm going to make you a daddy. One day, you'll hold our child in your arms."

He clutched her tighter, and long moments passed in a shared state of ecstatic wonder.

Zeph finally pulled back, but didn't let go. Shaking his head, he sighed. "I'm really sorry."

She frowned. In this moment of all moments, what could there possibly be to apologize for? "Why?"

"I'm just so sorry he didn't like you."

Ella froze. "What do you…that's not…"

Zeph's face broke out in an enormous, humored grin. He shook with restrained laughter.

She smacked his flat stomach with the back of her hand. "Shut up." His laughter burst free, echoing against the domed ceiling. "I can't help that I was worried."

Zeph's eyes watered as she glared at him. The harder he laughed, the more he tempted her smile. She put her hands on her hips. "Are you having fun?"

"Oh, love." He kissed her, long and sweet. "More fun than I've had in my entire existence."

Finally, she gave in to the urge to smile. "Me, too." And it was so true. With Zeph, she'd found her laughter again, and so much more.

How amazing that life could change so fast, in ways that seemed impossible and were totally unforeseeable. Moments before, it seemed, she was alone in the world, without direction or purpose. Now, she had a great love, a new family, and a purpose so important she nearly vibrated with excitement to get to work. But, in truth, what had most changed was inside her. She had come back to life—not just when she awoke as a goddess—but now she was a being filled with faith and belief and hope for the future.

She pulled Zephyros down for another kiss, holding in her arms the man, the god, responsible for it all. No matter what happened, what came at them, what problems they encountered, they'd always be together. In that—in Zeph—she trusted. With all her heart and soul.

ACKNOWLEDGEMENTS

What fun it is to have gods frolicking in your brain! I have Heather Howland, my editor extraordinaire, to thank for encouraging me to give each of the Anemoi their stories. Without her, Zephyros Martius, the beautiful, broken man so in need of love, might never have had his chance. And now that I've written him, I'm struck by what a shame that would've been! Thanks also to my best friend and YA paranormal author Lea Nolan, who critiqued the whole manuscript in lightning speed. In the dictionary next to "awesomesauce," you'll find her picture. Thanks also to my many friends and fellow authors in the Maryland Romance Writers, the best group of writing friends a gal could have. Given how deep into the writing cave I descended for this story, I have to thank my husband and kids for their patience and willingness to go it on their own for a few weeks as I wrapped things up. And, as always, I have complete love for the readers, who welcome characters into their hearts and minds and let them tell their stories over and over again. ~LK

HEARTS OF THE ANEMOI
BOOK ONE

NORTH
OF NEED

*Her tears called a powerful snow god to
life, but only her love can grant the
humanity he craves...*

LAURA KAYE

Keep reading for an excerpt from
NORTH OF NEED
*book one in the Hearts of the Anemoi series
by Laura Kaye*

*Her tears called a powerful snow god to life, but only her
love can grant the humanity he craves...*

Desperate to escape agonizing memories of Christmas past,
twenty-nine-year-old widow Megan Snow builds a snow family
outside the mountain cabin she once shared with her husband,
realizing too late that she's recreated the very thing she'll never
have.

Called to life by Megan's tears, snow god Owen Winters
appears unconscious on her doorstep in the midst of a raging
blizzard. As she nurses him to health, Owen finds unexpected
solace in her company and unimagined pleasure in the warmth
of her body, and vows to win her heart for a chance at humanity.

Megan is drawn to Owen's mismatched eyes, otherworldly
masculinity, and enthusiasm for the littlest things. But this
Christmas miracle comes with an expiration—before the snow
melts and the temperature rises, Megan must let go of her
widow's grief and learn to trust love again, or she'll lose Owen
forever.

CHAPTER TWO

"Merry Christmas," Megan murmured to the empty bedroom.

Gray light filtered through the two windows on either side of the king-sized bed, enough to illuminate the outlines of hundreds of glow-in-the-dark stars on the ceiling. She'd once remarked offhandedly that her favorite thing about spending time at their cabin was the huge glittered dome of the rural night sky. Up here, no city lights dimmed the stars' brilliance, so even the smallest, most distant ones beamed and twinkled. The next time they'd visited, John redecorated their bedroom cciling. Just for her. He wanted her to have her stars, inside and out.

She didn't bother wishing on them anymore, though. Not in two years. Two years, today.

In spite of the circumstances, the holiday filled the air with a special, magical buzz that set her stomach to fluttery anticipation. A ridiculous reaction, of course, since she was alone. No surprise gifts or family-filled dinner awaited. Just a quiet, empty house.

Wallowing in bed all day sounded appealing, but a burning

sensation on her cheek demanded attention. She patted the area. The skin felt rough, like a scab. *Lovely.* Turning back the cocoon of the thick down comforter, she slipped out of bed. She followed a path from one hooked scatter rug to the next, avoiding the cold, wide-planked wood floors.

The navy, mahogany, and white color scheme of the bedroom carried into the adjoining bathroom. Megan squinted against the brightness of the mounted light and leaned toward the mirror. Her left cheek bore the deep, dark red of frostnip. Her skin looked almost sunburned, except the angry mark was localized to the cheekbone. The spot where, yesterday, she'd leaned against the snowman, crying until the unceasing flow of her tears froze the wet flannel to her face. At least her nose and other cheek, pink from windburn, didn't hurt.

She gently prodded the mark with her fingers again. Last night, it had been cold to the touch, but now it was hot, chafed. So stupid. She slathered moisturizer over her face and smoothed ChapStick over her dry lips, and brushed and clipped her loose blonde curls on top of her head in a messy pile. What did her looks matter?

Megan slipped a pink fleece robe on over her flannel pajamas and threaded her way across the large great room, past the grouping of buttery leather couches and the floor-to-ceiling stone fireplace, to the open kitchen. Coffee was a must. She tapped her fingers on the counter as she waited for it to brew. Giving up, she walked around the long breakfast bar to the one concession she made to Christmas.

There, next to the raised stone hearth, a small potted Douglas fir stood in darkness. She reached behind and found the plug. A rainbow of colored lights shimmered to life, brightening the dim gray that still dominated the room despite the number of large windows. She stepped back and gazed at the small tree. Plain balls of every color mirrored the riot of lights, but the basic ornaments also spread an impersonal cast over the tree. She hadn't unpacked their collection of ornaments—where every one had meaning or told a story—since her last Christmas with John.

She turned away, sucked in a deep breath, and promised herself she wasn't going to think about that. Not until she had to. And she had almost eleven hours.

She curled into a wide armchair with a warm chenille throw and a mug of strong coffee. The ringing phone startled her and she almost spilled it in her lap. "Oh, hell," she murmured as she unburied herself and rushed for the cordless.

She knew who it would be before she answered.

"Merry Christmas, dear."

"Hey, Mom. Merry Christmas." She settled on the edge of her seat and dragged the blanket over her lap.

"How are you doing up there? The weather looks bad."

Her mom wasn't really worried about weather, today of all days, but Megan permitted her the ruse. "I'm just fine. It's been snowing steady. We've got well over two feet, I'd guess." An earlier peek out the front window revealed the storm had undone all her hard work from yesterday, reburying the stone sidewalk she'd shoveled. The snow family still stood there, though.

"I wish you weren't up there alone. You should be with us. Especially today. I mean, who's going to keep your father and brother from sneaking bites of ham and stealing cookies while I'm trying to cook?" Her chuckle sounded forced.

Restraining her emotions made Megan's throat tight. "I just...I'm not ready." Not ready to walk away from the annual holiday tradition of a cabin getaway she and John had created, even before they were married. Not ready to be around people actually happy it was Christmas. Not ready to pretend so others could be comfortable.

Her mother's sigh made its way down the line. "I know. I know you have to grieve, and I know how hard this has been. But, damn it, it's been two years. You're twenty-nine, Megan, so young, so much life ahead of you, so much to offer. You can't spend the rest of your life mourning John." She paused. "Nor would he want you to."

Megan forced her eyes to the ceiling to pinch off the threatening tears. "I'm trying, Mom. I am. But, please, I can't do this. Not today."

"I'm sorry. I told myself I wasn't going to say anything. I'm just so worried about you."

Megan nodded and swallowed around the lump in her throat, unable to do much more in the face of her mother's emotional outpouring.

"Oh, shit," her mother muttered.

"What happened?"

"That was uncharitable, wasn't it? Mrs. Cooke is tottering her way up the front sidewalk, annual fruitcake in hand."

"You need to go?" Their neighbor had been dropping by the inedible bricks since Megan was a kid, though this was probably the first time Megan felt grateful for it—Mrs. Cooke's timing provided the perfect distraction from this line of conversation.

"Yeah. I'm sorry, dear. Let me go help her. Your father hasn't been out to shovel yet, and God help me if she falls and breaks a hip on Christmas morning."

"Okay. Enjoy your fruitcake."

"Keep it up, smarty. I'll save you some."

Megan managed a small smile. "No, please. Don't do me any favors."

"I'll be thinking about you, Megan. I'll have Dad give you a call later." The squeak of her mom's front door sounded in the background. "Hello there, Mrs. Cooke."

Their quick good-byes overlapped their neighbor's high-pitched chatter. Megan could so easily imagine the scene unfolding at her parents' house. Christmas there was comfortably predictable. An enormous real tree filled the living room with the scent of fresh-cut pine. More decorations than a Hallmark store. Mrs. Cooke's visit. Her dad's buttermilk pancakes for anyone who had stayed the night before. The savory aroma of baking ham. A small army of visitors—Megan's older brother and sister with their spouses and kids, occasional aunts and uncles with their families, and even a few neighbors without other plans. Enough food to feed said army, and then some. A mountain of presents. More food. An evening of games around the big farmhouse table.

Much as she had always loved it, she couldn't face it. Not yet.

By ten in the morning, she'd talked to her sister Susan, amazed to learn her two nieces had been done opening presents for hours already, and her brother Aaron, who quickly handed her off to his wife. She liked Nora well enough and enjoyed talking to her, but knew her brother's cursory greeting stemmed from his continued discomfort around her. He didn't know how to make things better for her, and his instinct, as a man, as the big brother, was to *fix* it. Not being able to help her put him at a complete loss. Megan didn't hold it against him.

As noon approached, Megan talked herself into getting dressed and having a bite to eat. She was about to dig into a bowl of chili and homemade cornbread when the phone rang again.

"Megs! Merry Christmas!" came her best friend's voice.

Megan smiled. Kate always did that for her. "Merry Christmas to you, too. You just wake up?"

"Damn straight. Well, Ryan woke me up with some yuletide cheer earlier, but we fell back to sleep after." Kate snorted.

"Aw, too much information, woman. I don't need to know about his little yuletide cheer."

"Who said it was little?"

"Argh. La-la-la, so not listening."

"All right, all right," Kate said. "So, how are you? The truth."

"Meh."

"That good, huh?"

"Pretty much."

"Oh, Megs, what the hell are you doin' way up there by yourself?"

"Honestly? I couldn't face Christmas at my parents'. I know they want me there, but I hate feeling like the elephant in the room. Everyone tiptoeing around me. It sucks."

"Big hairy balls."

"Exactly." Kate's goofy side had often been a lifesaver, but not today. Megan sighed. "I can't believe it's been two years."

"Me neither. It's so hard to imagine."

"They say the first year is the worst, because every sunrise represents the first time you experience that date without the person you lost." The first Valentine's without him, the first birthday without him, the first summer alone, the first Thanksgiving without him to be thankful for. The first Christmas. Megan stirred her cooling chili and struggled to put her thoughts into words. "But, honestly, the only thing different about the second year is you feel like you can't talk about it anymore. Everyone expects you to move on."

"You can always talk to me. You know that, right?"

"I do. Thanks." She huffed. "Jesus, I'm sorry to be so damn morose. Maybe we should talk about Ryan's yule log again."

Kate barked out a laugh. "Hmm…yes, that is a *big*, happy subject."

"Shit, on second thought."

They hung up with promises to talk later in the day. After.

Despite their joking, the honesty of the conversation chased away Megan's appetite. She wrapped the bread and chili for later and wandered around the cabin, relocating from one seat to another without any real purpose. A lull in the storm brightened the afternoon. Needing fresh air and a little distraction, Megan bundled up and shoveled the sidewalk for the second time, estimating perhaps ten new inches covered it.

She was officially snowed in.

As she stomped back up the cleared path, her eyes looked where her mind told them not to. The snow family remained, though the constant snow had weighed so heavily upon the woman's arms that they'd collapsed to her sides, her pink gloves presumably buried somewhere beneath the new snowfall. Megan frowned when she looked at the man. Both his hat and eyes were gone. Blown away or, like the gloves, buried.

Back inside, her eyes drifted where she didn't really want them to go, to the clock on the microwave. Little after four. Her stomach clenched. About two and a half hours until the anniversary came and went, until John had officially been gone for two years. She found herself glad she hadn't eaten that chili.

Mismatched picture frames drew her to the mantle. Smiling faces shined out from the past. A candid of her whole family. Her and Susan kissing Aaron's cheeks at his wedding. Mom and

Dad's portrait from their twentieth anniversary. And half a dozen shots of her and John—their wedding, skiing, her sitting on his lap. Happy and healthy. Alive. She turned away, but he was everywhere. In the rustic moose throw pillows he insisted they had to have, despite the fact no moose resided in these mountains. In the beautiful Mission-style lamps they found at an antique store outside D.C. In the stars on the bedroom ceiling, in the closet full of his clothes.

By five o'clock, the snowstorm returned with a vengeance, dumping more white fluff while the wind whipped through the surrounding trees. When the lights flickered for the first time, Megan groaned. No way the electricity would hold against the storm's relentless onslaught. At least she'd stocked the firewood rack when she first arrived. She built a strong fire, providing a blazing source of illumination should the lights fail completely.

The flickering continued at uneven intervals. She'd never seen the electricity falter so much without simply failing altogether. Despite the crackling heat of the fire, the great room air chilled. She tugged on a fleece hoodie and checked the thermostat. The LED screen flashed. She frowned as she reset the program, but the screen just kept flashing. Jeez. First the Freon leak in the air conditioning unit and now the heat was on the fritz. Not much she could do about it with this storm, though. She'd have to schedule a repairman before she headed back to D.C.

A fresh pot of coffee would ward off the chill. She wandered to the kitchen and froze. "What the hell?" All the LED screens—on the microwave, the oven, the coffeemaker, the digital alarm clock on the counter—blinked. Odd. Especially since the clock had a battery backup and, like the thermostat, the coffeemaker wouldn't reset.

A high-pitched tinkling, like a small ringing bell, sounded from somewhere outside. Goose bumps erupted over her arms. She didn't have a wind chime, and the next nearest house was over a half mile through the stand of trees to the west.

The hair on the back of her neck prickled.

She dashed to the entryway and peered through the glass panes on both sides of the door. Without light, her effort was useless. A wall of darkness swirled beyond the glass. She reached to the side and tripped the light switches, then turned back to the window.

A strangled scream stuck in her throat.

CHAPTER THREE

Out of the darkness, from the heart of the howling snowstorm, a hunched-over man staggered up Megan's front steps. She wrenched back from the door, her heart pounding in her chest. Panicked, she skittered behind a couch.

Who the hell could he be? Nobody could have walked or driven here in this weather. Her breath came in fast rasps. The lights flickered again, then again. Her eyes trailed to the fireplace tools on the hearth. Maybe she should grab the iron poker. Just in case.

The lights wavered, struggled to hold on. From outside, a solid, deadweight thump startled a gasp from Megan.

Help him.

The words were so quiet they might've been a thought, but in her current state she still whirled, fully expecting the impossible—that someone else was crouched next to her behind the sofa. Of course, she was alone. She peeked around the corner of the couch, her panic subsiding into a feeling of absurdity.

Help *who?* The man. Just a regular, ordinary man. Who

must be in trouble. She remembered how he seemed to stumble on the steps and the thump. He'd fallen. She rushed from her hiding place like a sprinter at the sound of the gun. Peering through the sidelight, she whispered, "Oh, shit." She was right.

She tore open the door. Jesus, he was big. No one she knew from the neighborhood, though there were always tourists renting surrounding cabins to take advantage of Deep Creek Lake and the Wisp Ski Resort. God, he wasn't dressed to be out in this weather. No coat. No shoes. What the hell was she going to do with him?

Cold wind buffeted her and nipped at her skin, making her nearly frostbitten cheek tingle uncomfortably. Her hesitation wavered, then dropped away completely. What choice did she have? She couldn't leave him out in this blizzard.

The bitter wind sank into her bones as she stepped shoeless and coatless—like him—onto the porch. She didn't have to check for a pulse. Each shallow breath sent up a small fog from his mouth. Megan crouched behind his shoulders and wedged her hands underneath. Two fistfuls of red plaid flannel in hand, she pulled. He barely budged as she grunted and tugged. She tried two more times.

Shit, but it was mind-numbingly cold. "Come on, dude. Work with me, will ya?" she muttered, her hair whipping around her face.

Megan rethought the problem and stepped around to his bare feet. How could someone walk to this cabin without shoes? She shook her head and crouched, back facing him, between his legs. Securing an ankle under each armpit, she cupped his heels and pushed herself into a standing position. This time, when she moved, he moved. The guy was so big and heavy, she felt like Rudolph pulling Santa's sleigh without the help of the other eight reindeer.

The warm air from inside the cabin embraced her body, its comforting tendrils drawing her over the threshold and into the slate-covered foyer. The lights flickered again, sending out a quiet electrical hum that raised the hair on her arms and the back of her neck. She tried to drag the man carefully, but his head still thumped as it crossed the shallow ridge of the doorjamb. She winced. "Sorry."

As soon as he was clear of the door, she set his feet down and ran to close it. The indoor temperature had probably dropped twenty degrees while she'd been outside figuring how to lug his sorry butt in. She engaged the dead bolt, and the lights died. She gasped and pivoted, flattened her back to the door. He lay, right where she left him, melting snow all over her hardwoods.

Knowing he needed warmth, she recommenced with the lift-and-drag routine until she had him right in front of the fireplace. The crisis of his exposure to the elements behind them, she looked him over more closely. The first thing her eyes latched onto was the shirt and scarf—John's clothing. The pieces she'd used on her snowman. Was it possible this guy had walked here...in what? The pair of faded jeans he wore and nothing else? And then...he'd grabbed the clothes in desperation before collapsing at her door? Everything about that was two kinds of strange.

Well, she wouldn't know anything for sure until he woke up and could tell her what had happened to him, so for now she'd concentrate on warming him back up.

She grabbed the thick chenille throws from the sofa and draped the first over his torso, tucking it as far under his body as she could. His crisp, clean scent, like snow on a spruce, filled her nose. Long as the blanket was, it still didn't reach below mid-shin.

With the second blanket, she started at his feet. Amazingly, while his feet were red, they didn't seem to suffer any of the telltale signs of serious frostbite. She wrapped his legs completely, trying to give him a little extra cushion against the floor's hardness. While she was at it, she sacrificed her comfy down pillow to the cause, flattening it out with her hands before sliding it under his head. His hair was a mess of longish strands that hung onto his forehead and down to his collar. It looked pitch black, but then it was also sopping wet.

Maybe she should call 9-1-1. Could an ambulance even get here in this weather? She shook her head.

Megan stood and stretched, admiring the man's surreal good looks. Even asleep, unconscious, whatever, the guy was ruggedly handsome. Mop of shiny black hair, strong brow, square jaw, fair skin, full red lips. A male Snow White.

Her eyes traced down. Very male. No wonder she hadn't been able to lift his shoulders. They were broad and well muscled, which the tight wrap of the blanket emphasized.

Jesus. She hugged herself. What was she doing? She was all alone, stranded in a blizzard, with a strange man in her cabin. A why-this-was-stupid ticker ran through her mind.

But did she have a choice?

⊰⊱

Hot. Too damn hot.

Sweat soaked into Owen's shirt and jeans, making the latter rough and heavy against his sensitive skin. His hair was heavy and damp where it covered his forehead. He tried to lift a hand to wipe his forehead, but it wouldn't move. Something restrained him. He struggled, moaned.

"Hey, hey, it's okay. You're okay."

Owen's eyes snapped open at the sound of her voice. An angel hovered over him in the darkness. He sucked in a breath and flew into a sitting position, tearing out from under the tight blankets. She gasped and yanked herself back from him.

"Where am I?" He looked down at his hands, turned them over, practiced flexing his fingers and making fists. He wiggled his toes against the weight of the blanket.

"You're at my cabin. I found you on my porch."

He dragged his gaze over her. The fire illuminated the halo of loose golden curls that framed her face and covered her shoulders, made her inquisitive blue eyes sparkle and dance. He frowned at the crimson puffiness of her cheek. His fingers itched to trace the wound. His lips puckered as he imagined kissing it. Her beauty reminded him of the first snowfall of winter—clean and new and bright. Full of possibility. Far from diminishing her, the injury highlighted her fairness by contrast.

"It's Christmas," he said.

She eyed him and nodded. "Uh, yeah."

He pushed the covers off his lap and yanked the suffocating wool from around his neck, relieved to be rid of their warm weight. The fire crackled beside him, drawing his gaze. He shrank back and swallowed thickly.

"How about something nice and warm to drink?" She rose to her feet, words spilling out of her in a rush. "I've, um, I've got a Coleman coffeepot just, uh, out in the garage. Operates on batteries, so—"

"I'd like something cold. If you don't mind." He followed her movements with his eyes. She was tall and thin. Too thin.

"Oh, okay. No problem." She turned and strode into the

kitchen.

Following her lead, he stood, testing his body, getting his bearings. He took a few tentative steps, enjoying the chill of the floor against his bare feet. He rolled his shoulders, twisted his neck from side to side. His muscles came to life as his body made its first halting movements.

He glanced to the kitchen and found her watching him. Her gaze lit on him like a caress.

"Want water, juice, or soda?" she called.

"Water, please."

She returned with the glass immediately. He downed the whole thing in one greedy gulp.

"May I have another? Colder, if you can?"

She gaped at him. "Ice?"

"Mmm, yes."

A blush bloomed on her face. Curious. He liked it. Wanted to touch the flushed skin.

She handed him his second glass and gestured to the couch. "Would you like to sit down?"

He took a smaller drink, his eyes following the sway of her hips as she walked around the sofa. After a moment, he joined her. The leather was cool and comfortable.

"So"—she clasped her hands together in her lap—"why were you out in this storm?"

He frowned. Tried to think. "I don't know." He couldn't remember much before waking to the vision of her over him.

"What? You mean, you don't remember?"

He dragged a hand through his wet hair. Concentrating made his head ache. "Uh, no, I guess not."

"Oh. Well, are you hurt anywhere?"

He looked himself over, moved the parts of his body in

sequence. "I don't think so."

"You collapsed on my porch. No shoes or coat."

The image of a swirling snowy nightscape flashed behind his eyes. He blinked, tried to hold on to the image. "I did?"

She nodded. Fidgeted with her fingers. Stuffed her hands between her thighs. "So, uh…"

He watched, fascinated by all her small nervous movements. Such a pretty woman. "Why are you here all alone on Christmas?"

She paled, her mouth dropping open. Then she gasped. "Oh, my God." Her eyes cut to the dark components under the TV. She cursed and flew from the couch. More curses came from the kitchen. He rose, regretting his question, and went to where she was rooting through a bag on the kitchen counter. She pulled out a small cell phone, pushed some buttons, then groaned. "Why is nothing working?"

"Can I help you?" A pit of guilt took root in his stomach. Though he didn't understand the urge, he would've done anything to ease her apparent panic.

"The time. Do you know the time?"

He shook his head. "Sorry."

"I can't have missed it. Please tell me I didn't miss it." She ran across the broad open space and disappeared into a dark room, then returned moments later carrying a small glass-domed clock with a shiny brass pendulum. She placed it on the stone hearth, face toward the undulating flames, and settled onto her knees.

Something stirred deep in his gut, niggled at the back of his mind. A feeling like déjà vu gripped him. His forehead ached as he struggled to concentrate, to make sense of the odd sensation.

A low moan yanked him out of his thoughts. The woman curled over the stone hearth in front of the clock, her head buried in her arms, her shoulders shaking.

Her tears called to him. Down deep, on some fundamental level of his psyche.

Just as he stepped toward her, images and words flooded his consciousness. The panel of gods, the pleading man. He sucked in a breath.

All at once, he remembered his purpose. He remembered himself.

BLOOD
of the
DEMON

DEMONS OF INFERNUM

*The only woman he wants
is the one he's been sent to kill...*

ROSALIE LARIO

Keep reading for sample chapters of
BLOOD OF THE DEMON
book one in the Demons of Infernum series
by bestselling author Rosalie Lario

Keegan lives to exact revenge on the evil demon who sired and abused him. When his father devises a plan to bring on the apocalypse, he and his three half-brothers, interdimensional bounty hunters for the Elden Council, are charged with capturing and delivering their father for punishment.

Art gallery owner Brynn Meyers has no idea that her ability to read memories embedded in objects and drain people of their life force means she has demon ancestry. Unfortunately for Brynn, she's also the key to raising an ancient zombie army, which puts her on every demon's Most Wanted List.

And no one wants her more than Keegan's father.

Keegan must protect Brynn from his father by any means necessary, but he'll have to learn to harness the other half of his genetics—the far deadlier, uncontrollable half—when he starts to fall for the one woman standing between him and the vengeance he so desperately seeks. The one woman he'll never be able to resist.

CHAPTER ONE

She wasn't what he'd expected.

Keegan crouched on a nearby roof, watching, waiting for her gallery to clear out. A stray gust of cold wind whipped through the night air, ruffling his jacket. It didn't matter. Considering where he'd come from, the cold was a welcome relief.

The woman had looked fragile when he'd caught a glimpse of her through the store's large window front. Undeniably beautiful, with her long, honey-brown hair falling in waves around her heart-shaped face—but fragile nonetheless.

It was the perfect cover. No one would ever believe what she truly was, what lived inside her. But the blood never lied. She wasn't what she seemed.

Despite the gravity of the situation, Keegan had felt a stirring of lust rise within him at the sight of her, blindsiding him with its unexpected force. It had simply been too long since he'd gotten laid, something he'd have to remedy soon. Didn't have anything to do with the woman. It couldn't.

After all, she might very well be dead by the end of the day. Because if he received the order, he'd have to kill her.

He fished his cell phone out of his jacket pocket and called his brother. As expected, Taeg answered on the first ring. Skipping the useless chatter, Keegan said, "I've got an eye on the target."

"That's perfect." Even over the phone, the relief in Taeg's voice was palpable. "What now?"

"As soon as she's alone, I'll grab her."

"You don't think Mammon has managed to find her yet, do you?"

Keegan gave a short laugh. "If he had, he would've taken her already. Waiting's not his style."

"Yeah, right," Taeg muttered. "Don't I know it?"

"I'll keep you posted." He hung up without waiting for a reply.

Even though he couldn't see her from this vantage point, he wasn't worried about losing her. Not after he'd tagged her scent. He closed his eyes and inhaled, giving himself over to his sense of smell. Sorting through the various odors he'd picked up—the rich aroma of coffee, the ashy smell of a discarded cigarette, the pungent stench of rotting food—he discarded them, one by one.

Yes. There she was. Her scent was unique. Like strawberries and cream. Something he'd tried only recently and discovered he loved.

Would she taste just as sweet?

Shit. What was he thinking? She wasn't a potential lay, but a dangerous and powerful weapon. Maybe even the enemy. He'd do well to remember that.

Finally, the store emptied of everyone but her. He supposed

the right thing would be to go in and question her. But what if Mammon was no more than a few steps behind him? He couldn't take that chance. Not when the stakes were so high.

He would take her back to the apartment with him. There, he could question her at leisure and decide what to do without having to worry about Mammon or his henchmen discovering them. But what were the odds of her going along with him willingly?

Well, he couldn't worry about that now. He'd simply take her.

The night had grown dark enough that he didn't bother heading for the roof exit. Instead, he walked to the side of the building facing the narrow alleyway and stepped off. He landed the six-story fall with a thud that shook the ground. A cracking sound, followed by a twinge of pain shooting up his right leg, made him pause, but he ignored it as the fissure healed itself. The homeless man lying unconscious in a puddle not ten feet away mumbled and stirred before growing still once again.

Keegan crossed the street, his gaze singlemindedly locked on the figure of the woman visible through the window as she buzzed about the front of the gallery. A ray of light from a small lamp decorating the window caught her hair, spinning it into a web of gold. In that lighting, she looked almost like an angel.

But why was he thinking about the color of her hair? She wasn't an angel—not by a long shot.

And her luck was about to run out.

ഠററ

Brynn Meyers stifled a yawn as she tidied up the eclectic space of her showroom floor. With its old furniture and traditional chandeliers, the space more closely resembled an antiques shop than an art gallery. She'd started it several years ago with the inheritance she received following her father's death from a car accident, just a short time after her mother died of breast cancer. It seemed like she spent every waking moment here. If she wasn't working, she was painting in her small studio located in the back.

"Just two hours of painting tonight, then I'll go to sleep early for a change," she told herself. "This time I mean it."

God, how pathetic was she? Was she so lonely that she had to start bargaining with herself?

No, not lonely, Brynn. Just a loner. There's a difference.

Really, there was. Even if deep down inside, part of her wished she wasn't quite so alone. So unique.

Her hand grazed the easel holding the painting that had arrived earlier today. She turned to examine it more closely. Created by her favorite artist, she was drawn to it because of his tendency to incorporate unusual materials into his work, such as the tattered pieces of muslin glued to this painting. It was an amazing work of art, and the cloth obviously old and worn.

Brynn brushed her hand against the gathered fabric. Closing her eyes, she focused on the feel of it at her fingertips, on the shadows of memories that whispered to her, begging her to uncover them.

The muslin yielded beneath her touch, revealing its deepest secrets. Her vision narrowed, focusing in on the fabric as its memories hurtled toward her. Several hundred years old, its journey to her began as part of an elegant dress worn by a Frenchwoman. Images of the woman's trembling fingers flowed into Brynn's mind, and she smiled at the impressions of the woman smoothing the material down, eagerly anticipating a visit from her secret lover. Then, in a scene years later, someone tore apart the dress for scraps. Even later, the bits of fabric were twisted and crafted into a rag doll, cherished for many years by the little girl who lovingly slept with it until she became too old for dolls.

The flashes of memory faded away. Taking a deep breath, she slowly returned to the present.

It's just a bit of fabric. She often had to remind herself of that. The memories embedded in inanimate objects tended to make them seem alive to her. But they weren't. They were just conduits for energy. And for some reason, she had the ability to sense this energy. This was a gift she'd had her whole life, and what had initially drawn her to art. Each piece had a story, an experience, rooted within it. Older art pieces could be positively overwhelming.

Of course, her so-called gift wasn't limited solely to art. There were times when it didn't seem like much of a gift at all — like when she discovered something she wasn't supposed to know. Case in point: when she'd touched her last boyfriend's cell phone and learned he'd recently used it to make an assignation with his ex-girlfriend.

The front door opened with a loud chime and Brynn snatched her hand away. Not like anyone would ever know what she'd been doing, but for some unexplainable reason, she always feared her gift would be discovered. Life was difficult enough without being branded a freak or a psycho.

She lifted her gaze to find a tall, well-built man standing in the doorway. Her breath caught as her eyes traveled from his skintight black shirt, highlighting every curve of his muscular chest, to the dark, shaggy hair framing his olive-toned face. A shiver ran through her. He embodied Dark and Dangerous, with the leather jacket to match.

And *crap*, she was ogling him like a slab of meat in a lion's den.

She wiped her suddenly damp palms against her slacks before moving forward to greet him. "Hi, welcome to Meyers Gallery. I'm Brynn."

He stared at her outstretched hand for so long that she fidgeted. Maybe he'd noticed her wiping her palms and had gotten grossed out. Great.

She started to pull her hand back, but he stopped her by at last reaching out to clasp his hand over hers. A tingle of awareness flashed across her palm, so sharp she had to struggle to hold back a startled gasp.

"I know," he said.

"What?" Brynn took a second to remember what they were talking about. Once she did, she flushed anew. This hunk of a man was making her lose her train of thought. "You mean you know my name? Have we spoken on the phone before, then? Are you here about one of the new art pieces?"

"No," he said, without releasing her hand.

His grasp was warm, heating Brynn from the inside out. The sensation was so disconcerting she needed another long second to process his response. "No? Well then, how can I help you?"

The man smiled, but something resembling regret flashed through his bluish-green eyes. Lord, they were amazing.

"Sorry," he said, the sound curling around his lips like a lover's caress.

Her gaze drifted to his full, luscious mouth, and she couldn't look away. If she didn't get him out of here soon, she was afraid she might jump his bones. Never before had she felt so viscerally attracted to a man, and to say the least, it was unnerving. This was the sort of distraction she didn't want or need.

"You're sorry? About what?" She tried to tug her hand back, but the man's grip held firm.

"About this."

His left arm came at her so fast she only saw a flash of it, right before his fist connected with the side of her face. There was a burst of pain. Then, she went blissfully numb.

CHAPTER TWO

He'd made it all the way Uptown with an unconscious woman in his arms and hadn't been spotted once. Not bad. Then again, he did have a few assets at his disposal. Like not having to use the ground.

Keegan carried the woman's limp figure into the Upper East Side penthouse apartment the Council had lent him and his brothers. The place was a far cry from the tiny shack he lived in back at home. The office alone was bigger, not to mention the four sizable bedrooms. And the amazing view of the city skyline from the wall of windows in the living room was nothing to scoff at. Too bad the magnitude of the situation didn't allow him to enjoy the view.

Taeg and Dagan, however, seemed to have no qualms about living it up. Sprawled out on the huge leather sectional in the living room, beers in hand, they watched some sports game on the large plasma television. The two of them didn't even look up when he entered the room.

"Glad to see you two douchebags can relax when this

whole world is on the verge of being destroyed," Keegan said.

"No problem," Dagan said, before turning his attention back to the screen.

Smartass.

Taeg shrugged and kicked his feet off the coffee table, swiveling his head in Keegan's direction. He was wearing a T-shirt emblazoned with the words *Why Do Today What You Can Put Off Until Tomorrow?*

Keegan stifled a snort. "Nice shirt."

Taeg rose and started toward him. "My favorite thing about Earth so far is the shirts. Followed closely by the supercool lingo. Did you know 'Fuck off' is practically a greeting in this city?" He stopped a few feet away and examined the figure of the unconscious woman lying in Keegan's arms. "Wow. She's a real looker. What did you do to her, anyway?"

Keegan would've thought that was obvious. A dark purple bruise in the shape of his fist marred her otherwise flawless cheek. He swallowed past the flare of emotion that tightened his throat. "Knocked her out. How else was I going to get her back here?"

"I could have gotten her to come with us willingly, if you'd let me go with you," Taeg said. "But no, you wanted to go off and be Master of the Universe all by yourself."

"She was my responsibility."

"Yeah, and we all know how much you love responsibility."

Keegan ignored the unreasonable stab of irritation his brother's words provoked. He was only annoyed because Taeg was an ass. No other reason. Of all his half-brothers, Taeg especially knew how to push his buttons. The only way to win this battle was to ignore him.

"She's a job, and nothing more," he told Taeg. "And don't

forget what we might have to do to her."

"I haven't forgotten." Taeg smiled, though there was no humor in it this time. He obviously dreaded this as much as Keegan did. Taeg wasn't a monster. Not like their father.

Keegan's irritation melted away. His brothers didn't want to be here any more than he did. It wasn't their fault, what they were born into.

"Where's Ronin?" he asked.

"I'm here." Ronin appeared in the doorway leading in from the kitchen. He was the second youngest of his half-brothers, older than Dagan but younger than Taeg. "So you got her, huh?"

"Yup."

"Did she seem to know anything about Mammon or her ancestry?"

"I haven't questioned her yet. But there wasn't a trace of demon activity surrounding her. I figured I'd get her out of there first and ask questions later."

"Good idea." Ronin waited a beat before saying, "So…are you going to hold her all day, or what?"

Shit.

Embarrassment flooded through Keegan. He hadn't even considered letting go of the woman. Holding her in his arms eroded his ability to think straight, like the blood kept trying to rush out of his brain and into other parts of his anatomy.

I really need to get laid soon.

That was it. Nothing more.

Keegan turned and strode into the room they'd specifically prepared for her. For Brynn. As he carefully laid her on the bed, he couldn't help but think how well that name suited her. It was just as interesting and unusual as she was.

With her figure encased in tight wool slacks and a fitted black sweater, the outline of her slim form was clearly visible. Small, firm breasts. Flat stomach. When she'd looked up at him back at her art gallery, her eyes had been a soft, calming green.

She was beyond enticing.

The sound of a throat clearing roused Keegan from his slow survey. He looked behind him to see Ronin and Taeg crowding the doorway.

Ronin nodded toward Brynn. "Looks like you hit her pretty hard."

"Didn't mean to." What a dick thing to do, hitting her like that. But he'd had no choice. Not really. There was no knowing how close Mammon was to finding her, or if he hadn't gotten to her already. Either way, he'd needed to get her out of there fast. "I'll heal her."

"That's not necessary," Ronin interjected. "Not when I can do it with a simple touch."

Ronin started toward Brynn, but Keegan surprised himself by letting out a low growl. "I said I'll do it."

Shock registered on Ronin's face, and he held up his hands, backing off. Not that Keegan blamed him. Where did he get off being angry at the thought of his brother touching Brynn?

He must be losing his mind.

"Let him do it." Taeg's smooth voice dispelled the tension in the room. "You know how Keegan likes to suffer for his sins."

"Fuck you," Keegan said, taking a seat on the bed next to Brynn. He withdrew his iron pocketknife, flicked it open, and cut a shallow groove in his palm. After pressing his hand to her cheek, he drew it away. His blood seeped into her pores, healing her blood vessels. The swelling went down, and within a few seconds she was good as new.

He wiped the remnants of his blood off her cheek, trying not to think about how soft and cool her skin felt beneath his hand. She was just a woman, and a human one at that.

Well, mostly, anyway.

"So what now?" Ronin asked him.

"Now, we wait for her to wake up and question her. Then we'll decide what to do with her."

Taeg gave a soul-weary sigh. "Sounds great. I'm gonna go drink some more." He did an about-face and disappeared.

Unable to help himself, Keegan turned back to the woman. So soft and feminine.

The sound of Ronin moving behind him barely registered. "You did more than just walk tonight, huh?"

"What's that?"

Without another word, Ronin poked his fingers through the jagged slits in Keegan's jacket and shirt, making contact with the bare flesh of his back.

Keegan fought back a flush. "Oh. Almost forgot about that." Which was unusual for him, something his intuitive little brother had no doubt picked up on.

"I had a feeling," Ronin replied dryly. "Might want to change before she wakes up."

"Yeah, good idea." If she didn't settle for outright panic and screaming when she awoke, she was bound to have questions for him. He didn't need to add any more to that list. Standing, he followed Ronin out of the room and clicked it shut, and then slid the lock on the outside of the door into place.

⋙⋘

Brynn opened her eyes to taupe satin wallpaper, dark wood furniture, and the faint smell of fresh, clean linen. She turned her head to the side, confirming that she was lying on a bed. A soft, comfortable bed with silky, chocolate-colored sheets and a faux fur bedspread folded across the bottom. Where the hell was she?

Wait. What happened?

It all came back in one blinding rush. The gallery, the too-hot-to-be-real man. His fist shooting toward her face.

Oh crap.

Brynn jerked up off the bed. Her first instinct was to panic, but she forced herself to calm down. She'd been through something like this before…and she'd learned from that horrible incident that she was stronger than she looked. That was something the creep who'd dared to take her was about to find out…

She lifted two fingers to touch the spot where the man had hit her but, amazingly, didn't find even a hint of pain. What the hell? He *had* hit her, that much she knew. So why didn't she feel it?

She couldn't believe that the man had hidden behind his gorgeous exterior and managed to totally catch her off guard. Had knocked her out. And apparently brought her here. To his…to his…palace?

"That *asshole.*"

The amazing skyline view from the tall windows on one side of the room, as well as the lush décor of the massive space, told her the word *palace* wasn't too far off. She was obviously in an exclusive luxury apartment, one on the Upper East Side if she didn't mistake the view.

What kind of criminal brought his victim to a place like this? He was probably a rapist. Or a serial murderer. Well, it didn't matter. Whatever his reasons, he might have caught her off guard once, but it wouldn't happen again. And she wasn't scared of him. She wouldn't *allow* herself to be. Not with what she could do.

"Once I get my hands on you, you'll regret it," she muttered. No doubt he'd regret it.

The hollow sound of her heels clacking on the wood floor vibrated in her ear as she stalked over to the door on the far side of the room. She tried the knob. Locked. Great. Just great.

The walls seemed to close in on her, the surrounding space shrinking until she once again felt like she was inside the trunk of that car, fighting off her nausea and wondering what *he* was going to do to her. She forced herself to shake the feeling off and then pounded on the door. "Is anyone there? Hey, where are you? Let me out."

When there was no immediate response, she pounded louder. "Come on. Hello? Let me out!"

Brynn was about to lift her fist for a fresh bout of knocking when the doorknob turned with a *click*. She scampered back as the door swung open.

The hunk from the gallery stood on the other side, *sans* leather jacket. He wore an impassive expression on his face.

Her fingers clenched into fists at the sight of the man who'd imprisoned her. He was about to pay. "*You.*"

He opened his mouth. "Let me explain—"

Without further thought, she rushed him, pummeling her fists into his chest. He didn't flinch, didn't even budge. He was like a freaking steel beam. But that was okay. She'd get him, anyway.

She lifted her hand to his throat and dug into his bare skin. Giving herself over to her senses, she willed the flow of energy through her body, just as she'd done so many times before. Her arm grew hot with the familiar sensation of energy drawing through her fingers, working its way inside her with an electric sizzle.

But instead of collapsing as she expected, the man merely lifted one perfect brow. "Ow."

That was it. That was all he said.

"Ow?" Brynn repeated, going numb with shock. She'd felt it! She'd felt the familiar draw of energy. But instead of falling to the ground in an unconscious puddle, he just said, "Ow"?

Ow?

"Impossible," she gasped.

He tilted his head to one side. "What exactly are you trying to do?"

This couldn't be happening. That particular ability had never failed her before.

She brought both hands to the bare skin of his muscular arm, right below the sleeve of his shirt, doing her best to ignore the spicy, masculine scent emanating from his body and the heat of his rigid flesh beneath her palms. Seriously, the man must be running a fever. He was scorching hot.

Squeezing her eyes shut, she once again concentrated on summoning her energy. Again, she felt it flow, but he stood still in front of her. He didn't even flinch.

She staggered back. "Oh, crap."

It didn't work on him.

For the first time in a very long time, a strange sensation stirred in the pit of Brynn's stomach, churning her insides to a rolling boil.

Pure, unadulterated *fear*.

She was stuck in a room with a psychopath who'd knocked

her out and kidnapped her, and she had no way to defend herself. No way to fight back.

Oh, God, she was totally screwed.